THEY C▓▓▓▓▓▓ THE

C

Chapter 1

C hris Boylin had driven the stretch of Interstate 412 between New Mexico and Tulsa for going on twenty years now, since only a month or two after he'd gotten his license at sixteen and left home for good, chasing a pipeline job in Oklahoma and leaving behind a stepmother who couldn't have cared less about anything in the world than she did for Chris. He could almost hear the pop of the champagne cork that day as he'd crossed the state line into the panhandle of Sooner State.

Chris looked over at his daughter beside him. Her tiny body was strapped tightly into the front seat of his pickup, and the sight of her suddenly evoked images of crash test dummies, the slow-motion replays of the mannequins snapping forward in a cloud of chalk and debris. And though he'd driven the interstate a thousand times, today was the first time he'd been on the road with Jaycee, and the memories of his former life on the pipeline—as well as his shitty childhood in Pueblo, Colorado—were at once almost too much to manage. Plus, Jaycee was only six, and she had no business sitting in the front seat like a real person. But his Tacoma was crammed to the brim with crap of all types, some

1

of it needed (Chris had become an EMT during his current life and carried with him a stockpile of supplies), most of it not (that included everything else that either didn't fit in his apartment or that he was too lazy to sort and discard). And with Jaycee's haul of luggage for the month-long stay before she returned to her mother to begin the first grade, there was nowhere for her to sit but up front. But at least he recognized the danger, Chris reasoned, a trait that would keep him more focused on the road.

Still, though, Chris couldn't quite shake the nerves. He felt more vulnerable since the separation, and though he'd obviously been alone with his daughter countless times since she'd been born, it had always been as a married man, stable and secure in his relationship. But that was no longer the truth, and though his split from his wife was technically only a separation—Calista having moved back home to New Mexico until they sorted things out—he knew in his heart it was over for good.

And now, for the next thirty-two days, Jaycee was his responsibility alone, and for whatever the reason, the obligation terrified him. And the more he worried, the more he worried. The cars passing him on the left felt like jet planes taking off beside him, and he couldn't help but fret about what would happen if he got a flat on this stretch of road, or if the temperature gauge suddenly started climbing to the right, signaling the radiator was about to give. He was driving a 1995 Toyota Tacoma, after all, not exactly the year and model showcased on AAA's safety brochure.

"What's wrong, daddy?" Jaycee asked.

"Hmm? What do you mean, baby? Nothing's wrong." Chris gave a forced smile, his voice high-pitched on the too-quick response.

"Why are you so sweaty?" Jaycee scrunched her nose to show she thought her father's perspiration was gross.

Chris reflexively wiped his brow with his fore and middle fingers and then sighed, trying to calm himself. Jaycee had just turned six, not a baby anymore, and if he showed he was nervous about something, she would fret too. He had to relax; there was nothing to bother about. He was in control, feeling as healthy and alert as ever; he just needed to allow his anxiety to run its course. The more he fought it, the worse it would get. "Just a little hot, I guess. You hot?"

Jaycee shook her head. "I think it's kind of cold."

"Okay, baby, I'll turn the air down."

The fan knob on the climate control panel hadn't been in place for four years—at least four years—and the simple act of turning the air flow from three to two to one required a squeezed pinch of his thumb and index finger and then a snap to the left. He'd done it a million times, of course, but today his hand was shaking like a hypothermia patient, and the moisture from his sweaty fingers made the move nearly impossible. He wiped his hand on his thigh and shook it out, trying to dry it to get friction, but when he tried again, it slipped once more.

What is the problem? Why am I so edgy?

Chris considered himself to be a calm person most of the time, especially in his work, where such a trait was mandatory, the literal difference between life and death. In his personal time, however, away from the nerve-wracking drives and decisions he had to make for other people, he'd always had difficulty keeping the scary thoughts at bay. It was something he had to be conscious of, something that took work. And for the most part, his work had paid off, at least for the first several years after his marriage. He was the husband he'd always imagined he would be when he was younger, working and saving money and fixing things around the house, always with a stiff upper lip and an attitude of stoicism.

And then Jaycee was born, and his confidence began to slide. He worried a lot now, and most of it was to do with her. It hadn't taken him but a month or two after her birth to learn that the "sleepless nights" he'd always heard talked about when it came to children was not a metaphor, but rather a literal thing. He would lie in bed and grind over thoughts of his daughter, first about whether she was breathing in her crib, and then, when she graduated from infanthood, about her future in general. Would she make friends easily? Would she still be talking to him when she was fourteen? Could he help pay for college when that inevitable time arrived, especially considering he might soon be under a mountain of debt when the divorce finally went through? And maybe most of all he worried about the divorce itself. Would Jaycee blame him when she was an adult? For her father not being there all the time, even if it wasn't exactly his choice?

"I still feel the cold air," Jaycee said, not whining, just making the fact known.

"Okay, I know, I can't get a grip on this damn—"

"Daddy!"

Chris' first thought was that Jaycee was scolding him for the curse word, which wouldn't have been for the first time. But the sound that had come from his daughter's mouth was one he'd never quite heard before, her voice like the shattering of an ice block dropped from a twenty-story building. He snapped his head up until the back of it was flush against the driver's headrest as he locked his focus on the road ahead.

But the road was gone.

The black frame of the pavement, which only seconds earlier had seemed to snake subtly and infinitely into the horizon, had suddenly been erased, as had the horizon itself and the air and sky that bled into it. The world ahead, some five-hundred feet in the distance, in an instant had been cut off from Chris and Jaycee and their ten-year-old Tacoma pickup, blocked off now by a wall of dust that was as thick as it was high. It was as if an enormous brown curtain had abruptly dropped down from the heavens, sent to earth by some divine stage manager, arbitrarily, dividing audience from actors at a random point on the interstate.

Chris's mouth fell open at the sight of the mammoth wall, rapt now by this new, impossible addition to the world. And as the scenery finally registered in his mind, he hesitated for a beat; it was a pause that he realized only later could have been the difference between another day on earth and the end of both their lives.

But then, through the thick blanket of risen earth, shrouded in the haze of brown that had not existed ten seconds earlier, he saw two letters appear in the sky, floating ten feet above them, both P's, one green, the other yellow. To most, the appearance of the letters would have seemed a mirage, a trick of the mind, random images conjured by a frightened brain to settle it back to reality. But to Chris, having sat on a dirty carpet five feet from a television for most of his childhood, it took only a second for him to make the connection to the lettering on the back of the eighteen-wheel delivery truck: Penelope's Pickles.

Chris threw the full weight of his body in reverse, pulling back on the steering wheel as if he were attempting to elevate an airplane out of a canyon the moment before it struck the mountainside. Simultaneously, with all the pressure he could muster, he pushed the brake to the floor; had it been possible, he would have sent the pedal of rubber and steel straight through the floorboard.

But the distance now between the Tacoma and the big rig was too short—Chris was traveling close to seventy miles per hour and had started braking no less than four-hundred feet from the trailer—and at the point in the road they were currently, there was no way to avoid impact.

But there was no quit in Chris' mind, and an instinct inside him said that a direct collision with the back of the semi would be fatal, at least for one of them, and it might even decapitate them both if the strike were perfect. So, with this unconscious revelation guiding him, he yanked the wheel sharply to the right, more quickly than he'd ever turned a steering wheel in his life, even having driven an ambulance for the last eight years.

The Tacoma reacted hysterically, its rear end fishtailing forward (perhaps coming up on two wheels, though Chris would never know for sure), sending the driver's-side door of the pickup in a flat trajectory toward the Penelope's Pickles delivery truck. The course of the Tacoma almost guaranteed Chris' demise, and in that second or two, a type of melancholy overwhelmed whatever fear he might have felt, sorrow about the days and years he would never spend with Jaycee. That was okay, though, he thought. His death was also a sacrifice, one he'd made for his daughter without hesitation. Now that it mattered, he was the father he'd always prayed he would be. He could die proudly.

But as Chris's mind prepared for the afterlife, the tailgate of the Tacoma continued to rotate, gliding past a quarter turn so that the back end of the truck was now heading toward the rear of the eighteen-wheeler's trailer. And when the collision finally occurred, it was the rear driver's side panel that took the brunt of the impact—not the door—a distinction that no doubt saved Chris' life, and maybe Jaycee's as well.

Still, though, the impact was brutal, and Chris was thrown like a bean bag toward the dashboard as the truck bounced off the giant wheel and whipped around, spinning for what seemed like a dozen times but was probably only once or twice. Chris instinctively flung his arm out uselessly across Jaycee's chest, feeling the full thrust of her mass against his forearm as she flung toward the front of the car as well. But she was strapped tight, so Chris brought his hand back to the wheel, fighting to steer the truck as it swerved off the road and hit the eastbound guardrail, where the airbag exploded, and the Tacoma finally came to a stop.

Chris might have blacked out for a moment, but he opened his eyes and screamed, "Jaycee!"

The cab of the truck was crushed, and the dashboard was nearly hanging over the truck's front seats, though not quite. Thankfully, Chris could still turn his head, and when he did, he nearly began to cry at the sight of his daughter. Jaycee's seatbelt had held, of course, and the airbag deployed as designed, and though there was no safety feature to stop the glass that had exploded all around them and into both of their faces, he could see that she was blinking, alert. Alive.

"Jay—!"

A sonorous pop rang from somewhere behind them, and Chris's eyes flashed to the rearview mirror. The glass was cracked down the middle but still functional, and there he watched as steam began to hiss from the front of a Mercedes Benz sedan, the latest victim of the blinding dust that had arrived from nowhere like a biblical tempest. Unlike the Tacoma, however, the Benz had struck the rear of the semi head on, and though Chris knew the difference between a Mercedes and a Tacoma were many, especially when it came to safety features, unless whoever was driving got very lucky with the angle they'd struck the rig, there were going to be severe problems for the people inside.

Chris kept his eyes in the mirror, and after a lull of silence that lasted only seconds, the air was pierced again, this time with the violent sound of screeching tires. And then the sickening, twisting thump of metal, as the Mercedes was plowed from behind by another car, one Chris couldn't identify in the dust, but looked to be a smaller sedan, a Honda or Toyota maybe. It was this second rear collision that finally turned the small pricey German car into an accordion, and

most entirely devoured the interstate and the land around it in every direction.

"Jay, baby!" Chris coughed out, "you okay, sweetheart?"

Jaycee turned to her father now and blinked, and then she nodded.

"Are you sure? You're not bleeding anywhere? Nothing hurts?"

Jaycee shook her head.

Chris was reluctant to move her, even touch her, for fear that doing so would somehow undo the miracle that his daughter was unhurt. "Okay," he answered, smiling, trying to keep his voice reassuring yet stern and in control. He looked back through the windshield, where the burst of lighted forms had just appeared. But there was nothing now but brown air and the slowly diminishing world. It was his concussion, Chris knew; he'd seen stars only one other time in his life, when he was eleven and took a knee at second base from a sliding Joey Wharton, the bully bastard trying to stretch a bloop single into a double, directing his leg forward toward Chris' head at the precise moment of impact. Chris had finished out the inning that day (and the tag was perfect, thank you very much), but he'd had headaches for a month after, and he wondered how much damage had been done to his brain that day. But today wasn't that. He didn't remember hitting his head with much force during the accident, and the figures of light he'd just seen weren't the sudden, shocking type as during the shortstop incident. They were animated. Alive. Like thin forms of shimmering children.

But whatever Chris had seen didn't matter. Not now. He was alive, able to walk and talk; and, more importantly,

Jaycee looked to be okay as well, though he would have liked to hear her actually say so.

The dust storm outside wasn't quite raging anymore, but the air was still swirling and heavy, and Chris would have been best off simply remaining in the truck and waiting for help to arrive. But first he needed to make sure the Tacoma wasn't on the verge of exploding, and second, he couldn't simply ignore the injured couple behind them, or anyone else who needed help for that matter. This was his job, after all, and he was obligated to do it, even when he wasn't on duty.

Chris scanned the length of his daughter one more time and then stood fully outside again, looking now toward the hood of the truck. The front end of the pickup looked like a burgundy raisin, the metal crumpled and creased to a total loss. But there was no smoke coming from the hood, and more importantly, no fire. He got down on all fours and inspected the ground beneath the undercarriage, looking for any fluids that might have leaked and that could become flammable upon a spark. But there was nothing of real concern to be seen there either. Despite the Tacoma being half the length it was when they'd left the house that morning, it seemed to have held up, at least from the inside.

"Okay, listen, baby, there are some people back there that might be hurt. I'm going to go help them. I want you to stay here, okay? Just sit right like you are and I'll be back in a minute."

Jaycee said nothing.

"Jay, are you sure you're okay?"

Jaycee nodded now.

"Nothing hurts?" He paused, and when no answer arrived from his daughter, he added, "Jay, I need you to look at me."

Jaycee hesitated for a beat and then turned to her father, her face as flat and emotionless as an accountant's.

"What is it, JJ? Can you say something, please?"

Jaycee's face suddenly came to life, her eyebrows bending inward, her mouth dipping to a despondent grimace. "I don't want to go," she said, softly, defeated, as if the decision had already been made and she was waging one last plea to prevent it. "I don't want to go with them."

Jaycee was more rattled than Chris had realized, but she was conscious, and at least partially responsive, and there was nothing he could see that suggested she was physically injured. He slowly glided his hands and fingers over her head, searching for any sign of trauma beneath her hair, the back of her neck. But she was clean and clear of injury; he was sure of it now.

"You don't have to go anywhere," Chris said, keeping his voice low and firm, a technique he used to keep trauma victims calm. "You don't have to go anywhere until help arrives."

On cue, the first of the sirens sounded in the distance, and Jaycee turned her eyes back to the windshield and continued to stare forward, directing her gaze to the place where the shape of light had danced in Chris' head only seconds earlier. Chris lingered for another moment, continuing to study his daughter, and then, reluctantly, he said, "You stay right here, baby. I'll be right back."

Chris walked quickly toward the Mercedes, which was smashed upon the rear bumper of the Penelope's Pickles rig like a galleon on a Caribbean rock formation. He held both hands high in front of his eyes as he tried to keep the dust and dirt from blasting his face. The storm had thickened in just the past few minutes, it seemed; what was thirty feet of visibility earlier was now five or six at most. After a few steps in the general direction of the pile up, however, he could finally see the front end of the Mercedes again, and when he arrived there, he traced the fender back to the passenger door and the site of the injured woman. He could hear movement inside the car, shuffling (*struggling?*), and though the noises should have been a good sign, an indicator that the occupants were alive, something about the clatter made Chris uneasy.

The window was coated with dust now, making it impossible to see inside, so Chris took a breath and opened the door.

And then he screamed.

The woman, the passenger who only minutes earlier had been recognizable to Chris even from a distance, her face seemingly undamaged despite the unnatural shape of her posture, toppled from the seat to the pavement below, the right side of her face smacking the road at Chris' feet with a tampered thud. Her knees and feet remained upright, however, staying hoisted inside by the height of the seat, keeping her waist slightly elevated from the street below. She was clearly dead, however, a determination Chris made in a matter of seconds.

But how could that be?

Chris had seen her sitting upright just moments after the crash with her seatbelt strapped across her chest. It was the only way she would have had a chance to survive the accident at all. But here her corpse was now, strewn across the street like a side of beef, which meant the belt had been released.

Chris kneeled slowly to the pavement so that his face was only inches away from the dead woman's cheek, and there he placed two fingers on her carotid artery, just to be sure she was indeed expired. And as he touched her neck, the rest of her body slipped from the cabin of the Mercedes, legs and feet flowing to the pavement like thick butter, flipping the woman's corpse to the back so that it was now facing up.

The dead woman's blank face stared toward the sky, unconcerned with the dust and wind swirling around it, and in an instant, Chris knew that whatever pain she had felt at the end—at least as far as her face was concerned—had nothing to do with the accident.

The woman's right eye, the socket of which had been face down on the street seconds ago, was missing, and in its place was a key, one of many on the ring that dangled beside her cheek. It was as if someone had tried to start the woman's brain like the ignition of an engine, going right through her eye like some medieval surgeon turning the tender organ to pulp. The thought riled a sick bubble of humor somewhere deep in Chris' gut, but instead of a laugh, bile spewed to his throat and into the back of his mouth.

Chris looked up toward the driver now, and though the man was alive and conscious, his face was a sheen of shock, emotionless. It wasn't a look that was unusual to Chris, not under the circumstances, and he softened his own look, hoping to bring the man down easily as he spoke. "Sir, are you okay?" he asked.

But the driver didn't turn, and instead he kept his eyes fixed on the windshield, past the ruined glass into the back of the Penelope's Pickles truck and the smashed front end of his sedan.

"Hey mister? Can you look at me?"

The man remained silent, continuing to hold his gaze forward, and finally Chris turned and followed the direction of his eyes so that he was looking through the windshield too. And as his eyes penetrated the dusky air, he saw them again—the lights—their color and sharpness as brilliant as the ones he'd seen earlier. Except there was new detail now. The lights had formed into distinct shapes, structures of something familiar, alive, with frames or physiques that looked almost human, with torsos and shoulders, and the thinnest of light rays that protruded downward the way arms hang beside a body. Where a head might have been on each of the forms there were only bright curtains of orange, but then both curtains turned toward Chris in unison, and a pair of faces that seemed to have been formed by a welding iron stared at him from a place as dark as the blackness of space.

Two large opaque ovals pulsed at the top of the head, the eyes of the face, as expressionless as those of the driver to Chris' left. And yet they sparkled with energy, hypnotically in their glow, their stares seemingly locked upon the dazed driver.

Chris was mesmerized by the faces, and though the world of dust outside appeared as an unkempt aquarium, even in that haze, he knew he was in the presence of something new. Or perhaps old. Older than anyone alive.

Chris finally stood now and attempted to view the light figures not through the broken windshield but in the open daylight. But as he cleared the cabin of the Mercedes and his eyes reached the smoggy air, the lights began to recede into the wreckage, slinking forward, beyond the crippled metal of the Mercedes Benz and the Penelope's Pickles truck. And then, before Chris' mind could fully process the figures, to calculate any sense of what he had seen or where the forms might fit into the matrix of the world, they were gone, blending finally into the storm that still swirled behind them, leaving no trace they had ever existed at all.

"Jesus Christ!"

The voice rang from somewhere behind Chris, and this time he lurched, feeling his heart miss a flutter as he sprang to his feet, clenching his hands into fists, ready to fight. Standing a few feet away was a burly young woman with dark features and a good-natured face. Chris saw instantly she was an EMT. She was frowning and shaking her head at the misfortune of the Mercedes passenger.

"You okay in there," she called, bending at the waist as she peered inside the car.

There was still no reply from the driver, and Chris peeked back inside to view the man again. His gaze was still magnetically focused through the windshield, and then it hit Chris like a killer whale to his chest: it was the same look Jaycee had on her face when he left her in the Tacoma.

Jaycee!

Chris stood and turned toward the pickup truck, which remained in the same position as when he'd left it, crumpled against the guardrail on the side of the road.

But something had emerged beyond the truck now, the glowing, human-like shapes from earlier, like Christmas lights around a wire frame (he'd seen reindeer decorations on lawns that used this method). But as quickly as they had appeared, they were gone, instantly, as if they'd been sucked into the atmosphere. And before Chris could bring all he'd seen over the past minute or so to a rational conclusion, they were gone.

Chris dashed back to the truck now, mouthing his daughter's name as he ran, though no noise came from his lips. And when he opened the door and looked inside, he turned his head to the side and vomited.

Jaycee was gone.

Chapter 2

Arthur Richland didn't hear the woman at first, the rap of her knuckles on the outside of his door—Room 42—but the high-pitched squeak of the expanding hinges snapped him to consciousness in an instant, snatching him from yet another version of the same dream he'd had for most of his nearly eighty years on earth. The main players in this recurring dream were always the same—him, Jimmy, and Ruby—but the details were never quite, and this time was no different. They had all three been the same age in this edition, teenagers, maybe sixteen or so. In the real version, of course, Arthur was only twelve, a full year older than his brother and seven years older than Ruby.

"Arthur? Are you awake, young man?"

Arthur opened a single eye, and with it he squinted toward the approaching nurse who glided past the foot of his bed insouciantly before reaching the window and sending the blinds to the top with a steady pull. It took him a moment, ten seconds perhaps, for him to recall where he was, but he squinted the memory to his mind. He was in a home for old people, and the woman in his room was 'Betty,' or at least that was what she called herself and what her nametag read, though Arthur suspected the tiny Asian woman had gone by something else as a girl growing up in Bhutan or Bangladesh or Burma, Arthur could never remember which. But he was back now, alert and cognizant of the world around him, and the elderly man gave a grumble and a quarter turn of his shoulders away from Betty, both to relay his dismay at her appearance and to demonstrate he was still alive, at least for that morning. At his age and condition, there was no guarantee he would see the afternoon.

"Meester Richland? Deed you hear me?" Betty asked in her usual sing-songy voice.

"No," Arthur snapped. "For Christ's sake, I was dreaming."

"That is good, Arthur! Dreaming is good!" Betty's voice was patronizing, her accented pitch lifting on the word 'good' each time she said it, the way a preschool teacher might talk to her students gathered at her feet during story time. "I hope it was a good one, your dream, but it's time to come for breakfast."

Arthur closed his eyes again and prayed for sleep to return, to have one more moment with his brother and sister. But the ship of slumber had almost certainly sailed for that morning. At his age, sleep now made up a large chunk of his life, but once he awakened in the morning and the day was afoot, it wasn't until well after lunch that he was able to drift off again. "I'll take it in my room like half the damn zombies in here," he rasped.

"No, no, Arthur. You are fully able to come join us at breakfast. If Meester Anthony can come to breakfast, you can come too. You are a healthy man."

Mr. Anthony only comes to breakfast because you plop him in a wheelchair and roll him to the table, Arthur thought. Instead, he said, "If I was healthy, I wouldn't be in this damn haunted house."

Betty ended the discussion on the subject. "You need to rise up now. I will give you fifteen minutes." She laid out Arthur's slacks and an oversized tee shirt on the top of his cluttered dresser. "You were somewhere nice, I hope."

"Hmm?" Arthur had closed his eyes again, trying to force himself to drift off for another minute or two.

"Your dream," Betty clarified. "I hope it was in a nice place."

It wasn't. Not on that particular day and for most of the ones after. It was anything but nice. Still, Arthur would have done anything to return there in real life, on the morning and early afternoon of that specific day, just before the storm arrived. It was a place his mind recycled and replayed in his dreams often, adding variety each time, yet always keeping the aftermath of what happened at bay. Arthur sometimes thought it was the only reason he stayed alive, just so he could see Jimmy and Ruby that way again, if only in his dreams. In this most recent version of the reverie, they had been standing in line at the fair, just as they had on the real day, restlessly chatting and grinning as they waited their turn for the Ferris wheel, all the while craning their necks and squinting up at the gargantuan hoop of steel and wood spinning above them. It was the first time any of them had ever seen one of the magnificent structures, and to each it presented the wonder and fear of an alien spaceship.

The fair.

It was the first one Arthur had ever been to, and it was a day he kept as close and active in his mind as any of the memories that remained from his childhood, one he prayed his brain would never relinquish to the ravages of age and disease. Perhaps when the day finally arrived and he was sent on from this world, he would spend his heavenly days in Albuquerque, reliving the first part of that day over and over.

The year was 1939, the exact date he couldn't recall, but the month was October, the day a Monday. It was only the second year following the end of the first World War that the state fair had returned to New Mexico, and Arthur's father, who typically lacked any desire to cross the boundaries of their own town, let alone to make a journey into the beehive of the big city, had been hell bent on finding his way to Albuquerque, even taking a day off from work to do so.

Whenever Arthur thought of that day, he could still smell the amalgam of odors as he and his family pulled into the dirt parking lot of the fairgrounds, the aroma of popcorn and grease, meat and manure, and even in his old age, whenever he recalled that precise moment, he closed his eyes with belief and inhaled, hoping to somehow strengthen the faded power of his olfactory sense. He and James had sat in the cargo bed of their pickup truck during the six-hour drive, their backs against the side panel, knees bent with hands flat on the metal floor. And when they'd finally pulled onto the grounds, they waited like coiled springs for the vehicle to come to a full stop.

And from the moment they'd hopped the tailgate and caused an eruption of dust around their knees and ankles, there was nothing but magic and possibility in Arthur's heart, and he couldn't have fought off the grin from his face if he'd been promised a hundred bucks to do so. In that moment, it was the best feeling Arthur ever knew, and he would have been hard pressed to find one that ever eclipsed it later in life.

"So, was it a good place, Arthur?" Betty repeated.

Arthur took a deep breath, startled by the suddenness of the question and the memory that glowed brightly once more. "Better than this damn place," he replied. There was nothing playful in his voice.

"Oh, Meester Richland, stop it. We are not as bad as all of that. And you know it is true. I have worked at many bad places, and this one is not a bad one."

Arthur supposed that was a fair statement from the nurse, though it was one he had come to agree with only gradually over the past few months. His opinion of the Stratford Manor Rehabilitation and Nursing Center had changed dramatically since the day his granddaughter had arrived at his home one morning the previous fall, brochure in hand, a telling smile of bad news on her face. And as Tanya unfolded the narrow glossy pamphlet and began to spell out the thrust of her proposal, Arthur could still recall the tears in her eyes. Each of her words had been carefully rehearsed, her speech concluding with the hypothetical scenario of Arthur happily moving into the senior center where he would be 'well taken care of.' At the time, Arthur thought any manifestation of the plan would be the closest thing to Hell on Earth he could imagine. He was a natural recluse, had been his whole life, and it was a label upon which he placed no negative value. So, the thought of him suddenly being thrust into a sea of human misery, abandoned in an environment where intrusion would be the standard and prodding—both physically and psychologically—would be a daily occurrence, was nothing short of unbearable.

But the signs of dementia were real, he supposed, especially the one that had broken the camel's back, the day he was spotted on the back porch of his neighbor who lived six doors down. He was watering the woman's plants at the time when another neighbor phoned Tanya; but, in fairness to Arthur, they were plants very similar to ones he owned, plants of which, by the way, he took very good care.

So, it was Stratford Manor or moving in with his granddaughter, and though it was clear Tanya preferred the former, Arthur would have died first before allowing the latter arrangement. He would live alone forever, and if that were no longer an option, he would live with those about whom he cared nothing and amongst whom he could hide.

But, of course, there was another option too.

Arthur had considered seriously on at least a dozen separate occasions, before the paperwork for the nursing home was signed and the luggage was packed, of popping the top on his little orange bottle and rattling what was left of the trazodone down his throat, washing the pills into his gut with the half-fifth of Bacardi he knew still lurked somewhere in the kitchen, standing patiently behind some cupboard door for just the right time to be of use. Yet, despite the allure of death and the promises of escape it offered, he feared it even still. There was more in the world than what was realized by the senses, astonishing malevolence that was kept at bay for the most part, but not always. Not when it was disturbed. Not when stones were overturned and storms arrived. Not when children meddled. Not when the hearts of men and women were exposed like a nest of ants beneath a rotting log. When those things happened, malevolence found its way into the world like thin mud through naked toes. And though none of what Arthur knew to be true had to do with the afterlife, per se, there was more to the world than what was advertised daily, a fact Arthur had discovered over sixty-five years earlier. What came after he didn't know, of course not—not yet—but if it contained the Skadegamutc, he would fight it off for as long as possible.

And thus, Arthur had acquiesced to Tanya's plan, albeit with a bit of feigned reluctance and confusion, an act he put on to assuage any guilt she might have been feeling. She was young, after all, and though not particularly attractive or bright, she had a certain ambition that suggested her life would be reasonably successful, if unspectacular, and he owed it to her not to be the burden he was bound to eventually become. Besides, even if she had been willing to care for him through his days of infirmity and incontinence, his granddaughter was no nurse, and the care he would need one day was beyond her. She had her own kids now—Arthur's great-grandchildren—and that was where her focus needed to be.

"Gimme a minute, huh?" Arthur asked Betty in a tone that was as close to pleading as he would ever get. He wasn't entitled to full privacy anymore, a luxury which, if he were to rank the things he missed most about being independent, would have been solidly in his top three. He could still request it, however, and though Betty wasn't obligated to honor the ask, she usually did.

"Okay, Arthur, that is fine. I am just outside the door at my station if you need me."

"Christ, Betty, I know where you are. I think you live outside my door."

Betty smiled, and Arthur couldn't help but give a chuckle himself. He didn't like what Betty did for a living, or to be more precise, the necessity of what she did, nor did he like the fact that he was at the mercy of nurses around the clock. But he liked the woman herself, and he knew he was lucky to have her. He was old and sometimes depressed, and though his memory was still better than most around him, some of it was barely hanging on by a synapse. But he wasn't ignorant, and he knew about the nightmares that took place in the interiors of homes just like his. No matter the cost of the facility—and Stratford Manor wasn't cheap—there was evil everywhere, and it sometimes came in the form of sadists and sociopaths in teal uniforms, butchers who liked to slap old people in the face for no reason, or scare them to tears with stories about how their children had died and weren't coming to visit any more, stories about which the residents had no way of verifying.

"Oh, and Arthur, before I go, you had someone who came to see you last night. He came in just after the visiting hours ended."

The only visitor Arthur had had since arriving at Stratford Manor was Tanya, and since her husband had been transferred to some outfit in Ohio three months earlier, Arthur hadn't seen anyone from the outside, at least not who had come there to see him. Letters still arrived from Tanya on occasion, each containing a vague promise somewhere in

as 1970, and Arthur's mother, who died a year later, had kept a private investigator on the case for a full decade after her son died. Jimmy as the source would have made more sense, Arthur supposed, but Ruby's name was the one that wouldn't leave his mind.

Arthur finished in the bathroom and stood at the door staring at the envelope, and then he walked and picked up the item, studying it like a lost relic.

Another knock at the door. "Come on, Arthur," Betty called from outside. "Time to eat."

Arthur stared at the envelope for another few seconds, and then he went to breakfast.

Chapter 3

As usual, Arthur took the maximum time allotted to get to the breakfast table, using his walker in a way that was almost hammy. It was a tool that was mostly unnecessary, of course, but Arthur utilized it as often as possible, not wanting to seem too healthy and then, as a result, be asked to participate in some mindless activity like dancing or stretching or, God forbid, tai chi.

But the main reason Arthur took so long was that he hated breakfast, both the food and the company. He ate it, of course, but usually only enough to satisfy the watchful eyes of the nurses who buzzed around the table like flies at a picnic. His appetite was next to nothing nowadays, and with the sight of his less fortunate inmates being fed, drooling as they stared vacantly toward the ceiling, it only made the experience worse.

As Arthur approached the already seated breakfast crowd, Lois Hernandez smiled at him from across the extended table. Arthur pretended not to see her. She was one of the more cognizant residents in his wing of the home, and Arthur wasn't in the mood to be cordial, let alone to have an actual conversation. Nothing against the woman, but, coherent or not, she was boring, and once she got going, it was like a word dam bursting inside her mouth. How many times was he supposed to listen to her talk about her grandkids and their goddamn swim meets?

"Hi, Arthur," Lois called, flapping a wave toward him.

Arthur met her eyes for just a beat and then averted them quickly. He nodded and muttered, "Lois," showing at least enough manners to acknowledge the gentle woman. After all, her charmlessness wasn't really her fault.

He lifted his eyes again and let them swing around the rest of the table, giving a moment to study each of the inmates. They were ten in all today, and at least four of them couldn't have told you the name of one of their kids, and probably not their own. It was depressing, and yet another reason to stay in his room and away from this company. Arthur had never reconciled the tragedy that was the end of life, nor had he accepted the fate of those who hung on well after their spirits had vanished. He promised himself—as many did, he supposed—that if he ever got to the point of merely existing, he would take every dime left in his bank account and use it to hire an assassin to take him out of the dreariness. Of course, once things got that bad, he wouldn't have the wherewithal to make such a dramatic decision, but he liked to believe that by inserting this choice into his mind, when the time came, the idea would burrow up through the disease and disrepair of his brain and then linger there in the folds just long enough for him to follow through with the order.

"There he is." The words came as a grumble from Roger Desormeaux, who was seated just to Arthur's left as he approached the table. He drew out the word 'There' as a raspy, snarky sort of introduction. "The guy who's too good to join us," he continued. "At least by his own choice."

Arthur pretended the old codger wasn't talking about him, but there was obviously little doubt. Roger was no fan of Arthur's, and he was famous for calling out people's sins and shortcomings. And Arthur's main failing, at least according to Roger since a week or so after Arthur moved into the center, was snobbery.

Arthur ignored him as he sat in the remaining open chair at the table.

"To what do we owe the honor of your esteemed presence at breakfast, Sir Arthur?" Roger continued, smiling around the table as he spoke, proud of the accent he put on the last two words, as well as the vague Camelot reference. No one seemed to care.

"Like you said, Betty made me come," Arthur answered matter-of-factly. "Just like on most days." He looked over at Roger. "You, on the other hand, I haven't seen all week. Glad to see you were able to find your dick today and make it here yourself."

Lois Hernandez and Camille Ostroski gave a stunned cringe at the insult, visibly shuddering in their chairs as their eyes burst open in shock. And then they both exploded in a heckling cackle; Lenny Weiss had to spit his food into his napkin for fear of choking on it.

"Arthur!" Betty scolded from the nurse's stand, never lifting her eyes. But Arthur knew she'd thought it as funny as everyone else at the table, everyone except Roger, of course, and the oatmeal zombies who weren't really there at all.

Roger tossed his fork down and crossed his arms like a five-year-old, his lips ballooning into a comical pout; for a moment, Arthur thought he was going to cry. He looked like a caricature of someone who'd been slighted, and this made it even funnier.

But Roger's reaction was purely sincere, though it wasn't the insult that had caused the childish reaction. Not per se. After all, the affront didn't even make any sense. Nor was it the embarrassment of the laughter from his peers that had so completely dismantled Roger. It was frustration that ruined people's days in Stratford Manor. And Roger's frustration was a typical one at the center: that he wasn't forty years younger and capable of dealing with assholes like Arthur in a proper way. In this case, his youth would have allowed him to stand and confront Arthur, challenge him, maybe even throw a punch to the center of his nose.

Well too bad, old fool, Arthur thought. *Everyone here has something to complain about.*

Arthur suppressed a grin and looked back to Lois, using her as a barometer to measure the strength of his verbal counterpunch, hoping to see that the joke was still ringing heartily. Lois was a drone most of the time, it was true, but her sense of humor was decent, and if she was still giggling, Arthur would know he'd landed a good one.

But Lois was no longer focused on Arthur or Roger or anyone else at the table. Instead, she was staring off to her right, out the window, to the eastern side of the rehabilitation center where the empty parking lot reflected the morning sun. On Saturdays and Sundays, Stratford Manor was standing room only with visitors, but during the week, when the kids and grandkids were back to work and school, the place was a true hermitage, and the bare asphalt of the lot outside was a dead giveaway.

Arthur followed Lois' stare, and as his eyes reached the blacktop, he noticed first the bend of the pines that functioned as the property border to the north. The trees were swaying in the wind like waifs on an acid trip, and the sky above them had begun to bleed to the color of dirty chalk. Arthur scanned the table to see if anyone else had noticed Lois and her newfound distraction, but the rest of the inmates were either still laughing at Roger or else had begun to console him. Betty had now arrived at the table to pat his hand and shush him back to even.

A feeling of déjà vu suddenly entered Arthur's mind as he watched Lois, one as strong as he could ever recall, and though he could no longer see the woman's face, he knew the expression upon it. The blankness of her eyes, the stare that went on until the bend of space. He had seen the look before, many decades ago, in the year 1939. It was the stare of Glenn Flannery and Sherman Caswell. Of Randall Richland.

Arthur cleared his throat nervously. "Whatcha looking at there, Lois?"

Lois said nothing in reply, but the question seemed to activate her, and she stood now, slowly, though with unsettling ease, displaying an adroitness in her rise that Arthur would never have thought possible, not from Lois or anyone else in the center for that matter. She walked quickly in the direction of the window, as if her eyes were attached to some taut line that was reeling her forward. She only stopped when her face touched the wall-length pane of glass that formed the north side of the center, and there she pressed up against the window until the cartilage in her nose was sufficiently smushed into her face.

Still, the rest of the nurses paid little attention to Lois, as inmates suddenly walking off *sans raison* was not exactly unusual in the confines of Stratford Manor. But Lois was known to be one of the more mindful members in the bin, and finally, it was one of the male orderlies, Khenan, who followed her to the wall and gently grabbed her by the upper arm, attempting to turn her and redirect her back to her seat. It was a task he'd done a thousand times over the course of his work, no doubt, and he looked barely alert as he attempted to guide her.

But Lois didn't turn with Khenan, and instead she leaned into the glass, pressing her cheek there now in resistance. Khenan gave a firmer tug on her bicep now, nodding his head toward the table. "Come on, Ms. Hernandez. Let's get you back now."

Lois nearly slammed her face into the window now, lunging her body toward the wall and losing her balance, almost falling to the floor. Still, no one seemed to notice aside from Khenan and Arthur, and as the orderly steadied her, his face quickly morphed into a combination of confusion and annoyance, and now he braced himself as he pulled her toward him. "Ms. Hernandez, we're going back to the table now!"

The young man had a hundred pounds on Lois, maybe more, but she dug herself in, shuffling her feet wider with each of his tugs, bending her knees to keep from moving.

Arthur pushed himself to his feet now and stood at the table, watching the emergent struggle between Khenan and Lois play out. His breathing was short and raspy, his eyes alert with terror as the feeling that things were about to deteriorate bubbled inside him. He prayed silently for Lois to acquiesce.

"What is it, Arthur?" Betty asked, but Arthur barely heard the nurse, so fastened was his attention to Lois and Khenan and their growing conflict. He knew Lois was about to be hurt, or that someone was, and thus it was his responsibility to call for the encounter to come to a stop. It was his fault, after all, a belief he wasn't quite sure how he'd come to, but that he'd arrived at just the same.

But as he prepared to shout Lois' name, to bring her back from whatever stroke or mental collapse she was experiencing (though Arthur knew it was neither of those things), his own stare drifted past her and Khenan to the parking lot beyond, to the place where Lois was staring like a child's doll from a dark closet.

It took a few beats, but Arthur's eyes finally adjusted to the glare coming off the black pavement, and as they did, he saw them for the first time in over six decades, the forms he had attempted to avoid since he was not quite a teenager, and which he prayed he would never see again.

But they were there—finally—the ancient creations of malice that had changed his life's trajectory so many years ago.

"No," he whispered.

He spotted only the wispy hair shape of the first one, a scribble of light that glowed like the outline of an illuminated figurine, and he closed his eyes and opened them immediately, hoping perhaps he had just been hallucinating. But the sparkle of light remained, left of center, barely in the frame of the window, so Arthur rushed to the wall now, hoping to catch the form in its entirety, the thing he knew to be both real and impossible, which now taunted him and Lois like a lure in a trout stream.

But before he could find his way to the window, the figure of light sent a spraying glow into the sky, and in a second, the sun and brightness disappeared from the day outside, as if a solar eclipse had suddenly taken place, a cosmic anomaly unannounced to the world.

But Arthur knew it was no eclipse, and that this storm was no accident or glitch in the forecast. He still remembered the storms of his youth, the wind and dust and arrivals of darkness, and though it had been several decades since he'd experienced any storm quite like those, he recalled them as if the last one were only days ago.

Had he seen reports on the news of such storms recently? Near the border with Oklahoma? That sounded familiar.

The thin figure of light was suddenly gone, but the rampant shade of the atmosphere had now seeped from the outside into the nursing home, bringing with it the feeling of night in an instant, as if a dam of darkness had suddenly broken outside and flooded the rehabilitation center. There was the chorus of "Whoas!" from the staff and some of the saner inmates (the oatmeal zombies wouldn't have noticed if an asteroid had fallen through the roof), and then the power flickered for a few seconds, threatening to cast a more immediate emergency onto the morning, though Arthur assumed the place had generators to keep the center going for at least a day or two.

But the transformer held, at least for the moment, even though the wind, which had been only a breeze twenty minutes earlier, was now a screeching off-key whistle, and the tripping pines around the parking lot now appeared to be struggling to stay rooted to the ground, like stranded hikers bracing in a blizzard.

The buzz from Stratford manor was a steady drone now, and most of the able-bodied residents were standing and staring toward the window, trying to locate the invisible source of the sudden storm.

Did anyone else see it? Arthur thought. *Besides me and Lois?*

Arthur scanned the center for the look, the vacant gaze he'd etched into his mind, the focus and fixation that no longer existed in most of the residents there. It was part of the reason he'd agreed to come to Stratford Manor in the first place, had not fought Tanya to continue living alone. He knew most of the androids in the center wouldn't see them if they came. Or if they did, nothing would change. They were immobile in this place, at least for the most part, harmless, so even if they could feel the torture of the witches' draw, they wouldn't become dangerous.

But Lois had seen them—or at least one of them—there wasn't a doubt in Arthur's mind about that. The expression in her eyes was unique, reserved for those who knew intimately the ghosts of his past. Lois was one of the few who had her wits about her, who was ambulatory, and it was this cognizance and mobility that was her weakness on that day.

Lois continued to stand her ground with Khenan, clenching her core in deep resistance, impossibly, keeping the young orderly—whose demeanor was growing baser with each second—at a standoff.

"No!" Lois finally growled, never taking her eyes from the window.

Khenan had a grip of Lois' arm with two hands, the tension in them increasing by the second. "Let's go, Mrs. Hernandez!" the orderly barked again, his voice now deep and commanding, businesslike, the nice-guy routine having run its course.

But before Khenan could dig his fingers any deeper into the old woman's arm, Lois Hernandez slipped a hand into her left pocket, and from it she pulled a thin metal instrument which appeared to be a coffee spoon, the proper kind with an extended shaft. She nimbly flipped the utensil a quarter turn so that she was now gripping the spoon by the bowl, leaving the long, narrow handle jutting from her closed fist.

"You go!" Lois cackled, almost laughing as she screamed the words, and then she plunged the steel shaft into the young orderly's right eye.

And then a flood of memory hit Arthur in an instant, a recollection he'd hoped and prayed had left his mind forever. But here it was again, returned to him, as if sent from a distant land, arriving on the wind that continued to howl outside.

Or perhaps it had come from a place closer to Arthur, a place he knew as well as any and that continued to appear in his dreams night after night. He thought of the envelope on his nightstand, and of Clayton, New Mexico.

1939.

Chapter 4

C hris stood in front of his crumpled truck shaking, hugging his shoulders, his eyes never leaving the vast landscape of the Oklahoma plains. It was a scenery that was as flat as it was desolate, and to Chris, that combination equaled hopelessness. He rotated and looked behind him now, to the New Mexico side of the terrain, which, somehow, looked even more forlorn.

Beside Chris, standing with his shoulders slumped, was a patrolman—B. Williams according to his nameplate—who was finishing off the letters on his latest scribbled note with the speed of an arthritic mannequin.

"So, just to be clear then," B. Williams started, not looking up from his pad, "you say you went to help the couple in the Mercedes, and when you came back, your daughter was gone?"

The patrolman had asked the same question three times now, and Chris was beginning to think it was a test to see if he would give the same answer each time without wavering. The officer was either trying to gauge the magnitude of Chris' head trauma or discover if he was lying.

Chris wanted to scream his answer for the third time, but instead he restrained himself and nodded. "Yes."

He swallowed and looked back to the drab green and brown of the roadside terrain, grass and dirt and ranchland as far as the eye could see. Twenty minutes earlier it had been consumed in a blizzard of loam and gravel and clay, dazzling in its density and force; and then the storm had simply ended, disappearing as if vanquished by some blessed rain. But there had been no moisture in the storm, not a droplet from the sky. The storm just stopped.

"And how old did you say she was?"

Chris sighed and gritted his teeth. "I said she was six. Both times you asked, I said she was six. And I'll say it again if that will move this search the fuck along! Six! She's six!"

Patrolman B. Williams looked away in disappointment, rubbing his forehead and frowning as he regrouped his thoughts. A beat later, he looked back at Chris, his eyes now mimicking softness and understanding. Whether he was feeling those things sincerely or not, Chris didn't know, but if not, he did a fair job of pulling off the sentiment.

"Everything is already moving along, Mr. Boylin. We have patrol officers scanning the area right now. On foot and in cars. We'll get dogs out here if we don't find her soon, and a chopper, if necessary." He hesitated. "In the meantime, that was quite a knock you took judging by the looks of this vehicle. I think it'd be a good idea to have one of the EMTs give you a once over."

"No, thanks," Chris replied, and then a swell like he'd never felt arose in his chest, bringing with it a surge to his eyes, a flush to his face. He thought of Jaycee, alone trying to find her way through the storm, at some point losing sight of the truck and becoming terrified, lost in the desert, probably calling for her mother, though it was her father who was on duty at the time, who was at fault for her disappearance.

Her mother. Calista.

Chris couldn't imagine the sound his estranged wife would make when he told her Jaycee was missing. It would be otherworldly. Filled with disbelief and terror. And then hate when she got around to questioning how he could have allowed it to happen. And with that thought, the figure of light appeared in Chris' mind, the eyes like rotten tangerines against a vacant black face. It was the quasi-answer to his ex-wife's theoretical question he'd just contrived. *How could it have happened*? It couldn't have. Not in any way he could conjure. He knew his daughter. She wouldn't have left.

He felt panicked now, light-headed and on the verge of fainting.

"I need to find her!" he coughed out. "She was here!" He wobbled back a bit as he motioned with both hands to the passenger seat, and then he took a step back to the truck, steadying himself against the hood. "She was strapped in. I told her to stay and she...she wouldn't just wander off. There was no reason to wander off."

"She might have been disoriented," the patrolman offered. "This was as bad a wreck as I've seen in quite some time. The whole scene, I mean, not just your vehicle. Nothing I've *ever* seen in terms of a pile up. Not in fourteen years on patrol and my whole life living out here. And we get snow out here as bad as anywhere in the country."

Chris grew up in the plains and knew the weather patterns there too, but he saw no reason to offer this detail.

"So just be grateful your daughter wasn't too badly hurt—"

Chris looked up sharply, ready to argue with the patrolman, but B. Williams held his hands out from his chest defensively, showing he understood there was still the matter of finding her.

"I know, Mr. Boylin, I'm just saying, there are fatalities out here today. That woman in the Mercedes being one of them."

With the shock of Jaycee's disappearance and the image of the glowing form still lingering in his mind, Chris had forgotten all about the woman in the Mercedes. "How...how did she die?"

Patrol B. Williams gave a curious look and a cock of his head. "What do you mean?"

"I mean, I know it was the accident, but she..." Chris paused and shook his head.

"She what?"

Chris met the officer's eyes, and for a moment he wanted to describe the faces in the window, and the forms of light who had seemed to walk off from the wreck like a pair of demonic phantoms. But he knew that would shatter his credibility with B. Williams, which was already shaky due to his presumed concussion. Instead, he said, "I saw her in the car. Earlier. Before I walked over. She wasn't dead. At least not from..." Chris cut himself off quickly, now feeling like he was trapping himself with each word, pulling the investigation in another direction, one that would detract from looking for Jaycee.

"You mean the key?" B. Williams said.

The flash of Chris' eyes gave away the answer. He nodded.

"Hell of a thing, right? Not quite sure how that happened if I'm honest. But I've seen some accidents that would make your—"

"I'm an EMT. I know about accidents and bloodshed."

B. Williams raised his eyebrows. "So, then you know?"

"Yeah." The answer was a reflex, and Chris quickly struck it with a shake of his head. "But no. Not really. Not that. I've never seen that before. I saw her face just after the accident, and she didn't have a key where her eyeball should have been."

"You saw her just after? You mean..." B. Williams nodded toward the Mercedes, "...from here to all the way over there? That's what, forty, fifty feet? And in a dust storm, after a bad impact like you had? Can you be sure she didn't?"

Chris *was* sure—at least mostly—but he realized his argument, based on the details as they were, would have been decimated in any court of law and thus likely dismissed by the patrolman as well. Besides, he didn't much care. Not now. Not with Jaycee still missing. And yet he did. It felt relevant. He *knew* it was relevant. With all he had seen in the carnage, the figures and the lights and the disappearance of Jaycee, the impossible storm and the strange death of the Mercedes woman, everything he believed to be true now felt in question, as if a cable had suddenly snapped causing a shift in his worldview.

"What about the driver?" Chris asked.

"What about him?"

"How is he? Did he say anything?"

"*Anything?*"

Chris was growing tired of the whole cop thing, the constant question-with-a-question answers. "Did you ask him if he saw how she died? His passenger? For Christ's sake, she had a key in her face, which, if you ask me, is impossible. I don't care if the car fell from the fucking Empire State Building, that can't happen."

B. Williams shifted his eyes for the first time, showing that he was ceding at least some control of the interaction, agreeing with Chris in body language if not actual language. "Like your daughter, he was a bit out of it when I questioned him."

"What do you mean, 'Like my daughter?' Did he say something unusual? Something that didn't fit?"

Chris had repeated to the patrolman what Jaycee had told him just before he left to help, about 'not wanting to go with them.'

Them. Chris connected the word to the light figures for the first time, and he felt the blood rush from his face to his heart.

B. Williams dropped his eyes again, and this time he held them there for several beats before lifting his head and staring past Chris to the empty road beyond. The pile-up was still hours from being cleared, and the interstate heading east looked apocalyptically empty. Finally, he met Chris' expectant stare. "Yeah, he said something unusual."

Chris felt chills and the nausea arrive simultaneously. "What was it?"

The patrolman shrugged and tucked his pad and pen in his pocket. "He said: '*They came for me.*'

"*They*," Chris asked, barely able to get the words out. "Who?"

"That's what we asked, but he didn't answer. He just shook his head and said: '*They came with the storm*.'"

Chapter 5

Arthur didn't dare make a move toward Lois and Khenan. Not now. An assault had just been committed by one of the Stratford Manor residents, and he feared any movement toward the scene would be viewed as aggression, the second move of a riot, and he had no desire to be blindsided by some densely built orderly overreacting to Arthur's place in the scene. Not that such a security measure would have been out of line, he supposed, but all the good that understanding would do once Arthur's vertebrae were shattered into a million pieces.

Khenan was now huddled in the far corner of the center, sitting upright, his hand on the spoon as he quivered like a Parkinson's patient in the late stages of the disease. He was in shock, clearly, but something deep in the reserves of his instinct to self-preserve told him not to pull on the utensil, that doing so might leak his brains all over the nursing home floor. Instead, he simply held the spoon like a child might a spyglass, gently, inquisitively, waiting as the nurses and orderlies encircled him, deciding how they should help.

"Call an ambulance!" someone shouted.

"Is Dr. Phan still here!" another one called, maybe Betty.

"I saw her leave already," was the answer by another unidentified staff member. "Maybe twenty minutes ago."

There were protocols and orders being barked and followed, but the scene was gradually unraveling into chaos, so Arthur quickly turned and walked from the breakfast area, passing through the double doors and into the main hall, allowing the screams and commands and demented laughter from the oatmeal zombies unfold around him. He entered the long hallway and from there began on the padded vinyl path to his room, walking more quickly than he had in years, stepping deliberately but steadily until he reached the midway point between the common area and the residents' quarters. At that section of the hallway was a door that led to the recreation yard, and though it was unattended, it was secured with an alarm, and only those with the secret code could exit without setting it off. But alarms were for emergencies, and Arthur knew if it were to erupt now, all who heard it would assume it was tripped intentionally, to indicate the matter of Khenan's facial trauma and Lois' meltdown.

Arthur took a deep breath and then gently placed both hands on the thick bar that bisected the door, and then he braced his shoulder against the glass, preparing for the resistance that was sure to come. And then he pushed with all he believed in him, forcing the door outward against the gale, and then he squeezed his body through the portal and stepped outside, onto the stone patio that led to the lush lawn of Stratford Manor.

The siren blared above and all around him, but now that he was in the thick of the gust, it sounded muted and distant. Arthur released the door and looked back once in reflex, but there was no one behind him, and he followed the cobblestone path that led from the building to the picnic area, and then finally to the wrought-iron gate that spilled into the parking lot.

Arthur bent forward at the waist now as he pushed against the wind, fighting to maintain his balance and footing, determined to make it to the parking lot where he had seen the ancient form only moments earlier. They were back. The evil from his childhood had found him finally, tracked him to the place where he hoped he could disappear. They'd been disrupted once more, the stones disturbed, and though so many decades had passed since Jimmy and his friends had brought them to life from the soil of the Sampson farm, Arthur would have been a fool to think the terror had ever truly ended. Evil like the Skadegamutc didn't simply dissipate over time. That kind of malevolence had to be gazed upon, challenged, and though its final destruction may have been a goal too ambitious, it at least had to be suppressed, stifled, crimped and contained like a genie in a lantern.

But this time it was he who had tempted them, and thus he who would have to end it.

The wind continued to howl like a she-wolf in estrus, spewing dirt and gravel and trash directly toward Arthur and the nursing home itself, blowing as if it had been ordered from the gods to wage an attack on both. And in some way, Arthur thought, that was true. The storms had returned for him, again ensnaring anyone unfortunate enough to dawdle in their wake. And whether they had been searching for him for all these years, prowling the ether and earth and universe before finally catching up with him in his old age, he didn't know. And really, it didn't matter. They were here now.

Again. The last two of the trio which had ravaged the citizens of Clayton in the early twentieth century. And though Lois Hernandez had been the first to feel the grip of their latest clutch, Arthur suspected she wouldn't be the last. His only hope was that he would be next. And perhaps the last. And with his death, they would vanish forever.

But he knew that wasn't true.

They hadn't come to kill him, not directly, about that he was almost certain. It was his suffering they lusted for, for him to witness the pain of others as much as possible before he finally passed away in his sleep, or from the stroke of the stress they would bring to his life. It had always been their motus operandi. To torture their targets with the deaths of others.

The storm still raged, and Arthur knew they were close. Close enough that he had seen them from the breakfast table inside the center. And whatever he knew about the past and pathology of the ancient beings, and the fruitlessness of trying to alter the course of his own fate and that of those around him, he had to try something.

"You came for me," he shouted, coughing as the grime from the pavement entered his mouth, landing on his gums and tongue and lips. "So keep coming! You found me! You finally found me. I have them! I have them both! I'll bring them to you if you end it now! So end it now!" Arthur held the back of his open hand to his eyes as the dust stung his face like a thousand tiny yellow jackets, and he stared desperately across the open lot for the thing that he knew would be gone in a matter of moments. At least for the day. He could already feel the wind begin to wane and the dust and debris begin to settle back to the earth as the storm came to a close.

Arthur brought his hands to his face now, clearing the light layer of rubble from his face as he searched the air for the monsters of his youth. But he saw only emptiness, and as he turned away from the pines to head back to the breakfast hall of Stratford Manor, where the damage caused by the Skadegamutc was no doubt still unresolved, he caught a glimpse of dirt rising to his left, a vortex of dust that signaled its final departure.

And then it was gone, the dust and the evil, both dissipating into the day as if they'd been but a dream.

But that was for now. Whether it would be another day or week until they returned, Arthur didn't know. But return they would. Both of them. And based on the events in Clayton, New Mexico in 1939—and perhaps Spokane, Washington in 1951—it wouldn't be long until they did.

And, in truth, it wasn't a surprise. He *had* seen the news recently. And he knew of the crash near the Oklahoma border.

This was only the beginning.

Chapter 6

Arthur awakened as he did most mornings to the sound of a rap on the door. If he was in the midst of his recurring dream once again—or if he'd had it already, earlier in the evening—he'd forgotten it by the time he opened his eyes. He could already feel the flush of his mind, the depletion, and he fought in vain to break the layer of glaze across his brain.

The knock again, and Arthur recognized a delicateness to the knuckling, a tapping that was considerate, one truly asking for an invitation. Had it been the nurse who was entering, she would have done so already, her quick footfalls accompanying the staccato commands of how and when Arthur's day should begin. And since the incident with Khenan several days earlier, the nurses had been on edge, and any playfulness they may have demonstrated once had been put on pause for now. Even when it came to Betty.

There was an intermission following the second knock, and Arthur held his breath on the silence. He knew it wasn't them, of course, the Skadegamutc, that wasn't how it worked; but even the idea of them made him quiver.

And yet it *was* to do with them. Somehow. Arthur just knew.

A final knock and finally the muffled voice of a man followed it. "Hello? Mr. Richland? Arthur Richland?"

Arthur couldn't bring himself to answer, and though he wanted nothing more than to see the man's face, to hear his reasons for having come, he prayed he would honor the fact that Arthur was asleep and abandon his entry. But after another beat or two, the door finally cracked open, the customary squeal of the hinges singing like whippoorwills.

Arthur saw Betty first, grimly nodding toward his bed before receding into the hallway. And in her wake stood a man, late thirties maybe, tall and thin with a kind face and a head of auburn hair that hung just to his shoulders. He had the look of an apology on his face, but as he met Arthur's eyes, he gave a measured smile. "Arthur Richland?"

Arthur swallowed and nodded, already feeling the burn of interrogation in his belly and chest.

"Hello, Mr. Richland, my name is Chris Boylin. Thank you for allowing me to speak with you." The man spoke lowly, almost in a whisper, though his voice was as clear as arctic ice.

Arthur struggled to catch his breath as he stared spellbound by the man, and he absently scooted himself rearward until his back was flush against the headboard. At once, he brought the covers with him, pulling them to his chin like a boy staring at his closet door, pondering the rattling dangers beyond it. *Had* Arthur agreed to see him? If he had, he couldn't remember doing so. Or maybe the man was just being polite. Arthur had never lain eyes on him before, and the name wasn't one he recognized. But there was something about his face that was recognizable, if not in the features themselves, then in the expression. It was as if he were observing the face of his mother the day Ruby disappeared. Or perhaps the day she returned.

"What do you want?" Arthur asked.

"As I said, my name is Chris Boylin, and I was...hoping to speak with you for a moment. Perhaps longer, if you'll allow me the time."

"Speak to me about what? I already talked to the police about what happened to the intern last week." Arthur searched for the young man's name but couldn't find it. "I don't know any more about it than what I said then."

The man's face wrinkled with confusion and curiosity. "I don't know anything about an intern, Mr. Richland. That's not why I'm here."

Arthur knew the moment the man passed through the door he hadn't come about Khenan's assault, or about the charges that had been brought and then dropped against Lois Hernandez. Though in a sense, that's exactly why he was there. He was there about the storm. About the Skadegamutc. He was there about the Ditches and the Hollow and the altar. He was there about Clayton, New Mexico. The same way all of those things had been the cause of a spoon being plunged into a young orderly's eye socket.

Arthur thought of the orderly again and a lump of guilt formed in his throat. According to Betty, Lois had jammed the spoon so deeply into the boy's eye that the stem of the utensil missed his brain by only a centimeter. Had she put just an ounce more thrust into the stabbing, the kid would have died on the spot. Of course (*Khenan! That was his name!*) Khenan would never see through that eye again. But at least he was alive, his brain undamaged.

Lois had been turned over to the care of her daughter and son-in-law the next day, claiming to have no knowledge of the assault or what had inspired it. And though Arthur had heard some of the nurses doubting these claims, calling the woman a liar and accusing her of playing up her dementia to avoid prosecution, Arthur had no doubt she was telling the truth. At least for the most part.

"What is it you want then?" Arthur asked. His words weren't intentionally curt, but they came out that way, nonetheless. He already knew why the man was there, at least in the broad sense, and he feared where the conversation would go once he started speaking.

"It's about my daughter, Mr. Richland."

Arthur swallowed, staring at his hands as he rubbed them nervously. *Ruby.* "What about her?"

"She's gone missing. I'm hoping you can help me find her."

Arthur had met the man's eyes only in a flash to this point, focusing instead on his own hands or the bed sheets or some spot on the floor as he spoke. But on the word 'missing,' Arthur looked into Chris Boylin's face, and as he searched the man's eyes, he saw the expression of his mother again, and his breath caught in his throat, inspiring a fit of coughing. When it subsided, he cleared his throat and grumbled. "I'm sorry. About your daughter. Where do they think she might be? The police?"

The question caught Chris off guard. He wasn't used to being asked about where the police thought his daughter might be, at least not so early in any conversation about her disappearance. The queries usually started with *How old is she? Where was she when she disappeared? How long has she been gone?* Questions such as the one Arthur had just asked, about location theories, for example, usually didn't arrive until rounds five or six.

"They, uh, they don't really have any guesses," he answered. "It's the reason I'm here now. Why I came to see you."

Arthur paused and collected himself, trying not to give away too much about what he might know. He just wanted this man to leave. Not forever maybe, but for the next few hours or so, a day perhaps, while Arthur came to grips with the reality that it was all happening again. The incident at breakfast a week prior was real, as was the scene that followed outside.

"Not sure what you could mean by that," he replied. He scoffed and added, "You don't think I took your daughter do you? I'm an eighty-year-old man in a nursing home. Probably not the FBI profiler's number one suspect."

It was a joke, but Chris didn't laugh. "No, I don't think you took her, Mr. Richland. But I do think you might know something about...where she might have gone." He gave a quiver of his head, as if 'where' wasn't the word he wanted to use. "Or how."

Arthur felt flush. "*How*?" he repeated.

Chris rubbed his forehead and closed his eyes, hoping to reset the conversation. "I came to ask you about the article."

Arthur shook his head. "Article?"

"I gave it to the nurse last week. In an envelope, along with my phone number. I was hoping you would have looked at it. And that I would hear from you. I'm guessing you didn't read it."

The envelope! Arthur had forgotten about it entirely, and as he recollected the day Betty had given it to him—the day of the incident with Lois Hernandez—the feeling of excitement returned. He looked to the spot on his dresser where Betty had placed it, but there was only a pile of clothes and other clutter there now.

Chris followed Arthur's gaze to the dresser and then stepped to it, moving the strewn items until he found the rumpled envelope. He grabbed it and opened it, withdrawing from it a thick square of paper, unfolding it once to a half size and then again, revealing a small stack of standard-sized pages, four sheets in all.

"What is that?" Arthur asked, sitting up now, trying to get a peek.

Chris walked to the bed and held the stack in front of him, just out of reach of Arthur's hand. "I was hoping I'd never have to come here," he said. "I was hoping she'd be found by now." And then, "If what you read isn't familiar, or if you don't remember any of it, I'll be on my way. But I insist you look at it." Chris held his gaze firmly on the elderly man for several beats, and then he looked around the room and asked, "May I sit?"

A small desk and chair sat in the far corner of the room, two items Arthur had yet to use since his arrival in the center. Arthur nodded toward the chair and Chris quickly grabbed it and brought it close to Arthur's bed. As he sat, he smoothed out page one of the packet and turned it toward

Arthur, revealing a heading at the top that read in thick black font: *The Mysterious Case of Ruby Richland*.

Arthur read the words twice, three times, but the concept of their meaning didn't quite compute. And as he read and re-read the heading again and again, trying to make sense of what he was seeing, he suddenly felt dizzy, as if he were going to pass out, maybe worse. He tried to breathe, inhaling three or four times, but the air only seemed to go one way. It was as if the sight of his sister's name had caused his lungs to seize, and for the first time in many years, Arthur Richland believed he was about to die.

"Are you okay, Mr. Richland?" Chris took careful measure of the man, gauging the seriousness of his breathing difficulties.

"Huh?" Arthur now raised his stare to Chris, who was wearing a look of compassion and mild concern, his body slightly turned, preparing to rise and call the nurse if Arthur didn't get it together soon.

"Just take a couple of deep breaths," Chris instructed. "Do you need me to call the—"

"No. No, I'm fine. It's just. Ruby. I haven't seen her name in so...she was my..." he stopped, unable to get the word out of his esophagus.

"Your sister, right?"

Arthur nodded, and then he followed the earlier instruction to breathe, taking in three deliberate breaths and then exhaling through pursed lips.

"That's it, Arthur, nice and slow. You're okay."

Arthur reached for the first page of the packet, the one in Chris' hand, taking it as gently as he would a stick of dynamite. He held the page at eye level and read the words again. Finally, he asked, "What is this?"

"It's a page I printed from a website."

Arthur heard the words, but they made little sense by the time they reached his brain.

"Do you know what I'm talking about, Mr. Richland. The internet?"

He had a general idea. "The internet? I...why is my sister on the internet?"

It was Chris' turn to take a deep breath now, and after a slight pause, he said, "As I said, my daughter is missing, and the police have been less than effective in finding her. Though, I guess to be fair to them, it's not for a lack of looking. She was there one minute and gone the next. It happened almost in front of my eyes."

Chris paused again and studied Arthur's eyes, ensuring he was following the story so far. The nurse who had escorted Chris to the room had given a snapshot of Arthur's challenges, so Chris knew there might be some rapids along the river, some rocky portions of forgetfulness and quietude, even aggression. But so far, the elderly man seemed to be following and engaged.

"So, because they couldn't find her, I started doing my own research, looking for any incidences, events throughout history that might match what happened to my daughter." After a pause, he added, "Or the things I saw." He swallowed and reset his tone. "It was a lot to sift through, a lot of dead ends. Until I found this story on a website, about what happened to your sister when she was a kid. When she disappeared and came back. It was a long time ago, I know, but do you remember any of that, Mr. Richland?"

Arthur was as confused as he could ever remember, and a stray thought arrived to him, that the look on his face must have looked exactly like the oatmeal zombies. But unlike the zombies, he thought, his confusion was rational. It felt impossible. How could anyone even know Ruby's name, let alone the story of her disappearance? "How could...? How is it possible? How could anyone know about any of that? It was...so long ago."

Chris gave a sincere nod, acknowledging that the story was hard to understand, especially for someone who didn't grasp the full breadth and capabilities of the internet. "A lot of information is on the internet now. A lot of information that, before, would have only been known about by locals in the town where those things happened. Or maybe even to some scholar who took interest in the story. But even then, who would read it, right?"

Arthur nodded in response to the rhetorical question.

"It would get published maybe, in some obscure magazine or as a doctoral subject, and then buried in some esoteric section of the university library. But not now, Mr. Richland. The information is accessible to anyone. Anyone willing to look long enough." He paused and shrugged. "And I was willing."

Arthur was still stunned by seeing Ruby's name, but the words of the man were starting to sink in as the point was being made. "Is that what happened?" he asked. "Someone published a...paper?"

"Well, not exactly. In your sister's case, there was a newspaper article written about her sometime in the early forties, a few years after the incident at the fair. And it seems that whoever runs this website dug up the story and got a hold of the article. And...well...it's not as incredible as it might sound."

Arthur nodded, though he was far from grasping all of it. "What does it say about her?"

"The original article talks about how Ruby disappeared one day at the New Mexico State Fair. That was only a couple hundred miles from here. It's what grabbed my attention most of all. This was in 1939. It says she was with her brothers when it happened. That included you, right?"

Arthur nodded slowly, suddenly feeling the emotions of that day, and for the first time in several days, the sighting of the Skadegamutc slipped from the front of his mind and was replaced there by Ruby.

"But I think if that were all that happened that day," Chris continued, "that your sister went missing—though I'm sure it would have still made the news—it probably wouldn't have gone much beyond that. Kids go missing all the time, and even if they're never found, there's usually an explanation. Some working hypothesis that makes sense. But there was more to Ruby's disappearance, right?"

Arthur let the question hang unanswered.

"To read the article," Chris continued, "it sounded like that day was, well, unusual doesn't really describe it. There was a Ferris wheel accident that day also. A girl was killed. And several people were badly hurt during a stampede, fleeing one of the many dust storms that had recently sprung up in that part of the country. Do you remember any of this, Arthur?"

Dust. It was a word Arthur hated as much as any in his vocabulary. As much as 'Cancer' or 'Alzheimer's' or 'Abduction.' He nodded.

"And it was during that storm," Chris went on, "according to the article, that your sister disappeared." He paused again, waiting to see if Arthur had anything to add to what he'd already unpacked. But the elderly man continued with his silence, still rattled by what he was hearing. "It goes on to say that she was found...or else, she returned a couple weeks later, though that part was never quite clear. As weren't the facts about where she was or who she was with during the time she was gone. And so that's why this story is on this website, I suppose. Because there were a lot of questions that were never quite answered. Never answered at all really. Or at least not during the time she disappeared and this newspaper article was written." Chris shrugged. "And when things don't piece together properly, people like to fill in those gaps with their own theories. As I'm sure you're aware, Mr. Richland."

He scooted the chair forward until it was touching the frame of the bed and his face was only a foot or so from Arthur's.

"So, the reason I'm here, Mr. Richland, is I was hoping you had one. A theory, that is, about what happened to your sister."

Arthur stared coldly into Chris' eyes now. "How did you find me?" he snapped, suddenly feeling cornered. A conversation that to that point had been both startling and revealing now felt contentious.

"Your name is mentioned in the article, Mr. Richland. Yours and James'. Your younger brother."

"I know who my brother was!" The shout was unnecessary, but Arthur suddenly couldn't control his emotions. "I'm sorry, I just..."

Chris ignored both the outburst and the apology and got to the point. "There was a storm last week. A dust storm as bad as any we've had in these parts in a very long time. Maybe you saw it on the news."

It was a few days before the stabbing, the day before he'd seen them in the parking lot of Stratford Manor. Arthur was aware of the storm.

"Anyway, as you might have seen, during that storm there was a pile up of cars on Interstate 412. A couple of people died. And at a point during that storm, during the chaos of the accidents and the..."

Chris paused and closed his eyes, recalling the day once more, the day that he would have died a thousand deaths if it meant he could undo just one of the decisions he'd made that led to Jaycee's disappearance. He'd replayed the day in his mind so many times he sometimes felt like he was there again. Like he was *then* again. Except in his rerun of that day, he took 40 instead of 412, and he paid close attention to the road instead of screwing with the air control. And, most of all, he never left to help the couple in the Mercedes. He stayed in the truck with Jaycee. *Goddamn it, why didn't he stay with her?*

"Well...during the storm my daughter disappeared. She just vanished from my pickup truck like she'd been...plucked into the atmosphere by some invisible hand. You asked about the police. You asked where they thought she was. Well, to be honest, by the end of their interview with me, they all but accused me of making the whole thing up. Of making Jaycee up. Said the way I told it, it was impossible for her to have gotten so far away in that short span of time. That there was nowhere she could have gone that they wouldn't have found her. And though I was pissed at the time, terrified and angry and confused, I knew they were right. Still know it. There *was* nowhere she could have gone. If it wasn't for my ex-wife confirming that I had taken Jaycee that day, and that I would never have done anything to hurt my daughter, I would have either been dismissed as a schizophrenic or thrown in jail for abduction and murder."

Chris spoke with bullet-like rapidity now, as if all he was saying had been memorized in a specific way and then corked inside his mind, and if he didn't recite it in a precise cadence, he might leave something unsaid, something that might convince the man before him to help. He cleared his throat, resetting. "As it stands now though, they have nothing to go on. Nothing at all. The only rational theory is that at some point during those four or five minutes that I was away from her, someone came and took her. But there was no way a car could have gotten in and out of that part of the interstate during the pile up. The road was entirely blocked. And she's only six, so she couldn't have walked far. I just..." A tear was creeping toward the surface and Chris quickly blinked it away. "I'm just looking for other theories now, I guess. And the story about your sister is one I'm pursuing."

Arthur listened intensely to the man who was unloading his heart onto him, Arthur Richland, a stranger, some senile old nursing home patient who, for all the man knew when he first stepped foot into the room couldn't tell his big toe from his dick. Chris Boylin was a man who was desperate, as desperate as Arthur's mother had been during the two weeks Ruby was gone.

And the truth was, Arthur did know the answer. Or at least he knew the story behind the girl's disappearance. He knew it better than anyone else alive.

Arthur held out his hand, reaching for the additional pieces of paper. "May I?"

Chris nodded quickly. "Of course," he said and then passed the crumpled sheets to Arthur with a shaky hand.

Arthur read the remaining pages of the website piece in silence, stillness. Most of it contained information Arthur didn't recognize, details that were either grossly inaccurate or had simply been made up by whoever had written it. But there was something in between the words, a solemness in the theme of the piece that, though all the facts weren't correct, landed heavy on Arthur's mind. He handed the pages back to Chris and asked, "What is it you want to know?"

Chris was bolstered, but he tempered his excitement, not wanting his hopes to rise too high and then explode in a regurgitation of elderly confusion. "Anything," he said. "Everything. Everything you can remember about the day she disappeared. Anything you can about how...how she came back." The tears were streaming now, and Chris made no attempt to dam them.

Arthur gave a weary smile and nodded. He had always assumed this day would come, though he'd begun to doubt it with every passing year. The day when he would cleanse his mind of the wickedness from his childhood in rural New Mexico, of those days and weeks during the fall when he was only twelve. He was an old man now, his mind in less than perfect condition, but he still knew the importance of his tale, that he would tell it aloud one day, and thus he'd kept it fresh in his mind. Or at least moist and available. It was a strange thing about growing old, the way the mind purged itself of the more current events to keep space for the memories of old. And though Arthur wasn't as bad as some in the haunted house he now called home, he hadn't avoided dementia entirely. He forgot things almost daily, and he wasn't above the humiliation and depression that came with that. The name of his only child sometimes slipped, his son who had died almost two decades earlier in a small airplane accident, an accident he always loosely attributed to the spirits of the Tompiros, though there was never any evidence connecting the two.

And the memory of his wife had faded as well, the woman who had left Arthur the day after their son's graduation, leaving only a note that said she was sorry, but that she hadn't been happy in twenty years.

And yet most of what had deteriorated, the names and dates, were of things that had occurred since he'd become a seasoned man. And the more recent the name or event, the harder it was to recall. If you asked him the name of the current vice president, he would have scoffed at the difficulty of the question.

But he remembered Clayton in 1939. He couldn't have forgotten that section of his life if he'd been tortured into doing so.

"My first real memory of Ruby," Arthur began, "of really spending time with her, was when she was five. The day we went to Downes' Grocery."

Chapter 7

Clayton, New Mexico
1939

"ARTHUR, YOUR SHOES!"

Dotty Richland barked at her son without ever taking her eyes away from the ground below her and the wooden steps she swept with vigor. It was a chore she performed at least ten times a day now, sweeping as if Jesus Himself were about to walk up the stairs. And that was just the stoop. When you added in the interior floors of the home and the back porch, Dotty had a broom in her hand more than she didn't. If she wasn't eating or sleeping or washing the dishes, she was sweeping.

"I know, Ma," Arthur replied. "I'll leave 'em out."

"Storm last night. Another one. Grace of God we was all in bed by then. Take me a week to get this dirt up though."

Less than a month had passed since the first of the storms had arrived, but already Arthur couldn't remember a world without dust. There wasn't a morning that landed now when he didn't wake with it in his eyes and hair, when it didn't coat the bottom of his feet by the time he walked from his bed to the front door each morning—a trek that was no more than twelve or thirteen steps—and then outside to the outhouse to relieve himself. Dust was now as common to Arthur's existence as water was to a fish's, and in only a few short weeks, he'd gotten used to it. Or at least accepting of it.

And though the dust didn't bother Arthur so much anymore, the storms that brought them still did, making him as anxious as a crooked mayor each time one arrived from the east. He envied Jimmy's ability to sleep through them, including the one that came through the previous night, while he, Arthur, cringed beneath the covers like a kitten as he waited for it to pass.

But pass it did, and by the time school was over and Arthur was back at home, the only memory of it was the dust that coated the world, and the order from his mother to keep his shoes off in the house.

"How'd you do on that biology test today?" Dotty asked.

"It was civics," Arthur replied, now sitting on the porch bench as he removed his shoes. "Biology is tomorrow. I think I did good though. Got my math test back from yesterday and got a 48 out of 50."

"Hmmm. Well, we'll get those two the next time, yeah?"

Arthur shrugged.

"Where's your brother?" Dotty gave an aggressive trio of sweeps in the crease between the top two steps and then leaned on the broom, looking at her son expectantly, one eyebrow raised. "Arthur, did you hear me?"

"Yes, ma'am. He said he was going with Bucky?"

Dotty frowned and scanned the barren landscape suspiciously. "Bucky, huh?"

Arthur nodded.

"Hmm. Parents are fools, but I guess the boy's alright. If not a bit foolish himself," she added. "Just going to his house or what?"

Arthur shrugged again.

"Well, you should know that, Arthur. James is your little brother. He ain't by much, but he's younger'n you still. Means he's your responsibility when he ain't in the stead of me and your Pa. You get that?"

Arthur nodded. *Not really.*

"So, when your brother says he's going with Bucky, you ask him *where* he's going with Bucky. Who else is going. Anything to fill out the story. See?"

"Yes, ma'am." This concern for Jimmy and his whereabouts was nothing new, but it had certainly been enhanced since the first of the storms arrived three weeks earlier. News about their arrival in Texas and Oklahoma had spread quickly in the papers, and fears that they would be coming to New Mexico were well-founded. And though Jimmy was eleven years old and as resourceful as a combat marine, to Arthur, it sometimes seemed his mother still worried about him as if he were a toddler.

"We're heading to the fair in a few days, and I'ma trusting you kids to look out for each other while were there. Y'all gonna be able to do that, right?"

Arthur nodded with conviction, showing he was one hundred percent able to do that. He didn't want anything to risk the trip to the fair. It had been his one desire since his father had made the announcement at the beginning of the month.

"Mama?" The chirp came from behind Dotty, and she turned to the voice with a rapid spin, moving slightly to her left as she did, exposing Ruby, Arthur's younger sister. She stood at the threshold of the house like a giant doll, smiling.

"Well look at you there, baby girl," Dotty said. "A little early to be up from your nap."

Ruby had stopped napping two years earlier, but she carried out the ruse anyway, always staying in her room until a reasonable amount of time had passed to come out. Her mother knew she wasn't napping, of course, and Ruby knew her mother knew it. It was a charade, and Arthur could never quite understand why they played the game.

"I'm not tired," Ruby announced, a refrain that was almost a reflex at this point. She looked at her brother and waved. "Hi, Arthur."

Arthur glanced up at his sister, who was smiling expectantly now, hopefully, her mop of red hair falling unrulily over the front of her face, making her look both ridiculous and beautiful. Ruby was only five, but her size—she was quite tall for her age—and facial features suggested she would be stunning to look at when she was older. It wasn't something Arthur normally noticed in girls, even ones his own age, but Ruby was different in a way that even a kid from the plains could recognize.

But there was more different in Ruby than just her size and hair and beauty, and it was something Arthur had recognized in her before she turned two. She was smart, no doubt on that, but it was more than that: she was *aware*, cognizant of things around her that few others would have noticed, even adults. When she was maybe three—and Arthur was ten—their father had scolded Arthur for breaking the metal latch on his new lunchbox, and though Arthur had taken the scolding with his typical stoicism, the lash of the reprimand had landed on Arthur's heart with an unusual sting. But he'd only nodded at his father in conciliation and then began his walk to school, squeezing the tears back long enough to get out of range. Ruby had run up behind him that day and grabbed his hand, pulling her brother down with a hefty tug and kissing his cheek. Arthur never forgot the sad smile on her face that day, one which suggested she understood his pain, but also that everything would be fine.

And that was only one example of Ruby's uniqueness. Maybe six months after the lunchbox incident, she'd simply picked up one of her mother's Reader's Digests (which at the time was being used to steady the dining table and had slipped free from the foot), and the words on the page to which she'd opened simply began to spill from her mouth. Many of the words Arthur himself couldn't have read at the time, that was for sure, and it was probably true of their father as well.

"Arthur, take your sister inside and give her her snack please. And get yours too. I made some sandwiches with jelly. And..." Dotty gave a slight grin and cocked an eyebrow "...they had Twinkies at the market today, so I splurged."

"Twinkies!" Arthur repeated.

"Twinkies!" Ruby parroted with a smile, keeping her eyes on her brother. Arthur caught the look and was suddenly embarrassed. She didn't care about the Twinkies for herself; she was happy because Arthur was happy.

Arthur and Ruby ate their snack together, and by the time they were done, Ruby had a frown on her face, a look of indecision in her eyes.

"What's going on, Rube?" Arthur asked. "Did you have a good day today? What'd you do 'sides take a nap? You reading anything interestin'?"

She shook her head and shrugged. "*The Hobbit*."

"Again? What's that? Five times now?"

Ruby shrugged again and forced a smile. "I don't know. Prob'ly more than that."

Arthur smiled and shook his head, never ceasing to be impressed by his younger sister. But the grim look on Ruby's face remained. "What else, Rube? Somethin' wrong?"

Ruby looked up at her brother studiously, her eyes in a squint now. "Did you hear the storm last night?"

Arthur nodded. "Of course. Doozy. Did it scare you?"

Ruby thought about it and shook her head lightly. "Not so much. Not the storm really. It's what was in the storm that scared me more."

The slightest of shivers ran through Arthur, like a breath of breeze hitting his lake-soaked body on a warm summer's day. "What do you mean by that?"

Ruby paused, unsure of how to proceed. She was a smart kid—brilliant, maybe—but she was still only five, and the look was one Arthur recognized as frustration, the inability to explain exactly what she was trying to say.

"I heard somethin' in the wind last night. Or maybe not in the wind exactly, but...I don't know...between the wind."

Between the wind? Arthur couldn't even comprehend the phrase. "Heard what?"

Ruby looked at her brother shamefaced, reluctant to answer. Finally, she acquiesced and said, "Sounded like a voice."

Arthur flinched and stifled a cough, covering the nervousness by clearing his throat. He didn't know exactly what answer he was expecting, but it wasn't the one Ruby had given. He smiled uneasily and asked, "There's no voices in the wind Rube—or between it—but I know the feeling you mean. I hate the storms too. Hate 'em like beets and cabbage." Arthur lowered his voice and peeked outside, not wanting his mother to hear his criticism of her food. He then said, "But they's nothing but wind and dust, and sometimes those things get to blowing so hard it sounds like it's talking to you."

"But you said you didn't hear it."

Arthur cocked his head, ceding the point. "Yeah, but everyone's ears is different. I probably did hear it, it's just instead of voices, to me it sounded like the regular wind. You understand?" Ruby gave a genuine nod, and Arthur was proud to have set her mind at ease for now. "Did you wake Ma? Let her know?"

Ruby slept on a small mattress in their parent's bedroom, while Arthur and Jimmy shared a bed in the only other bedroom in the house. At Arthur's question, Ruby shook her head emphatically, as if the query were a preposterous one. She would never have woken either of her parents for something as base as howling wind, and Arthur knew it.

"I get it, Rube. I wouldn't have waked 'em either." He giggled and lowered his voice. "Specially Pa."

This caused Ruby to laugh too, but just for a moment. Soon, she was back to wearing the worried look from seconds earlier.

Arthur frowned. "Dang, Rube, you really are scared by them storms."

Ruby sighed. "But that's just it though, Arthur. I wasn't. Not until the one last night. The first ones didn't scare me much at all. But then, like I said, I heard the voice."

"Come on now, Ruby. Did you just hear what I told you or not? That was just the whistling of the wind." Arthur looked toward the door and their mother again, who had now descended the stairs and was looking out toward the landscape once more. "To be honest with you though, Rube, I can't sleep much at all when they come. And even though most people think the ones that come in the day are scarier—cuz we have to find shelter and all—I'd rather those than the night ones. Less scary in the daytime you ask me. Doesn't get in your head and make you see and hear things."

Ruby gave a sad smile at Arthur's confession, and Arthur thought the look almost patronizing, as if she appreciated Arthur's advice but that it wasn't quite right. "I guess," she said and then took a nibble of the crust left over on her plate from the jelly sandwich.

Arthur knew his sister wasn't fully convinced, and though she was bright, five-year-olds still made things up. It was the ideal age for that type of thing, he thought. So, he played along further, delving into the specifics. "What does the voice say?" he asked.

Ruby paused. "It said a name."

Athur furrowed his brow. "A name? That's what it said? '*A name*?'" Arthur started repeating the phrase ominously: '*a name,*' '*a name.*'

Ruby shook her head quickly, irritated. "No! It was the name of a person. I think. I didn't know it, but it soun—"

"Your father's home," Dotty announced, stepping briskly into the home. There was a brightness in her voice that she usually reserved for special occasions, which, apparently, at least on that day, their father arriving home by four o'clock counted as one. But Arthur knew the tone was manufactured, an attempt to offset the sullenness that was soon to arrive.

Randall Richland worked at Chester Sutton's Garage and Service Station, the one and only service station in Clayton, New Mexico, and one of the oldest of its type in the state. Arthur's father had worked there since he, Randall, was in high school, first as a store clerk, years before there were such things as 'service stations,' and later learning on-the-fly the trade of repairing cars, eventually establishing himself in the community as 'the mechanic' in town, a label which he both seemed to accept and resent. He was proud to be a mechanic, someone who could fix things that others couldn't, but he resented what he deemed a lack of appreciation for his services from the residents of Clayton, and certainly from Chester Sutton himself.

"You're home early," Dotty said nonchalantly, not looking up as she swept the area of the floor beneath the sink, which, if she swept it any further, the floorboards would have started to splinter.

"No point staying at work when there ain't nothing to do," Randall grumbled. "Coulda been home three hours ago, wouldn'ta mattered an eyelash."

"Guess that's right." Dotty had learned years ago not to try to inspire or look on the bright side of things when it came to Randall's dourness, so, as per usual, she changed the subject. "In other news, your son got an 'A' on his math test today. Isn't that right, Arthur?"

Randall looked at his son for the first time since entering the house, scanning the length of him as he frowned. "Gonna be a mathematician when you get older?"

There was nothing in Randall's tone to suggest the question was a joke, but Arthur snickered anyway. "No, sir. Not good enough at it for that."

"Then what am I supposed to do with the information your mother just gave me?"

"Randall!" Dotty snapped, one hand on her hip now, the other still holding the broom at her side like a staff. "Don't be taking your sullenness out on Arthur. Slow day at work ain't a call for that."

Randall looked away sheepishly; he was a rough-around-the-edges man, for sure, and often an asshole—no one in town would have argued that, as demonstrated by the moment at hand—but he was deferential to his wife on most occasions, and he took strides where possible to avoid fights with her. "Where's Jim?"

Of the three kids, Jimmy was Randall's favorite, a fact that, even at five years old, Ruby knew to be true.

"He went home with a friend after school."

"Hmm. He was s'possed to help with the truck today, so let me know when he gets in. Gotta get that wheel right. Thing's still wobbling like Darrel Crocker on a Friday night."

Dotty frowned. "Honestly, Randy," she scolded, "Darrel Crocker's a friend of yours and a good man."

"Didn't say he wasn't. Just a drunk is all."

Arthur could feel the burn in his mother to chide their father further, but that would have just kept the conversation going, so she clucked and shook her head and continued to sweep.

"In any case, we ain't making it to Albuquerque or anywhere else if it don't get fixed, so wake me up if I'm sleeping when Jimmy gets in, will ya? Just gonna hose off and lay down for a few minutes."

"I'll let you know," Dotty replied, and then she immediately smiled sadly at Arthur, who shrugged and smiled back.

Arthur knew he should have taken it as a slight that his father was waiting on his younger brother—and not him—to help fix the truck's bum wheel, but he was used to the preference by now, and it honestly didn't bother him. In fact, he was more concerned about how *his mother* would react in instances where his father passed him over for Jimmy. But his brother had a different connection with their father than Arthur did—or Ruby for that matter—and no amount of pandering or pouting was going to change that. Randall Richland cared for his two other kids—Arthur believed that to be true—but he loved Jimmy. And besides, when it came to things like the issue with the truck's wheel, love wasn't really the determinant. Jimmy was a natural with all things mechanical, while Arthur had yet to go near the toaster on the counter, the one his mother had won in a raffle a year earlier.

"You know what, Arthur," Dotty said, suddenly wearing an inquisitive look. "I forgot something from the store today. I knew I had a miss the second I walked out, but by the time I remembered what it was, I was already stuffing the cupboards with the things I bought."

"Whadya forget?" Arthur asked.

Dotty paused, clearly stalling for an answer. "Those jelly sandwiches you ate, I believe that was the last of it. The jelly, I mean. Got a little too excited about those Twinkies, I guess, and passed right over the Welch's." She gave a weak smile.

"We'll just have tomato and cheese tomorrow. It's okay."

"Arthur, I'm asking you to go into town to get me another jar."

Arthur knew his mother was trying to make him feel useful, and though he appreciated her concern, he could have done without the chore. "Uh, okay, sure. Now?"

"Well, yes, now. When else? You leave any later it'll be dark by the time you're on your way back."

"Yes ma'am," Arthur replied, half whining, half agreeing, wanting his mother to understand she wasn't really making him feel better. "I'll need money, won't I?"

Dotty shook her head. "I've still got a dollar and twenty credit at Downes', so you won't. And take Ruby with you. Give you both something to do until supper."

Arthur normally would have put up more of a debate—feigning homework or plans he'd forgotten about with friends—but with his father home and in a bad mood, a walk into town didn't sound so bad.

Downes' Grocery was at the far end of town—about a mile walk—and Arthur and Ruby reached the store in just under thirty minutes. A handful of cars passed them along the way, kicking up dust and honking their hellos as they sped by, and by the time the siblings reached the front of the grocery store, they were filthy. From hair to shoes they each looked as if they'd crawled out of the Ditches, and neither could help but laugh as they spotted themselves in the reflection of Downes' storefront window.

It was late afternoon by the time the kids walked into the store, and though the rest of the shops in town were closing for the day, Downes' had at least another hour until they shuttered for the night.

"Is that Arthur Richland?" a voice called just seconds after the bell above the door rang with a muffled tinkle, indicating Arthur and Ruby's arrival. It was Mrs. Flannery. She was standing at the counter, glasses low on her nose as she stared toward the kids. She had a pencil in her hand and an open book on the countertop below her.

"Hi, Mrs. Flannery."

Janet Flannery was the adult daughter of Raymond Downes, the entrepreneur who had come to Clayton in the 1920's and built his store from the ground up, ushering into their otherwise common town a new way for women to market, one in which many around the country even by the 1940s didn't enjoy. His idea had been to organize the food in aisles, and to allow people the freedom to walk around the store and pick their own items, as opposed to handing their lists over to a grocer. These were novel luxuries in those days, especially in rural New Mexico, as was the store's proximity to the butcher shop. Mr. Downes had purposely picked the location right next door to Belton's Meats, knowing that women would appreciate the convenience of being able to walk right next door to complete their shopping.

But Raymond Downes never realized his vision fully, having suffered a massive stroke in 1934 and dying a year later. And with the founder and pioneer of Downes' now deceased, many feared the store would close for good, or be sold and converted to the town's first hotel, or even another bar, and that the women of Clayton would be forced to drive to Harding County for their groceries. God forbid.

But Raymond's daughter Janet had been determined to keep the store running—and to improve it, where possible—and though her husband Glenn was technically the store's owner and manager now, being that he was a man and it was more proper that way, it was Janet, at least as far as Arthur could tell, who did most of the work. She was certainly the only one who did any managing. She never *wasn't* at the store when Arthur came in, while, when it came to Glenn Flannery, it was the opposite. Arthur couldn't remember a time he'd seen him in Downes', though he'd often spotted him coming in or out of The Patio, the only dedicated bar in town.

"Your mother was just in here this morning, Arthur. She forgotten somethin'?"

"Yes, ma'am. Jelly."

"Hmm. Can't be having no jelly in the house, that's for sure. Aisle is four. A quarter way down, middle shelf."

"Thank you, ma'am."

"Hi, Ruby," Janet called, ducking low with a wave and a stock smile she kept on tap for kids. But the exhaustion in the woman was palpable, and the smile waned in seconds, morphing into a sigh and a frown, a culmination of expressions that reflected both the things she had in her life, as well as those she'd sacrificed. Her nephew Ralph Brater was the closest thing she had to kids, and he was hardly her favorite person in the world.

"Hi, Mrs. Downes," Ruby replied.

"It's 'Flannery'," Arthur corrected through gritted teeth.

"Oh, it's alright," Mrs. Flannery chimed quickly. "Most in town wish my name *was* still Downes." And with that, Janet Flannery gave a genuine laugh, and though it was one that came at the expense of her husband, she didn't care. She was the one working, while he wouldn't be seen for another four hours, likely stumbling into the house with a plastered smile and grabby hands. "Aisle four, kids. Call me when you're ready, and I'll adjust your mama's tab."

The store was empty of customers except for Arthur and Ruby, and finding the jar of Welch's Concord took less than a minute once the search was afoot. But by the time the kids returned to the front counter and Janet Flannery had crossed off the $1.20 on their mother's credit list and replaced it with a .90¢, the sky had turned from cyan to taupe, and the dust from the whip of the wind made the air outside look like a cloud of sand had suddenly towered from the earth.

"Will you look at that," Janet Flannery said. "Another one already? Still got six inches of dust piled on the stoop from last night."

Arthur held the jar of jelly like a torch as he stared hypnotically at this new development in the atmosphere. And he knew this was just the precursor, the foreshadowing of the real storm that would be arriving in seconds. He couldn't see the approaching tempest from inside the store, but he knew just the same it was on its way. "We should hurry up, Rube. Ma's gonna be worried."

"Hurry where, Arthur?" Janet answered. "You're not going anywhere until this is passed. You think your legs is faster than the wind?"

Arthur shrugged.

"They ain't. If you was a mustang you couldn't outrun these dang storms. 'Sides, your mother's gonna know you took shelter and be glad you did. And she'd kill me with good right if I let y'all go. Y'all get a telephone yet?"

Arthur shook his head.

"Alright, well no use worrying then. Y'all are fine now, and you will be when you get home within the next hour or two. In the meantime, let's get on back from the door in case."

Janet shuffled the kids toward the aisles and then paced quickly back to the front door, bolting it locked before joining the kids again in the middle of aisle 3.

"We'll just wait it out here. Won't be but a few minutes. Hopefully, the electric doesn't leave us. Either way, y'all'll have a story to tell when you get home, right? Arthur and Ruby's Great Adventure at Downes' Grocery."

The heavy wind arrived within the minute, and Arthur watched through the window as brush and dust and sticks and trash blew past the store. All the while, he waited for the large pane of glass to give and then the rush of air to follow, filling the store in seconds, consuming them like a buggy in a twister. And then he thought of less dramatic things, all the dust and dirt that would be left behind, and all the sweeping his mother had done that day and would have to start again tomorrow. It was as if none of the work she'd spent all day doing mattered. It made him want to laugh and cry at once.

The whistling started now as the air began to fill the crevices of Clayton, hissing through porches and door cracks, fenders and fences, and Arthur looked to Ruby with a teetering smile that said, *See? I hear it too*.

But Ruby didn't see her brother, as she wasn't looking at anything at all. Her eyes were closed, and it appeared she was listening.

"Ruby?"

Something large and hard smashed against the storefront window, and Janet Flannery shrieked, causing Arthur to scream as well. The woman put her arm around Arthur and gave him a shake. "Sorry, hon, the noise just scared me." She sighed. "Whatever that was is gonna cost me something, I'm sure, though I can't see any scars from here. Here's hoping anyway." Janet looked down at Ruby. "Ruby, you alright, baby?"

Ruby opened her eyes and stared at the inheritor of Downes' Grocery, but there was no smile of reassurance. She locked eyes with the woman for a moment and then dropped them instantly, nodding weakly.

"It'll all be over in a moment."

And like that, it was. The storm ended with a final whistle—like a train coming into the station—and the beaver-brown air slowly turned to tan and then clear. In fewer than ten minutes, other than the debris and the newly added layer of dust that now coated the ground outside, it was as if the storm had never happened.

Janet, Arthur, and Ruby walked uneasily to the front of the store, and after a fleeting inspection of her window—which appeared undamaged—Mrs. Flannery unlocked the door and opened it wide, allowing in the dusky sunlight and surprisingly clean air. The storm was gone, and the sky above had returned to its natural blue.

Soon, the other shop owners and customers who remained in town made their way into the street, each wearing an expression that reflected both relief and foreboding as they scanned Main Street in both directions.

"Hey there, stranger," Janet said suddenly, clearing her throat.

Arthur didn't see who Janet was addressing at first, but then, through the lingering haze, he saw a man approaching the store from the direction of The Patio, which was one block down and one over. In a moment, Arthur recognized him as Glenn Flannery. He was a shortish man, ten years older than Janet, maybe more, and though Arthur had only experienced him indirectly, despite his perceived indolence, there was always a good-naturedness about him, never without a smile and a pat on the back to any chap passing by.

But his stride today was steady and focused, seemingly homed in on Janet, toward whom he marched like a wind-up toy soldier.

"You kids get on home now," Janet said, her voice distant and wary as she followed the steps of her husband.

Arthur didn't know the Flannerys well, and he knew even less about their relationship to each other. But there was a crackle in Janet Flannery's voice that was unusual, and Arthur knew she was unsettled by her husband's stiff gait and steady gaze.

"Don't let your ma worry any more than she has to," she added, and with that, Janet Flannery re-entered Downes' Grocery and closed the door behind her.

"Let's go, Rube," Arthur said.

Ruby hesitated a beat, and as Arthur grabbed her hand and pulled her along, she resisted, just for a moment, until her brother finally tugged her along. In minutes, they were back on the road and on their way home.

"HAVEN'T SEEN YOU WALK that straight in two years," Janet admonished, her eyes again on the accounting sheet that was spread out on the counter, not looking up when the bell rang again, her husband entering the store for the first time that day. "At least not at this time of day." The footsteps clicked steadily toward the counter, but Janet remained fixed on the numbers beneath her. "Did the Patio run dry or you ju—"

Janet's mouth stiffened on the final word of her question, hanging agape like a dental patient being checked for cavities. And just as Glenn Flannery drove the tip of the screwdriver into the side of his wife's head, sliding it in with a squishing plunge until the length of the shaft was covered with skull up to the base of the handle, Janet looked up from the ledger to see her husband's face one last time.

And then Glenn released his hand from the screwdriver, and Janet's head smacked down to the counter, her body hanging like a fish on a hook for just a beat before dripping to the floor, dead.

"THAT WAS PRETTY SCARY, huh?" Arthur said uneasily.

Ruby stayed silent, walking slightly behind Arthur, who had to keep downshifting his stride to stay beside her.

"Ruby?"

Ruby looked over at her brother.

"What's wrong *now*?" The question sounded harsh in Arthur's ears, uncaring, so he rephrased it. "What's wrong, Ruby?"

"Remember...remember how I told you I heard a name in the storm last night?"

Arthur sighed and nodded, reluctant to resuscitate this conversation but playing along anyway. "Yeah."

"I heard it again."

Arthur sighed and then stopped walking, and Ruby stopped beside him. "Heard it when?"

"Just now. When we were in the store. With Mrs. Dow...Flannery."

"What did you hear?"

"It was like before. A name, like I said. I didn't know who it was before, what it was saying really." Ruby paused. "But I think I do now. I *know* I know."

Arthur kept quiet, waiting.

"It was 'Glenn Flannery.' That was the name I heard last night. And today."

The revelation sent a wave of distress through Arthur, and he felt his throat constrict at the sound of the name that had just been released from his sister's lips. Had it been Jimmy who said it, or one of Arthur's friends from school, he would have shucked it off, assumed they were pranking him, riling him up like they all did with ghost stories at sleepovers. But Ruby was only five, and no matter how smart she was, she didn't have the wherewithal to pull up Glenn Flannery that way, a person whose name Arthur doubted she'd ever heard before that day. And she wasn't Jimmy; she didn't have the devious kind of mind that would have wanted to spook Arthur.

Glenn Flannery.

As the name registered in Arthur's mind, it triggered a thought of the store again, Downes', and then of their purpose for being there.

The jelly.

In the chaos of the storm and the insistence of Mrs. Flannery to head home, he'd forgotten it.

"We have to go back, Rube."

"What?" Ruby immediately began to shake her head, and Arthur could see she was terrified at the thought of returning.

"I forgot the Welch's. Ma'll have mine if I don't come back with it—especially after being docked for it—and it won't put Pa in no better mood neither."

Ruby's posture melted, but she acquiesced, hearing in Arthur's voice that she wasn't going to change her older brother's mind. And within minutes, the siblings were back at the front door of Downes' Grocery.

"Look at that," Ruby whispered.

At first, Arthur didn't catch it; his mind was focused only on the jelly as his hand gripped the doorknob to enter. "Look at wh—"

And then Arthur saw it. The storefront window—which had appeared undamaged when Arthur and Ruby left for home—was now a network of broken glass. The large slab was still in place, but it was completely shattered into a pane of mesh, the shattered shards webbing out in every direction.

"It wasn't even chipped when we left," Arthur uttered.

"What is that, Arthur?" Ruby's voice shook now, coughing and panting the way it did just before she was about to cry.

Arthur could count on one hand the times he'd heard Ruby cry since about the time she turned four, so when she made that sound, Arthur took note. "Ruby, what's—"

"Look!" Ruby shrieked.

For a moment, Arthur thought his sister's voice would send the precarious glass to the ground. But the pane held, and through the tangle of exploded crystal that was now Downes' storefront window, a shape appeared, or an outline of a shape, framed by a continuous line of yellow light. It glowed steadily for a few seconds, and then it began to move, upright and confidently, as if walking away from a task it had just completed. A second later, two more shapes appeared, identical to the first, but separate from each other, their shimmering bodies side by side.

And then one of the shapes rotated at the top, and Arthur could see a face, or the glow of a face, and then it turned back and was gone, disappearing with its companions into the empty space near the middle of the store, likely in the same aisle where Ruby and Arthur had taken shelter minutes earlier. The whole sighting lasted only three or four seconds, but Arthur would have sworn—if anyone had asked him at the time—that the lights were alive, organic.

"Arthur?" Ruby said. Her voice was calm now, and though she didn't ask the question aloud, she was staring at her brother with eyes that asked, *did you see that too?*

Arthur pressed his hand against his chest and took a deep breath, nodding.

"Okay," Ruby said, nodding back, as if consoled that she wasn't alone with the sighting. And then, to Arthur's surprise, she added, "Open it."

Arthur inhaled and opened the door, and as the two children stood at the threshold of Downes' Grocery, the remaining citizens of Clayton began to run toward the store, all of them coming to see why Ruby Richland was screaming.

Chapter 8

Chris Boylin hung on every word, and by the end of the story, he was nearly hyperventilating. The storm. The shapes of light in the store. He knew even before Arthur Richland described them that what he and his sister had seen through the window was the same thing Chris had seen on the interstate. "How could you know about that?" he asked breathlessly.

Arthur was perplexed by the question at first, but then after a pause of consideration, he said, "Then you saw them as well." With this he smiled slightly, as if a pesky missing part of some enigma had finally been answered for good, or perhaps a doubted memory had been validated in the present.

"Can everyone see them?"

Arthur nodded the way a professor might, one taking a query from a particularly curious student. "That question has always been a mystery to me. Whether everyone could see them or just...the ones who were affected."

"Are they alive? What are they? How can...how can they be?"

Arthur couldn't process the questions as worded, and he closed his eyes and put a hand to his forehead. And then, he asked, "You saw them where your daughter was? When she disappeared?"

Chris nodded, and though on some level he felt comforted that what he had seen outside the windshield of the Mercedes and by his pickup was real, and that the electric figures hadn't been the result of a concussion or stress or a combination of the two, he was also frightened now, more so than before, terrified that Jaycee was more than just missing.

"What is it? What did I see? Is it...are they the same things that took Ruby?"

Arthur looked toward his bedroom window now, and as his eyes landed on the lawn outside, they went blank and glossy. He opened his mouth to answer the man's question, but nothing came out. His memory, which had summoned the information about that day at Downes' only moments earlier, now felt depleted, his mind empty. It was funny, really: he had performed the act of forgetting for months with his granddaughter, gradually exaggerating his cognitive abilities with each week that passed, knowing she would only relinquish him to the nursing home if his condition worsened beyond her abilities. But now, as he began the story of Clayton and the arrival of the storms, it was happening for real. The fog over his thoughts felt heavy, like a dump truck full of mud had been deposited into his mind. He looked back to Chris, fear and pain in his eyes as he shook his head. "I don't know. I...I forgot. Who are you?"

"What?"

Arthur began to shake, and he hugged his arms close to his body. "I'm sorry. Where is Ruby?"

Chris stood and moved close to Arthur, sitting on the bed beside him. "It's okay, Mr. Richland," he said, comforting the old man. "Everything is okay." He put his hand at the top of Arthur's back and rubbed there gently until he could hear his breathing return to normal. "That's fine. You were telling me about that day at Downes' Grocery."

Arthur's eyes suddenly came to life again, and he blinked in relief as the thread suddenly returned. "Oh yes. Downes.'"

Chris didn't have a lot of direct experience with dementia or Alzheimer's patients, but as an EMT who'd answered more than one call responding to victims suffering from cognitive diseases, those who had fallen or wandered or became violent in some way, he had some. He knew about the good days and bad, times of fluidity and others of obliviousness. And though at first encounter Arthur Richland had seemed as fluid as anyone—certainly anyone his age who Chris had ever met—he was at Stratford Manor for a reason, and something in the retelling of his trauma at the grocery store had tripped a wire. Or maybe his mind was protecting him from dredging up of anymore past pain.

But Chris didn't have time for compassion, not now, not when Jaycee was lost somewhere in this world—or even in some other, if that's where this story was heading—and thus he wasn't prepared to let Arthur off the hook too easily. But he also knew scenarios like this were delicate, and simply imposing his will to hurry the elderly man along to some end of his own desire was pointless. His desperation to find Jaycee felt volcanic in his gut, but if he were to get the answers he wanted, he had to let Arthur proceed at his own pace. Chris knew he could get there, he just had to guide him along.

"Did they find him?" he asked. "Glenn Flannery?"

Arthur smiled, as if the gap in his story had never occurred. "There was no one to find," he said. "Glenn Flannery, he never ran."

Chris took a breath, relieved to have Arthur back on track. But the path was precarious, and though he needed to keep it direct, he tried to go slowly. "Did he ever say *why* he did it? Why he killed his wife?"

Arthur shook his head. "He said he didn't know. Didn't remember a thing in fact, not until a minute or more after he killed the poor woman. Just after he found himself under a pile of bodies that included Ray Smith and Jeb Neeble, neither of whom weighed less than two-fifty." Arthur shrugged. "That was his defense anyway, and it didn't work out too well for him."

"What about the lights, Mr. Richland? The shapes? Did he mention seeing them at all? You and Ruby saw them, so he must have too." The vacant stare from Arthur again, and Chris quickly brought it back to Arthur's current place in the plot. "It didn't work well, you said? Glenn Flannery's defense? He was found guilty then?"

With this question, Arthur nodded solemnly. "Died in the electric chair within ten months of his conviction. Wouldn't be another man executed in New Mexico for five more years. Made a bit of news back then as you might expect." He lifted the pile of printed paper from his lap. "I saw the execution was mentioned in the piece here, so your website guy got that part right."

Careful not to push too hard, Chris next asked, "What do *you* think, Arthur? Do *you* think he saw what you and Ruby did? Like the article suggests?"

"I can only tell you what *I* saw. And that it certainly didn't happen like it was written. That nonsense about Glenn Flannery spewing on about the Devil..." He shook his head in disappointment. "Janet Flannery was the only one there when it happened, and there was no way she could have told her story after the fact. And by the time me and Ruby got there, like I said, he was just standing there in a stupor, like he didn't know what planet he was living on."

Chris didn't mention that Arthur himself had described the killing, including the words Janet had uttered just before the screwdriver went into her temple. But that wasn't relevant, he supposed, and he assumed a certain local lore had worked its way into the story and Arthur had allowed for it. Besides, calling the man out on details like that not only wouldn't help the story along, it was likely to derail it.

"But you do think what happened at Downes' was connected to your sister's disappearance?" he asked.

Arthur shook his head slowly. "I don't *think* a thing, Mr. Boylin—about whether Janet Flannery's killing had to do with what happened to Ruby—I know it did. Glenn Flannery killed his wife that day, but he wasn't responsible for her death. No more than Lois..." he broke off the comparison with a shake of his head, not wanting to comingle the incident from the cafeteria with those of his youth. "And if anyone had bothered to ask me about it back then, I would've told 'em so. Though, if I'm honest, by the time I knew there was a connection to be made, with the Ditches and the altar and the storms that would follow, it was too late to change the minds of anyone who might have sympathized with Glenn Flannery."

Chris waited for Arthur to clarify this last segment of the story, but when nothing else came from the elderly man, he asked, "So, if Glenn wasn't responsible, who was?"

Arthur furrowed his brow, as if the answer were as obvious as the first letter of the alphabet. "It was my brother Jimmy's fault," he replied. "Him and his friends."

Chapter 9

Jimmy Richland turned right on Ranch Light Road, and based on the depth of the sun in the sky, he was very late for supper. And he was still a quarter mile from his house, having mistimed how long it would take for him to get from Lynnie Radich's house to his own on foot. If he had just been coming from the Ditches, the way he had a hundred times, there would have been no problem; but Lynnie Radich had come with the boys that day, claiming to have some special insight about the Ditches from her grandmother. Truth was though, even if she hadn't, not a one of the boys would have denied her the invitation. There weren't many pretty girls in Clayton, but Lynnie was one.

And after the exploration was complete, though Jimmy hadn't planned on walking Lynnie all the way home, she had asked him to, and he didn't take a second to oblige. He didn't get a peck or anything from her afterwards, but even still, whatever punishment awaited him when he walked through the door would be worth it.

Of course, Jimmy Richland wasn't going down that easily. He'd already planned his excuse for his parents and played it out in his mind a half dozen times. He'd hurt his knee falling off Bucky Mason's bike at the elementary school. *"We wasn't jumpin' or nothin' like that,"* he'd say, *"just hit a stray stick and it sent me soarin.'"* He'd even practiced his limp

on the way home—nothing too dramatic, he was no ama-
teur—just enough of a hobble to be noticed by a fussy mother.

But by the time Jimmy closed the gap to his house and
was fewer than two hundred yards away, he knew his parents
had more important matters to deal with than his fake injury. There was a car in the driveway that didn't belong to
the Richlands, and though Jimmy was too far out to see the
gold lettering and small red siren on the roof, he knew by the
shape and overall color it was Sheriff Brickell's police cruiser.

Jimmy stopped for a moment and stared at the scene in
front of his house, captivated by the spectacle as if it were
being projected upon the screen at the Lobo Theater in Albuquerque. He'd never seen a motion picture, of course, the
theater had only been open a year or two, but he'd heard stories from those who had, and he often imagined what his life
would look like from the seats of a cinema.

But this reverie lasted only seconds before he landed
back to earth, and then the adrenaline arrived, and Jimmy
began to run like he'd rarely done in his life, sprinting the
five-hundred feet or so to his property line as if his shoes
were on fire. And as he ran, he conjured other images, ones
of the sheriff telling his parents that Arthur had been found
dead. That he had fallen from a tree or a cliff and broken his
neck. Never felt a thing, thank God, but it was no less sad,
a boy so young. Or maybe it wasn't quite so gruesome as all
that. Maybe Arthur had just gone missing, and Dotty had
called the sheriff to send officers to look for him. And as Jimmy watched from afar, with the sheriff in the process of gath-

ering her statement, deputies where on the way now to Rabbit Ear Mountain to begin the search.

But Jimmy didn't *really* believe it was Arthur. God would never have been so cruel as to levy that news upon him. So, based on age alone, he assumed his father was the reason the sheriff had come. He had probably dropped dead at Chester's in the middle of his shift, pump in hand while some poor cross-country traveler looked around nervously, debating whether it was feasible for him to just drive away so as not to get caught up in some wild west police business. Sure, it was almost certainly Randall Richland who had died. Jimmy knew three kids his age whose fathers had all passed before turning fifty, and none from getting hit by a train or bitten by a rattler. The hearts of men in New Mexico were defective, or at least in Clayton they were, and even if no one talked about it, everybody knew it was true.

But as he neared their small house, Jimmy could see both Arthur and his father sitting beside each other on the porch bench, an old tree trunk that had been halved and preserved and propped with stones beside the front door for seating. Arthur's shoulders were narrowed and sunken, while Randall Richland leaned forward solemnly, elbows on his knees, hands clenched palm to palm. The sheriff sat in a dining chair across from them, while Dotty hugged Ruby from behind at the threshold of the door. It wasn't a setting that exuded celebration—Jimmy could tell that much—but at least his family was alive.

Jimmy approached the house nearly unnoticed, as the dirt drive came in from the main road on the side and was mostly blind from the front of the house. And when he reached a point about twenty feet from the porch, he stopped, standing beside the cruiser, winded and weary, watching the scene from this new angle as he waited to be noticed. Ruby saw him first (of course), and though she gave him a smile that was unhappy, it was also one that reflected she was pleased he was home. Jimmy only blinked and shook his head in return.

"James," his mother said finally. She glanced to the surrounding land, which was now only minutes from dusk. "You're late." There was no conviction in her voice; the admonishment was sheer reflex.

"I'm sorry. I..." He began telling the lie he'd practiced all walk but then aborted it in favor of the scoop. "What's happened?"

Dotty Richland swallowed nervously and looked at Sheriff Brickell. "Is it absolutely necessary you to talk to Ruby, sheriff? She's tired and still shaken. And what's she gonna say besides?"

"Fraid I do, Dotty. This was a serious thing happened today, and your girl was there. Saw as much as anyone."

"I know it, but Glenn...he admitted to it already. What else is there to know about what happened?"

"Admitted to what?" Jimmy jumped in. "What happened?"

Randall Richland looked at his watch and then to Jimmy. "Thought you was gonna help me with that wheel today."

"Huh?"

"The wheel on the truck. You remember? Needs fixing 'fore we can drive all the way to Albuquerque. You said you'd be home by five to help on it."

Jimmy looked at his father confused, and then he nodded. "Oh yeah. I...I'm sorry. I was down at the Ditches and..."

On the word 'Ditches,' Sheriff Brickell peeked up from his pad and gave a quick glance at Jimmy, letting his gaze hover for a moment before returning to his notes. As he wrote, he said, "Not supposed to be down those parts, James. Government's got a bead on that area. You know that. And they ain't gonna appreciate too much you kids dusting it up 'fore they even get to it."

Jimmy could have kicked himself for copping to the truth so easily, without even the slightest bit of pressure from his parents or the sheriff; but at least he didn't have to carry the burden of lying anymore. And he could lose the limp too, a part of the story that hadn't come up but which he'd continued playing out anyway.

"We're the ones that found it," Jimmy said under his breath.

"What's that?" Sheriff Brickell laid the pen flat on his pad now and locked eyes on Jimmy, waiting for an answer.

"Nothin."

"Cuz you found something doesn't make it yours," Sheriff Brickell replied. "Not necessarily, it don't. You understand that right?"

Jimmy did and he didn't. Maybe finding the Ditches didn't make them his, but it didn't make them the government's either. He nodded and gave a "Yes sir," though the look on his face conveyed his true feelings. But he still didn't know what the sheriff's presence at his house was about, so he shifted back to the subject, changing his line of questioning. "Did someone die or what?"

As all heads snapped toward him at once, Jimmy knew he'd hit the mark.

"Who?"

After a pause, Randall cleared his throat. "Janet Flannery," he answered, not looking up.

"Mrs. Flannery? From the grocery? That's Ralph's aunt?" He paused and then whispered, "Oh goddamn."

"James!" Dotty snapped.

"Sorry, I...sorry. She's really dead?"

There was another long pause until the sheriff finally confirmed. "That's right."

"And Ma, is it right what you said? 'Glenn did it.' That her husband's name, ain't it? Glenn Flannery?"

The sheriff cleared his throat and rested the note pad on the table beside him, and then he focused fully on the sixth grader who'd arrived unexpectedly to unsettle the interview. "Listen, James, I think I've gotten what I need from your brother here. At least for the time being. So why don't you two go on inside and let me talk to your sister a bit." He turned to Arthur. "Stay close though, Arthur. Might need to ask you a few more questions."

The relief on Arthur's face was palpable, and he quickly rose and pushed past his mother, entering the house where he instantly headed for the safety of his bedroom. Jimmy paused a moment as he watched his brother go, and then he followed behind, joining him in the bedroom where Jimmy quickly shut the door behind them.

"What the hell happened, Arthur?" Jimmy asked, taking a bouncing seat on the bed. "Is all that true? The killing and all?"

Arthur wavered his head slowly, giving a blank stare toward his bedroom wall as he attempted to fully process all that had happened that day, was still happening.

"Artie!"

"What?" Arthur snapped.

"What about it?"

"Yeah, it's true. Just like you heard. Glenn Flannery, he...he killed his wife. Stuck a screwdriver right through her head like he was puttin' a knife through a...a pumpkin or somethin.'"

"You're shittin'!? You saw that!?"

Arthur shook his head. "No. Didn't see him do it. But saw right after. Her body and all on the floor."

"Oh, goddamn! Was you scared? You musta been! Scared shitless you was!"

Arthur began to tear up now. In all the commotion of the murder scene—the blood and brains and the strewn body of Janet Flannery—and then the ride home and the questioning by Sheriff Brickell, he hadn't really had time to process all that had occurred. But now, in the confines of his bedroom, with Jimmy forcing him to retrace the events, the full impact of the murder began to land in his gut. And Jimmy's fascination with the story wasn't helping, talking about it like it was a comic book story and not a real thing that had happened. That and his seeming lack of compassion for Mrs. Flannery, it was making Arthur feel sick.

He wiped his eyes. "I guess I was. Scared that is. Specially cuz Mr. Flannery was still there when we walked in."

"You're shittin'?!" Jimmy repeated. "Still there? Are you...I mean did..." Jimmy was apoplectic with excitement, unable to form his thoughts and finish the sentence.

"But I was more sad than scared," Arthur continued. "At least once I realized what had...about the body. I didn't even see it until Ruby started screaming."

"So Ruby *was* there! I thought that's what the sheriff was saying.'"

Arthur nodded.

"Oh goddamn!" Jimmy let the story marinate in his mind and then gave a disappointed grin and a snap of his head, sorry to have missed the adventure. "Some guys, I'll tell you."

"It wasn't nothing you woulda wanted to see, Jimmy!" Arthur was angry with his brother now, disgusted. "A'right? It wasn't. A lady died. Died violently. And that's your friend's aunt for Christ's sake. You should be...I dunno...you shouldn't be like you's actin'!"

"Alright, alright, I don't mean nothin' by it. It's just fascinatin' that you was there. And Ruby too. Right in the middle of the biggest thing's ever happened in this town. Least since I been born." Jimmy was quiet a moment, understanding of his brother's point and letting the moment simmer. And then, sincerely now, he said, "You're right about Ralph though. His aunt didn't like him too much—least that's what he always said—but still, his ma's gonna be shook." He paused. "Why'd he'd do it you think? Mr. Flannery?"

Arthur shrugged. "I dunno. Ma thinks they must have been fightin' 'bout somethin'. Kids maybe. Pa thinks it had sumpin' to do with money and the store. They's just guessin' though."

Jimmy nodded. "Yeah. Did he come after y'all? After you saw him?"

Arthur shook his head. "Didn't make a move. Not at first. Just stood there with his hands at his sides, staring down at his dead wife, head looking down to the floor like he'd been hanged right there on the spot." This brought another thought to Arthur's mind. "You think he'll be hanged for it?" And before Jimmy could answer. "Prob'ly, right?"

Jimmy nodded. "For sure."

"Anyway, he didn't even seem to notice we were there 'til Ruby screamed."

"Then what did he do?"

Arthur swallowed nervously now and looked to the door as if hoping his ma or pa would enter, saving him from having to recall the memory. He looked back to Jimmy. "Body didn't move, but he lifted his head, real slow, and then he gave a smile as wide as anyone you ever saw in a magazine."

"Smiled?"

Arthur closed his eyes and nodded again. He was exhausted.

"What'd you do?"

"We ran, of course," Arthur answered without opening his eyes. "But he didn't chase us or nothin'. Thank god for that."

Jimmy smiled and shook his head slowly. "My god, Arthur. This was all today?"

Arthur nodded. "Right after the storm."

Jimmy' eyes flashed at this added bit of detail, and then he looked away, considering it.

"What?"

Jimmy shrugged off the question and shook his head. "Nothing. Not really. Just...reminds me of something Lynnie Radich told me today. Somethin' her grandmother told her."

"Yeah?" Arthur opened his eyes now and smiled, happy the subject had shifted from his day to Jimmy's. "You was with Lynnie Radich today? All while I was discovering a murder? My little brother got hisself a girlfriend?"

"Hell no, I don't!"

Arthur normally would have kept going, amping up the teasing to the point of bringing Jimmy to tears; today, however, with the shock of Mrs. Flannery's death still fresh in his mind, he only smiled and nodded. "She's nice anyway. Even if she ain't your girlfriend."

Jimmy paused and then brought the major topic of the day back to square one. "You discovered a murder. My big brother. And here I thought the fair was gonna be excitin'."

"Ain't gonna be no fair for us you don't help Pa out with that tire tomorrow."

"It ain't the tire, it's the wheel. And shit, Arthur, you could help him out. Why don't he ask you?"

"Maybe cuz I don't know the difference 'tween a tire and a wheel."

Jimmy snickered and dropped his eyes, knowing this was only part of the reason. Their father preferred Jimmy over Arthur, a fact both understood but neither really talked about it, especially Jimmy, who always seemed embarrassed by the favoritism. "Anyway, Pa'll be workin' all day tomorrow. He ain't gonna be able to get to the truck 'til Sunday. You want to come to the Ditches with me? It's Saturday. And I know you ain't got nothin' to do."

The Ditches.

Despite Jimmy's fascination with the place, and the claim—which was mostly true, Arthur supposed—that he and his friends had 'discovered' the site, Arthur never had much interest in going there. It seemed a little Cowboys and Indians to him, or a fantasy hideaway that he was too old for, especially at twelve. And after the state came in to inspect the site—and possibly the Federal government—Arthur had other reasons for not going there. It felt like trespassing (which it was), even dangerous somehow. Or maybe he was just scared of the mystery of the place and was too chicken to admit it. Of course, for most of the other kids in Clayton, even ones older than Arthur, the interest from the authorities had had the opposite effect, and Jimmy had become the de facto leader of The Ditches, a title about which he never shied away. "You'll be my esteem'ed guest," Jimmy declared.

"Very honored," Arthur replied. "What do you want me to go there for anyway? That place is washed up. No offense to you and Bucky and Ralph."

Jimmy grinned and shrugged his eyebrows. "Trust me, Arthur. You don't know the half of it. And I think it's time. Especially after today. And now that Lynnie knows."

"Time for what?"

"For you to see what the Ditches are really about."

Chapter 10

The day before Thanksgiving in 1938, Jimmy Richland and William "Bucky" Mason rode Bucky's bike to the edge of the Sampson farm where a large swath of land had been cleared for the spring planting season. (Jimmy mostly walked to the farm that day, since his bike had been 'stolen' a few weeks earlier, though everyone in the family was fairly sure he'd busted the frame doing jumps and had buried the evidence somewhere in the desert). The plan at the farm that day was to build a series of dirt ramps, each varying in distance and slope, and then to see who could jump the farthest while the boy not on a bike would lie in the gap to get a worm's-eye view of the stunt.

But on Jimmy's third jump, one which he landed utilizing a quick, wobbling shake of the handlebars, the ground beneath him suddenly softened, and Jimmy, along with Bucky's bike, sank into a perfect circle as the ground collapsed around him. When he stood, he was in the middle of what could only be called a crater—a dirt-brown version of the ones he saw in the moon each night—three and a half feet below the surface of the ground. By noon, as the kids bunny-hopped and wheelied and vaulted from ramp to ramp all around the property in search of other craters, Jimmy and Bucky had unearthed six more 'ditches,' each roughly the same size as the last, about ten feet across and three and a half feet deep. They didn't know what they were finding exactly, or whether the craters were the result of some geological phenomenon or man's creation, but they knew they were old, and that the kids in Clayton, New Mexico would come in droves to see them. And that once they did, they'd consider Jimmy and Bucky's Ditches the neatest things they'd ever seen in their lives.

And while the first part of the prediction came true, that curiosity would bring kids to the outskirts of the Sampson farm, the second part was less so. Every school-aged kid in Clayton had made the trek to the Ditches by the end of the week, but few took the same interest in them that Jimmy and Bucky had. There were a handful who did, of course, mostly the younger kids, but the older ones didn't pay much attention to the place, giving them little more than a raised eyebrow and a shrug as they stared at the holes for a minute or two before heading back to fix their cars or plow their family's fields or whatever.

But for those whose interests were sustained, the agreement they'd made was to keep it a secret from the adults, a sanctuary that no one over the age of sixteen could know about. Of course, the mystery of where kids were going each day after school and on Saturdays lasted less than two weeks, and by New Year's Day, the New Mexico Archaeological Society was on the scene, and then a reporter from the Union County Leader, whose article appeared on the front page of the paper, though only Mr. Sampson got a quote in it, a fact that Jimmy obviously thought unfair (it wasn't Jimmy's property, but it was his discovery).

And then the State government appeared a few weeks later, and within days, barbed barriers had been constructed around the perimeter, and signs with ominous warnings that blared at them in black and red lettering: DANGER! KEEP OUT! had been posted at the entry to the cratered land. And so, for those few kids who had been intrigued enough by the land to continue coming—kids that included Jimmy and Bucky, obviously—and who had spent hours playing war and tag and riding their bikes up over the rims to the middle of the ditches and then back up the other side with a wheelie, had been ordered by their parents to stay off the farm for good. It was trespassing, after all, and just because Old Man Sampson was no longer able to keep a close watch on his property, it didn't mean they were allowed to just schlepp all over it any time they pleased.

And then it all came to a halt. The interest and intrigue about a few holes on the far edge of Ty Sampson's farm disappeared as quickly as the Lindbergh baby, and what was a beehive of activity in the rural backlands of New Mexico for several weeks simply stopped. There were no more reporters or societies visiting, no more New Mexico government officials in black cars to claim land that wasn't theirs. Rumors that the Interior Department had sent agents to the area swirled—and even someone from the Bureau of Indian Affairs—but Jimmy had kept a close eye on the property, staking it out from afar over a series of weeks on Bucky's bike (when he could borrow it), and he hadn't seen anyone that looked like government since early February. The sheriff still talked about 'Feds' coming to excavate or whatever, but Jimmy thought this just a scare tactic to keep him and the other kids away.

And as spring came and passed, and the land—which now went by the name The Ditches to everyone in Clayton, a moniker which many took credit for, but no one could validate—continued to sit unexcavated or explored, Jimmy knew the time had come to return. And by the summer, the place was again open for business, at least as far as Jimmy and his friends were concerned, and a few others as well. Of course, the number who dared venture to the Ditches had been cut by three quarters at least, and now it was only Jimmy, Bucky and Ralph Brater who went there almost every day. Others showed up periodically, mostly on a dare, or else they were older teens who brought their girls there to impress them.

Arthur stood outside the wired-off area of the grounds, next to the sign that warned the area was under government surveillance. He did a full panoramic inspection of the grounds and chuckled. If the place was under surveillance, he couldn't see how. The landscape was as empty as the moon it resembled; there wasn't a place for someone to hide for a hundred miles, he guessed. "Alright, Jimmy, I'm here. What was it you wanted so bad to show me?"

Jimmy hesitated and stared at his brother, a look of reconsideration now occupying his eyes. Finally, he said, "It's over here. Come on." Jimmy snuck a leg between the middle and lowest of three barbed cables, and then his body followed naturally, avoiding with ease brushing either of the cables. He then walked to the edge of the crater closest to the fence, which was about ten paces out, and there he stopped and stared out over the fifty yards or so that made up the area of the site. Without turning, he said, "'Fore I show you though, just take it in, Artie. Just look at 'em there. It's pretty fuckin' swell, right?"

There was no reply, and Jimmy turned to discover that his brother hadn't followed him inside.

"Arthur!" he called. "What gives? Come on!"

"Yeah, I know, except...but...the sheriff. He warned you, Jimmy." Arthur shuffled his feet, knowing this reply wasn't really to do with why he hadn't followed. "Plus, I didn't know 'bout all these signs now. What if they really are watching us or something?"

Jimmy threw his head back and laughed, and then he turned in a full circle like a ballerina, arms out. "Where? Who? I come here every day, Artie. If they was watching us, I'da been tossed in Alcatraz months ago." Jimmy steadied his voice now, seeming to appreciate the reverence Arthur was showing, or the fear. He understood the feeling. "I agree it's a little creepy, but I promise it's safe. And the thing I want to show you, you can't see from way back there. We have to go to that far crater, the one yonder." Jimmy pointed to the ditch furthest from where he stood, Crater 7 as they'd come to call it.

Crater 7 was unique compared to the other six—which were arranged in columns of three and rows of two—in that it was out of position, asymmetrical.

"Why? What's so special 'bout that one? Except for where it is?"

"Gotta *show* you that," Jimmy replied, and then he shrugged and put his arms out again, the move this time indicating they were at a stalemate unless Arthur came along.

"Fine," Arthur said, and then in a sort of huffy advance, he tried to duck beneath the barrier headfirst, snatching the fabric of his shirt at the neck.

"You gonna get stuck that way. Leg first like I did."

Arthur backed out and followed the path of his younger brother, ducking his leg through the bottom two cables, avoiding the barbs this time, albeit with less adroitness. And once he was inside, Jimmy turned and began walking again toward Crater 7, and though Arthur hesitated for a few beats, getting a new angle of the Ditches from inside the wires, he soon followed.

As Arthur navigated the natural paths that ran alongside and between the craters, he looked down into each of them, seeing little more than rocks and dirt and simple farmland that had once been three feet higher and had since imploded into a footprint. But aside from their depth, the holes were unspectacular in every way, and by the time he reached the end of the main set of craters, mystique had turned to tedium, and he suddenly felt humiliated at having balked from the beginning.

What was the big deal with this place anyway? The government obviously wasn't that interested, he thought, *or else they'd have been out there months ago with shovels and pickaxes and magnifying glasses.*

Arthur stared toward Crater 7 now, which was offset from the other six by a good ten or fifteen yards, and as Jimmy neared the edge of the ditch, walking casually, Arthur followed. He watched his brother stand at the rim for just a moment before jumping down inside, and then he saw him head to the left.

And by the time Arthur reached the edge of the crater himself and looked inside of it, his brother, impossibly, was gone.

Chapter 11

"Jimmy!"

Arthur stood at the edge of Crater 7 in frozen confusion. He stared down at the empty hole with his jaw dangling in disbelief, hanging open until finally a gust of dirty wind passed his lips, polluting his mouth with dust and brush and gnats. He shook his head as he spat and blinked, clearing his eyes with his fists, an act he hoped would somehow make his brother materialize. But when he removed his hands, there was only the chasm in front of him, empty but for the collapsed dirt, as well as several large rocks that had collected in a pile inside the hole to his left.

Where was Jimmy?

The hole was barely the size and depth of a tiny pond, and the sun was shining like the brightest of lamps above him. It was impossible that Arthur wasn't seeing him; there was nowhere to hide. And he had watched his brother enter the depression—about that, he was sure. He was simply gone.

"Jimmy!" Arthur called again and then waited, receiving only the whistle of the breeze in reply. He thought of Ruby again. Of the voice in the storm. And just as he was about to call again, he heard his own name spoken on the light wind.

"Arthur!"

The word came out muffled and distant, and Arthur screamed at the sound of it, taking several steps backward, swiveling his head dramatically as he searched for the source of the cry. He felt his breathing begin to race, his heart thumping in his chest like thunder. He put his hand there now, his palm flat against his sternum, pressing firmly, reflexively measuring the pace of his heartbeat. It was a habit he'd developed when he was only six or so, and one which he still fell back on occasionally, especially in the most stressful of times.

"Arthur!"

This time Arthur snapped his head in the direction of the voice, which was at the ten o'clock position from where he was standing currently, the side of the crater where the rocks were piled. "Jimmy?"

"Jump down inside."

Arthur stayed silent, hesitating.

"Trust me, Arthur. You can't see it from up there, only when you're standing in the ditch."

Arthur shook his head now and blinked wildly, at once trying to make sense of what exactly was happening while also denying the invitation from his brother's voice. There was no chance he was stepping inside only to disappear into some void.

"It's alright, Arthur. I promise it is. You'll see it when you come down. It's just hidden from up there. Not sure how, really, but it is. You'll see it once you're inside."

"Come out first. So I can see you."

There was a pause, and then, as if from some magic act performed at the fair, or a miracle from God, Jimmy suddenly appeared in the crater, emerging as if birthed from the side of the indentation, materializing from the dirt like Adam.

Arthur took a step backward and threw his hands over his mouth, gasping.

Jimmy stood in the hole smiling, and then, like a traveling tonic salesman, he threw his hands up in a *ta-da!* gesture.

"Devilry," Arthur whispered.

Jimmy laughed. "It's not magic, Arthur. At least I don't think so. It's just a disguise. If you'll stop being chicken and come on in, I'll show you."

Arthur's curiosity finally took hold, and he stepped back to the edge of the crater, where he paused once again. And then he climbed over the edge of the hole, his stomach against the rim, dropping his leg so that he barely brushed the toe of his shoe on the bottom of the crater, testing the dirt as if he were stepping into a lake in early April, gauging the temperature before committing to the plunge. But as he let his foot finally settle flat, the floor felt as solid as the ground above, and he brought his other foot down until he was standing inside.

And, just as Jimmy had promised, now that he was inside, he could see the place of mystery where his brother had been hiding.

It took him a moment to spot it, however, since, at first glance, most of the crater's interior appeared no different from the other holes. Except for in one section, on the side where the stones still rested. There, Arthur could now see a thin gap, a carved-out section that was about half the width of a normal door. From the surface, the gap was invisible, blending in with the rest of the crater in some way Arthur didn't quite understand. Now that he was standing level with it inside the ditch, knowing the gap existed, the blindness of it from above didn't make sense. But it was a fact, and he wondered now if this cloaking had been done intentionally, or if it was just some trick of light and angle. In any case, it was amazing.

"Pretty swell hiding spot, Jimmy," Arthur said, chuckling nervously. "Scared me half to death though."

Jimmy grinned. "Oh, it's a bit more than a hiding spot, Artie. You ready?"

"I don't know," Arthur answered with a raised eyebrow. "For what?"

Jimmy cocked his head and sidestepped back toward the gap, and then, like a cat burglar through a jimmied door on a wealthy manor, he bent his knees into a hunch and slipped through the crater's slit in a single motion, keeping one hand outside for just a beat, using it to wave his brother to follow.

Arthur's curiosity standing at the top of the crater was profound, but it was nothing like what he felt now that he was inside of it. There was a secret cave—an invisible secret cave—and he was now overcome with inquisitiveness.

Jimmy was gone again, impossibly, having disappeared somewhere beneath the ground of Clayton, New Mexico in a single step. And the look on his face just before he entered the gap was one Arthur had never quite seen before from his brother. Arthur realized now that this was something new—whatever *this* was—and not just to him or the town of Clayton, but maybe to the world outside as well.

Arthur swallowed once, a hulking gulp, and then he followed Jimmy's route and method through the entrance, ducking below the height of the hollow's rim and turning his body in the same way his younger brother had, similar to how he'd crossed through the barbed fencing. And as he entered the void in the side of the crater, he slid through the dirt wall with ease, barely brushing the edges as he entered the earth.

Inside the cave, the darkness was profound, and Arthur felt an instant rush of cool air from his left that enveloped his entire body. And though it was too dark for him to see even his hand before his face, once he cleared the width of the wall fully, a sudden sense of openness consumed him. He could breathe without effort (which was one of his fears before entering), and the dull noises that resonated around him gave off the slightest of echoes, like he was in a proper room, albeit one built for dwarfs and children.

Then the strike and sizzle of a match, and Arthur could see his brother's face once more. Jimmy's tongue snaked above the corner of his top lip in concentration as he held the match steady, placing the flame just so against a frayed piece of cloth. And then fire erupted as the torch in his hand was lit, and Jimmy's mouth sprung to a smile as the world in front of him became bright, thrilling. "Come on and sit, Arthur," he said, patting the ground beside him.

But Arthur was still in the throes of mesmerization, and the words from his brother sounded distant, dreamlike. They were inside a cave, a three-foot-high fissure that spanned out for several feet—yards maybe—though Arthur couldn't see beyond the glow of the torch.

"Arthur, you're gonna bust your back if you stay hunched over like that. Come on and sit." Jimmy patted the ground again, and then, as if he'd done it a hundred times, he wriggled the base of the torch into the ground, standing it upright into a tight hole, one that had obviously been designed for just that reason.

Arthur finally sat, and as promised, he felt the relief in his lower spine immediately. "Did *you* make that hole?" He nodded toward the torch holder. "For the torch?"

Jimmy shook his head. "Nah, it was here already. The torch was in it just like it is now. All we had to do was bring the kindling and the fire."

This detail unnerved Arthur, but he put it aside for the moment and scanned the dirt room around him, amazed. "This is...this is goddamn incredible, Jimmy. I can't believe you never told me about this place."

Jimmy shrugged. "You never liked the Ditches, and me and the boys promised to keep it a secret." He paused. "But this ain't all. Not by a lot."

"What? Not all? What else?"

"I'll show you what else, but it means you gonna have to trust me one more time. Maybe two."

Arthur let the last of his scan finish, and then he brought his attention back to Jimmy. "Fine, but before that, you're gonna tell me how all this came to be." Arthur was only a year older than Jimmy, but he was still his elder, and before they started exploring any more of this secret grotto, he needed more information. His mother had taught him that from when he was as young as he could remember and had just reminded him of it a day earlier. Arthur was responsible for Jimmy when it was just the two of them, or three when Ruby was along, and he was going to get up to speed on the details. "Who else knows about this...what do you call this place anyway?"

"Which place?"

"*This* place. This cave where we's sittin' now. You knucklers got a name for everything, and I doubt this room is any different."

"We call it...the Hollow." Jimmy grinned, as if this were the most creative thing anyone had ever concocted.

"The Hollow, eh? Regular buncha Hemingways y'all are. And who else 'sides you knows about this Hollow?"

"Just Ralph and Bucky and me as far as I know." He paused and looked away guiltily. "Oh, and now Lynnie Radich, I guess. And you."

Arthur gave a frown and a nod. "Mmhmm. And how is that possible?"

"What part?"

"The part where no one else knows? There was three dozen kids came over here them first weeks after the Ditches was discovered."

"Yeah, but me and Bucky was the one's that did the discoverin'. We found 'em all at the same time. Somethin' we don't get enough credit for you ask me."

Arthur didn't care about Jimmy's credit, just the story.

"Anyway, when this'un came down—Crater 7 we called it—it took us a few hours to find it cuz it was so far out from the others. But find it we did. And there was somethin' different 'bout this one. We knew it within the first minute we was inside. None of the other holes had anything like it. The gap that is. And you know Bucky don't care one way from up. He was the first one through. And then me and

Ralph followed him in. Then, after, we covered it up with the stones."

"Why? Why cover it up?"

Jimmy shrugged. "Just seemed like somethin' to keep secret. Even from you. I mean look at this place. You know damn right them older kids woulda' just bullied us outta here once they found out about it. Made it their own. You know how Tim Jennings and his crew get. We'd a never seen inside here again."

Arthur let this explanation settle, knowing it was a valid one, and then he asked, "How'd ya do it? Cover it up, I mean."

"Easy, really. You saw how thin the gap is. We thought if we could get a bunch of good rocks and stack 'em high enough, all the way to the rim, it would cover it up fine. And that was right too. Hardest part was quarrying the rocks. Had to get 'em from inside Old Man Sampson's barn and haul 'em here. Then we just filled in the space 'til you couldn't see it no more."

"Hell," Arthur muttered, "I couldn't see it anyways. Not from up on top."

"Weird, ain't it? But that's right, so it's not like this little crevice was grabbing anybody's attention who was just walking by anyway. And even when you're standing on the inside, if you do happen to notice it, who would think to crawl through such a tiny space. Not like you can see into the hollow from the outside, just like you can't see out of it right now."

"*You* went in though. What made *you* go in?"

"I told you: it wasn't me. Not first. It was Bucky. 'Course it was. He's a crazy sonofaone, Arthur."

Arthur smiled. Bucky was no doubt a bit off. Off in a way that would likely cause him trouble later in life but now just seemed kind of funny.

"He just started squeezin' hisself through like it was on a dare, 'cept no one dared him to, he just did it. And then he was gone. Poof! Like a rabbit in a hat. It was the craziest, Artie. Me and Ralph just started screamin' for him. We thought he'd fell into the middle of the earth or somethin'."

He kind of did, Arthur thought to himself. "And no one else tried to get in? None of the other kids noticed the gap."

"A bunch of the kids was jumpin' in and out of the crater during those first couple of days of course, but we'd covered it up by then, so no one really paid any attention. And it wasn't the main ditch anyone wanted to play in anyway. They liked the first six'uns cuz a how close together they are. It's more fun jumpin' bikes in and out of 'em the way they's lined up. Any time I saw anyone in Crater 7, it was usually older boys comin' there to smoke."

The explanations from Jimmy were plausible, but Arthur's questions were many, and he wasn't ready to lose the thread just yet. "What about all those government people? You tellin' me they didn't see this place either? This Hollow?"

Jimmy shrugged. "Can't say if they did or they didn't. Doubt it though. All them suits have done so far is walk around the site and claim it for themselves. Don't agree with that last part—the part about them claimin' it—and neither does Pa, by the way. But that's somethin' else to talk about another day, I guess. In any case, they ain't done no excavatin' or nothin'. I been watchin' for it since they came that first day, and I ain't seen a one that looks like they's ready to get dirty."

Arthur sighed and shook his head again, staring around the room, still not having processed quite where he was exactly or how he'd come to be there.

"You ready then?" Jimmy asked. "The torch ain't gonna last forever, and I ain't got any more rags with me to keep it goin'.

"And the way you lit it? You stole Pa's matches, I'm guessin'? Those'll be missed, you know?"

Jimmy gave his signature pirate's smile once more. "They haven't been yet."

Arthur smiled back and snickered. "Alright, fine, show me what else."

"You sure?"

This time Arthur gave a definitive nod. He'd seen too much wonder now to back off from whatever came next.

"Alright, but it's better to crawl though. Save your back from crampin'. Just follow me." Jimmy plucked the torch from its holder and then led the way for about six paces on his hands and knees. At that point, the boys came to a sheer wall of dirt, which looked to have been reinforced with crudely cut wooden beams and cross-stitched with twigs and sticks. Jimmy ran his hand along the ground now, patting to his left until he felt what he was looking for. He held out the torch now and shined it on what looked to be a ledge that dropped precipitously down into blackness, the depth of which Arthur couldn't tell from his perch above but that he assumed was severe.

"Crap my pants!" Arthur shouted and then covered his mouth, fearing that any noise too loud might bring the ground down on top of them.

"Don't do that in here," Jimmy laughed. "Crap your pants or shout so loud."

"What's down there?" Arthur whispered, overcorrecting his volume.

With the question now asked, Jimmy moved the torch a little more to his left, hovering it over what appeared to be a steep flight of steps. He looked back to Arthur and asked, "If you want to find out, I'm ready when you are."

Chapter 12

Arthur went silent now, giving a gravid pause in the story, something he had done with increasing frequency throughout much of his tale. It was usually to recall some detail of the story that had gone blank or else didn't sound right when he said it aloud. He wanted to be accurate, specific, and not spin that fall of 1939 into one of fiction. Of course, he had no doubt that grains of false memories had found their way in, filling in parts of the story that had been forgotten over time; but the important parts he refused to invent just to get through, and if it took him thirty seconds or a minute to piece some event together properly, then that's what he was prepared to do.

But the silence he was displaying now was one born of exhaustion, and though it was his real desire to continue, he simply didn't have the strength to keep dredging up recollections from sixty-five years ago. He was tired now and wanted to sleep. "I'm sorry, Mr....uh..."

"Boylin," Chris answered. "Please, call me Chris."

Arthur smiled and nodded. "That's all I can recall today, Chris. Perhaps tomorrow you can come back? And I'll tell you about the rest of that day then." Arthur gave a shameful look to the side, not because he was embarrassed that he couldn't go on, but because he feared what he had told his visitor already had been of no comfort, and that he would feel tortured as he walked out into the night, just as his mother had suffered every second of the two weeks that Ruby was gone.

And about that he was correct.

"Mr. Richland, I'm begging you," Chris replied. "Please, sir. My daughter is missing. And...it's a miracle I found you. Right here in New Mexico. It's impossible, but I have. And I...I appreciate everything you've told me today. I truly do." He paused and added, "And I believe you. I believe every word." He sighed now and gave a pleading look of despair. "But nothing you've said so far helps me find Jaycee. Where is she, Arthur? And what does her disappearance have to do with Ruby? Arthur, please!"

Arthur felt the close of his eyes on the sound of his name, and as the clouds of sleep began to cover his mind, he felt a jostle of his wrist. "Mr. Richland!"

Arthur grumbled back to consciousness, but just for a moment, long enough to see Betty now standing in the doorway.

"He is very tired, sir," Betty scolded. "There is nothing left to tell you tonight. He is an old man and must get his sleep. I think it is time for you to go. And maybe you don't come back tomorrow, eh?"

With one last thread of awareness, Arthur registered the suggestion by Betty and opened his eyes. "No, please. Come back tomorrow, Chris. The altar. The fair. We haven't gotten to the fair. That's when I really saw it for the first time. That's when I knew the evil was here to stay."

CHRIS BOYLIN ARRIVED the next day a half hour after breakfast. He had made a point to smooth things over with Betty on his way out the door the previous night, not wanting to risk permanent banning from the center for his badgering of the patients. And during this leveling-over discussion, he discovered that late morning was the best time to come, the hour when Arthur was most lucid and amiable, willing to talk.

And as Chris entered the room, he could see immediately Betty's recommendation was correct. Arthur looked alert and relaxed, his eyes alive and open.

Arthur flashed a sober smile at his new friend and waved him into the room. "It's good to see you, Chris," he said. "Please sit."

The chair from yesterday was still positioned by Arthur's bedside, or else it had been repositioned there, and Chris gently took the seat as instructed.

"I promised to tell you about the fair, yes?"

Chris nodded.

"Well, then that's where I intend to get us to. Eventually."

"Before that," Chris said quickly, "may I ask you about something else? Something that came to me last night?"

Arthur gave a look of disappointment, as if he'd prepared exactly how he was going to begin the day, the place in the story where he would commence, and it had now been hijacked by this unforeseen inquiry. "Of course," he replied, somewhat suspiciously.

"It's a follow up really. Yesterday, you thought I was the police. You mentioned something about an intern. Do you remember that?"

Arthur nodded quickly. "Yes, I'm sorry for that. I mistook you."

"No, it's fine. I was just...curious. Wondering what happened that you were talking to the police? With the intern?"

Arthur shifted his eyes, first to the floor, and then to the door, letting his gaze hover there for several beats, as if summoning Betty to appear there and rescue him from having to engage in this off-topic dialogue. But there was no one coming to save him, so he replied, "There was an attack here. It happened a day or so earlier. Or perhaps it was longer than that. It's a bit of a blur now. It happened while we were at breakfast."

"An attack?"

Arthur nodded, not making eye contact.

"What happened exactly? Who got attacked?" Chris could feel his heart pick up speed, his blood pressure and breathing increase. There was something in the shiftiness of the elderly man that signaled whatever had happened wasn't unrelated to his daughter. "Mr. Richland?"

Arthur cleared his throat and stared toward the window. "One of the...uh...residents here. She...um...she had an incident with one of our young staff members."

"An incident? Was anyone hurt?"

Arthur met Chris' face now, and he stared unblinking for several seconds. Finally, he nodded and whispered, "Yes."

Arthur began to shake, and his eyes began to well, and Chris knew if the man broke down now, he might not get him back. Not on that day anyway. And perhaps not again. And if Arthur flipped his lid entirely and started to cry inconsolably, or even scream like a howler monkey, it might be the last time Chris set foot inside Stratford Manor. And then he would never hear Arthur's story to the end.

It didn't matter, Chris decided, not then; if something criminal had happened at the center a few days earlier, an incident that involved a police investigation, Arthur Richland wasn't the only source of that information. It would be a matter of public record, and he could find out about it later.

Regarding Ruby Richland in 1939, however, Arthur Richland was the only person to whom Chris could turn.

"You were talking about the Ditches yesterday," Chris said, turning the narrative back in Arthur's direction. "Just before I left. You remember that, right?"

Arthur blinked quickly and nodded.

"Do you want to finish telling me about that now? Or do you want to get right to the fair? It's your choice Arthur. Whatever you want to do."

Arthur took a breath of relief, as if happy to be brought from the precipice of having to reveal what he'd seen at breakfast days earlier in the common room and later in the parking lot. He smiled contentedly. "Do you have a picture of her, Chris? Of your daughter?"

Chris was caught off guard by the question, but he nodded quickly and pulled his phone from his pocket, flipping up the screen.

"No photographs, eh?"

Chris shook his head. "Nothing that shows her at the age she is now."

"Only baby pictures, I'll bet?"

Chris gave a forced smile of acknowledgement and pulled up the latest picture of Jaycee on his phone. Six years old, taken the day she disappeared. Her thumbs were against her temples as she waved her fingers in the air in the classic teasing pose, an ear-to-ear smile on her face, a gap where one of her bottom incisors used to be. She was sitting in the front seat of Chris' Tacoma, which was still parked outside Calista's house, only minutes before they left for Oklahoma. Chris had thought often of that exact moment—which now seemed like a lifetime ago—when the traffic report had indicated there was an accident on 40 and that 412 was currently the quickest route. It had been fine with him at the time, this alternate trek, as he hadn't been along the northern route in several months and was looking forward to breaking the monotony of 40. Who could have known?

He turned the phone toward Arthur, who wrapped his hands around the device and gently pulled it toward him. Chris released it reluctantly.

"Look at that smile," Arthur said, shaking his head and chuckling at the clownishness. "She is something beautiful, I'll tell you that." He looked at Chris and said, "Must get her looks from mama!"

Chris chortled and nodded. "Yeah, she does."

Arthur's eyes softened. "I'm sorry about it. Her going missing."

Chris took his phone back and nodded. "Thank you."

"And I know the police are doubtful about finding her, but I am not."

A single tear had begun to stream down Chris' face now. "Thank you," he said again, this time with a splintered pop in his voice. He could sense the coherence in Arthur's words now, see the soberness in his eyes, and he wanted nothing more than to get back to his story, to press the issue of Ruby and her disappearance now while the neurons were sparking. But he'd learned his lesson by now, and whether the man was drawing out the story intentionally (something Chris was beginning to suspect), or if he really was limited by the linear nature of his own narrative, it didn't much matter. He would go at his own pace, and nothing Chris could do was going to change that. All he could do was sit and listen.

Arthur handed the phone back to Chris and then reached his other hand out and said, "Would you mind giving me a hand?"

Chris extended his forearm for Arthur to use as a brace, and the elderly patient pulled himself up to a sitting position, at once aligning a pillow behind his back for support. He took an exhausted gasp and with some effort reached for the plastic cup of cranberry juice beside him, lifting it from his night table and taking a sip. He took a heavy swallow, which he followed with an 'ahh,' and then he said, "We were in the Hollow, if I recall correctly. So, let's start there today."

Chapter 13

Arthur stood at the bottom of the short flight of stairs that led to the Hollow's basement, still fascinated by the shallowness of the area. What looked to be a bottomless chasm from the precipice above was little more than four or five feet below the main surface of the secret spot. If he were in a swimming pool, Arthur noted, he would have been able to breathe standing on his tip toes.

But then Jimmy began to walk forward, away from the staircase to the interior of the underground room, and after several paces, as the torch in his brother's hand grew smaller and dimmer by the second, Arthur knew the space they were now in was far more vast than that above them.

Jimmy finally stopped and turned, his face glowing like an imp's in the radiance of the fire. "You comin' or what?"

"How far does it go?"

"Not far. A couple of steps from where I'm at now; but the thing I want to show you is down here."

Arthur looked back up to the stairs, which he could barely see now that Jimmy had walked away, and as he stared at the short but steep incline, a feeling of constriction and ensnarement suddenly flooded over him. His breathing became fast and short, and as he was about to reach for his heart again, he regained his composure, taking in a full breath before heading toward the torch, moving as fast as he could without risking a trip and a fall. If he broke his leg in there, he thought, it might very well be the spot of his grave.

The path to the end of the corridor was narrow, tapering sharply with every step Arthur took until he finally arrived at a spot barely wide enough for both boys to stand. But he reached Jimmy in seconds, and when he did, his brother was standing just outside an opening in the dirt wall, staring into a carved-out section of the basement at the end of the room. He was holding the torch at eye level as he peered inside, and Arthur silently followed the direction of his gaze.

The room was large, ten feet by six maybe, with a vaulted ceiling, one that was several feet higher than those in the rest of the basement. Arthur instantly got the feeling they were standing beneath the underside of the ground outside. "What's up there? Is that the ground up top?"

But Jimmy's eyes were fixed on the contents of the room, never wavering. "Don't worry 'bout that. Just follow me."

Jimmy entered the room and Arthur followed him step for step, no longer wanting to be left behind, fearing that if the path they were on led to a series of turns and dips and more staircases, he would end up lost, dead.

But only four or five paces in, Jimmy stopped suddenly, the torch now illuminating a large table that looked to have been carved out of a single piece of wood. It was probably five feet long, two or three feet wide, the wood as dark as it looked old.

"What is this place?" Arthur asked, spinning in a slow circle, trying to get a feel for the size of the room. "And what's this table for?"

Jimmy shrugged. "At first we thought it was for eating. Then for sex stuff. Like this was a bed or somethin' where they brought virgins for doin' it."

Arthur couldn't help but snicker.

"But Lynnie Radich said that wasn't right."

"What'd she say it was for?"

"She said it's a altar?"

"A altar?" Arthur scanned the room, looking for a cross or a picture of Jesus, something to validate the theory. He could just make out some markings on the far wall, the one near the foot of the altar, but nothing that reminded him of Sunday mornings in Clayton. "Like at church?"

Jimmy shook his head as a first reaction, and then he cocked it to the side in reconsideration. "Well, sorta like that. But to hear her tell it, Lynnie, this one ain't for consecratin' the bread of Christ."

Arthur swallowed. "What is it for then?"

Jimmy walked to the far end of the room and then turned and faced Arthur again, waiting a beat while his brother's eyes adjusted to the light that he held there. And then he lifted the torch, placing it close to the wall. "Look at this."

Instantly, Arthur noticed that the wall beside Jimmy was different from the other three in the room, as the dirt that formed it had been plastered over with some type of stone or clay. It appeared gray and polished, and within the clay, the carvings Arthur had noted earlier suddenly came to life, glowing like fireflies in the dancing flame, depicting scenes that, despite their simplicity and faded detail, made Arthur's stomach churn.

The first image that struck him was of a man on his knees atop the altar, his torso high as if he were praying. Except he had been decapitated, or nearly had, his head hanging behind him like a flower that had been split from its stem with a razor blade, leaving just enough of the stalk to keep the bloom aloft. In the case of the depicted man, of course, his head was attached by a final flap of neck skin, while his eyes stared in wide anticipation, alert, as if awaiting something awful approaching him from behind. Another image showed a woman, also upon the altar, lying on her back with her stomach opened like a knifed orange. And in the void of her belly was the crude outline of a young girl, her body nothing more than a stick figure, though her face showed expression, her eyes wide and vacant like the man in the previous image. She too was staring toward some encroaching object in space, though this one appeared to be approaching from the front, somewhere beyond her mother's sprawling legs.

And there were other depictions as well, perhaps a dozen in all, each one as grisly as the next, with death and torture the theme, all of them bizarre and wicked in their creativity. But it wasn't so much the violence of the pictures that frightened Arthur, it was the reaction of the subjects. Their eyes. Their stares. And as much as Arthur tried to bury the thought, he couldn't help but conjure the image of Glenn Flannery standing over his wife's corpse.

"My god," Arthur whispered. "Did y'all make these?"

"Hell no, we didn't!" Jimmy yelped. "Whadya ask a question like that for?" He lowered his voice. "We ain't...whadya think I was, Arthur? A monster of some kind."

"Sorry, I just...who did make 'em?"

Jimmy was quiet for a few beats longer, not ready to let the insult slide so easily. Finally, he answered, "Lynnie says it was the Indians who used to live in these parts. The Tompiros tribe they was called."

"Tompiros?" Arthur shook his head. "Never heard of 'em."

"It's cuz they ain't around no more. Not for a long time."

"Extinct?"

Jimmy nodded. "Over two-hundred years now."

"Two hundred? How's she know about 'em then. Lynnie, that is?"

"Her grandmother knows about 'em. Like I told you earlier."

"Her grandmother's two-hundred years old?"

"No, but half her blood is Indian. Pueblo. And it's a lot of people think the Tompiros—at least a few of them anyway—got mixed in with the Pueblos. That they didn't really go extinct. Not all the way. And they kept the stories going. Lynnie says her grandmother's got stories that go back even older than two hundred years. Told by her grandmother and hers before that."

Arthur took in the information and reflected on it for a moment. "Hell, I didn't even know Lynnie was a Injun."

"She don't tell people cuz she's only a bit a one. A quarter, I think. And she don't like being called no Injun neither."

Jimmy didn't hide his defense of Lynnie Radich, and Arthur respected him for it. "Sorry, I ain't mean nothin' by it."

Jimmy nodded. "It's alright."

"So what did these Topporos Indians do in here?"

"*Tompiros*?" Jimmy corrected. "And take a look at the pictures on the wall. What's it look like they did? It was for sacrifices. At least that's what *this* room was for."

"Sacrifices?" Arthur took a couple of steps toward the wall now and studied the images closer, and then he ran his fingers over the second one from the left, the image with the woman and child. He felt the cold, gritty indentation of the picture and rubbed the soot between his fingertips. "Musta been a scary thing to be the one, eh? The one gettin' killed?"

"Yeah, 'cept Lynnie says most of 'em volunteered for it. That's what her grandmother told her. It'd still be scary though, even if you chose it."

Arthur shivered at this idea. "Volunteered? Why...why would they do that?"

"Crops was dying. People was too. And not just from starvin'. Mother Nature brought the drought and the famine, and the White man brought the disease. Tompiros thought they had to do somethin' to fight off their extinction. Or at least they had to try. Sacrifices was part of that."

Arthur considered this and said, "Guess it didn't work in the end."

"Nope. I guess not. But like Lynnie said, they had to try somethin'."

"Why down here? What's with all the crypts and darkness and all?"

Jimmy shrugged. "Hide from the White man, I guess. There ain't a lot of places to hide in New Mexico 'cept underground, especially round here where there ain't no peaks. Some tribes built pyramids and killed the victims at the top, ones in Hawaii tossed 'em into volcanos. Tompiros did it like this. That's what Lynnie's grandmother says anyway."

"So her grandmother knows about this place? This specific spot? Thought you said it was just the four of y'all knew about it."

Jimmy shook his head. "Don't know if she knows about it or not. Probably just speakin' in general." He then shook his head. "I doubt she does though. Being that it was buried underground since who knows when, and we swore Lynnie to secrecy. And even if she does know, she don't know that *we* know about it. Hell, we didn't even know Lynnie had a Indian grandmother 'til she started talking 'bout her. Everything I'm telling you was things her grandmother had told her over the years she was growing up. About sacrifices and things. She recognized the images right quick. Knew all about the altar and everything."

Arthur turned back to the images on the wall and studied them, and as he did, his eyes soon drifted to a series of dark outlines in the top corner. "What's that?"

Jimmy hesitated, but then he moved toward the corner of the room and held the torch a foot or two below the pictures, instantly illuminating a row of images. They were of faces and bodies that were long and gaunt, with hair that straggled like dry stream beds from the top of the head to halfway down the wall. The depictions were simple, sketches, outlines of heads and torsos; but the haggard looks of the faces, the wild, serpentine nature of the hair, and the malevolence that oozed from the large, oval eyes, made them unmistakable as to what they were. They were witches; nobody would have argued that.

"Goddamn," Arthur said breathily, "those are some nasty looking bitches."

"Hey! Watch it!"

Arthur snickered. "Watch what?"

"Your language."

"Are you kiddin' me? Hell, you got the filthiest mouth of anyone I know."

Jimmy frowned and nodded, resetting his demeanor with a sigh. "Yeah, I know, but..."

"But what?"

Jimmy's eyes got shifty, unsure whether to reveal what was on his mind. Finally, he said, "It wasn't just the sacrifices."

"What wasn't? What's that mean?"

"It means the Tompiros came up with more than one idea to keep the White man from comin'. To keep the crops from dyin'. More than just fightin' on the plains with weapons and loppin' off heads in here."

"What *ideas*? The hell you talkin' about, Jimmy?"

Jimmy looked back to the sketches on the wall, allowing his eyes to view them for only a beat before turning away. "Ideas like..." He nodded toward the sketches now, averting his eyes entirely. "And it just...it don't seem right to talk about 'em like that. To call 'em names and such."

"*Them?* Don't seem right to talk about *them?* What the hell are you talkin' about now, Jimmy?" Arthur snickered. He tried to remain nonchalant, but the fear in his voice was obvious. "They have names?"

Jimmy swallowed and nodded and then stared up at the pictures again. Reluctantly, he held the flame close to the wall, nearly touching the carvings now, and as he did, something tripped in Arthur's gut, and he nearly choked on his fright. The primitive clay etchings, which were barely visible in the dull glow of the cave, suddenly began to glow like fireflies, as if the etchings in the clay were absorbing the very fire of the torch now, soaking up the flame, creating a shade of orange Arthur had seen only once before in his life, a day earlier at Downes' grocery, just before he discovered Janet Flannery's body.

"She called them the Skadegamutc," Jimmy said, pronouncing the word with the care of someone carrying nitroglycerin down a flight of stairs.

Ska-de-ga-moo-zee.

And then Jimmy swallowed once more, slowly now, as if he were ingesting an elixir, unsure of its toxicity. "They're witches," he said. "Or was witches, I guess." This last sentence Jimmy said doubtfully, hoping that somehow simply speaking the words would create the truth, overturn reality.

Arthur couldn't take his eyes of the picture now, and he could only reply absently. "Witches?"

Jimmy nodded.

"So, what do they have to do with these other pictures?"

Jimmy took a deep breath. "Lynnie says when the sacrifices didn't work, when the crops kept dying and the White man kept comin', the Tompiros started makin' their sacrifices crueler and crueler, hopin' to appease whatever god or nature they believed could help them. They was lookin' for a formula, I guess, like a recipe or combination."

"And so...you're tellin' me they found it? The recipe, I mean? These witches was the combination?

Jimmy shrugged. "I think that's right. The cruelty, the pain of the sacrifices, it brought out...or maybe *up* is the right word...something terrible. Something worse than terrible."

Arthur gulped. "The Skatter...sacaker—"

"Skadegamutc," Jimmy said, nodding.

"It's not real though, right?" It was almost a plea.

"You wouldn't be able to convince Lynnie of that. All she wanted to do was leave. Demanded it. Said she was gonna tell everyone about this place if we didn't get her outta there right then. Said we best never come back here either. That we was gonna stir things up that shouldn't get stirrin'."

Arthur had begun to sweat now, the tight space of the hollow now feeling oppressive, constricting, as if the full weight of the ground above him had begun to weigh down upon his shoulders. In an instant, he knew exactly how Lynnie Radich had felt. "How...how could she know about any of this?" he asked.

"I told you, her grandmother. She's been tellin' these stories her whole life. The Skadegamutc, I think that was one told when she was little. Type of thing to scare kids to get to bed or whatever. But her face when she saw the picture..." Jimmy could only shake his head, the suggestion that she had always considered the witches more than a story.

Arthur stared up at the pictures again, and with Jimmy no longer directing the flame toward them, a darkness now embraced the sketches. And in that dim light, the images of the witches seemed even more menacing, bleaker, and somehow more focused on him. "So y'all left then?" he said, still rapt.

"Yeah, she made me walk her home. That's why I was late last night."

Arthur finally drew his eyes away from the etchings and pondered all his brother had just told him. "Maybe Lynnie was right," he said, no longer trying to hide the fear in his voice. He wasn't yet willing to make the full connection between the sketches and the figure he and Ruby had seen the day before, though somewhere in his subconscious it had already been made. "Maybe y'all should stop comin' here, Jim. I'm serious. This don't seem like the kind of place to be messin'. Not that I believe in all that Injun...Indian stuff, magic and whatever, but it's no use temptin' it. You don't wanna start disturbin' the dead or whatever, messin' with things sacred. That's true of anything sacred you ask me. Don't care if it's Christian or Indian or what."

Jimmy dropped his head and looked to his left, shamefully. "Yeah, well..."

"What is it?"

"Might be a hair too late for that."

The words landed in Arthur's ears like cannonballs. "Too late for what?"

Jimmy held the torch out toward Arthur. "Hold this."

Arthur took the torch, which was now beginning to burn dimly, the fire quickly devouring the rope and cloth keeping it lit. Jimmy stepped back to a spot in front of the altar and stood there a moment, facing the massive top of the table like a priest beginning the consecration, and then with a deep inhale and a bend of his knees, he pressed the heels of his hands against the edge of the wooden slab and pushed, driving his legs as he shoved the table surface some eighteen inches, careful not to go too far and topple the surface to the ground.

"What in the holy hell?" Arthur muttered.

The altar top, which at first glance looked to be part of a single block of wood, was, in fact, detached from the lower part of the platform, capable of being moved, as Jimmy had just demonstrated. From where he was standing, Arthur couldn't see what was beneath the tabletop, but he knew instantly there was an opening there, that the altar was hollow.

Chapter 14

"Come on," Jimmy said.

Arthur followed his brother's instruction and navigated the few steps until he was again standing beside Jimmy. He looked into the chamber and saw nothing but emptiness at first, a chasm as black as a coal mine, and for a moment, Arthur guessed it a tunnel to hell, the place from which the hags from the wall had ascended to Earth.

But as the torch light flickered forward and Arthur's eyes adjusted, the bottom of the altar's opening illuminated, and he could now see what appeared to be three large rocks, each as black as the coal he'd imagined in his hypothetical mine seconds earlier. They were arranged off center, not stacked, but rather positioned in a kind of pyramid shape, with one rock at the top and two beneath it. The two rocks which comprised the bottom of the formation each touched the stone above it, but not one another.

"What is this?" Arthur asked. "What...went on inside this thing?"

Jimmy shook his head. "I don't know."

"What about Lynnie Radich?" Arthur couldn't take his eyes away from the chasm, the words originating from his mouth unconsciously.

"We never showed her. Not this part. It was her first time ever comin' and...well...I guess we wanted to keep some stuff to ourselves. Plus, it's like I told you, she wanted to leave soon as she saw the pictures of the Skadegamutc. And somethin' tells me seeing this would've made her want to leave even faster."

Arthur nodded in understanding, and then he glanced down toward the rocks. "What are those? Them stones at the bottom?"

"We call 'em the Orange Rocks."

Arthur leaned in closer, squinting. "Orange? They look blacker than the Devil's soul."

"Yeah, but they's as big as oranges. Look at 'em." Jimmy shrugged, noting the absurdity of the name. "I dunno. Ralph called 'em that the day we first saw 'em in there and it just stuck." He paused now, chewing his lip. "I wonder if Ralph knows about his aunt yet? Still can't believe Mrs. Flannery's dead."

"He's gotta know," Arthur replied. "Sheriff woulda sent someone over by now. To inform the family and all."

Jimmy nodded. "Yeah, I guess that's right." He stared back into the altar and then back to his brother. "You want to take one?"

Arthur squinted, baffled. "Take one?"

Jimmy swallowed and nodded, giving a nervous smile. "Yeah, one of the rocks."

Arthur turned toward his brother now, the expression of bewilderment now glaring on his face. "No, I don't want to take one. And you shouldn't be touching 'em either." He looked around the room again. "Shouldn't be down here at all more I think about it."

Jimmy nodded. "Yeah," he said absently, not addressing either part of his brother's statement specifically.

Arthur turned toward his little brother. "You didn't touch 'em, did you Jimmy?"

Jimmy shook his head.

Arthur closed his eyes and sighed, nodding. "Okay, good."

"Not these ones anyway."

Arthur's eyes shot open as he felt the blood drain from his face and rush toward his heart. "What do you mean '*these ones.*'"

"There was six in all."

"*What?*"

Jimmy chortled and shrugged. No big deal. "We figured if...if we each just took one, it would still leave some for the government to find. The archoligists," he mispronounced. "Whenever they got around to it."

"*Each took one*? Jimmy? You tellin' me you and your freak friends each took a stone from a goddamn burial altar? Or whatever this is!"

"It ain't no burial altar, it's for sacr—"

"It don't matter!" Arthur clenched his teeth now, seething. His mother had been right all along; he couldn't let Jimmy out of his sight, not really, or at least not without knowing where he was going and what he was up to. "I'm guessing y'all still have 'em then, right?" Arthur tried to get calm and not provoke his brother too much, which would either scare him to tears or turn him on Arthur with a straight cross to his chin.

"I have mine," Jimmy replied. "Guessin' Ralph and Bucky got theirs too."

"How long since you took 'em?"

"A few weeks after we started comin' here again. I don't know. Beginnin' of the summer, I guess."

Arthur closed his eyes and shook his head. "Jesus Christ, Jimmy. You gotta bring 'em back. You know that, right?"

Jimmy nodded unconvincingly.

"I'm serious, Jimmy."

"Okay!"

Arthur didn't back down, but he knew he had to diffuse the subject, so he switched gears and said, "Do you remember when we were in our room yesterday and I mentioned somethin' 'bout the storm. And that it was right after when we saw Glenn Flannery comin' toward us? And then...the killin' happened?"

Jimmy nodded. "Yeah, I remember."

"You gave me a look then. And when I asked you about it you said it was cuz of somethin' Lynnie Radich told you. You remember all that?"

"Yeah." Jimmy dropped his gaze and stayed quiet.

Arthur gave his brother a few beats to tell, and when he didn't, he asked, "Well, dammit, Jimmy, what was it? What did Lynnie tell you?" The subconscious connection Arthur's mind had made earlier was now surfacing, about the lights and the etchings on the wall, and though he knew he was fighting headwinds, he prayed Jimmy would answer with something to prove him wrong.

He looked up again. "The Tompiros is gone, but the things they...I don't know...conjured up, I guess, they don't disappear so easy."

"That ain't helpin' me, Jim."

"The Skadegamutc. They lay sleepin' for a time. Waitin' to be woke up. And when they do, that's when the storms blow."

The fire from the torch was nearly gone, and all Arthur could see now was the grim expression on his brother's face.

"And they're back now?" Arthur asked. "These conjured things? Comin' with the storms?"

Jimmy nodded. "All the dust storms that's been happening in these parts this past few weeks, Lynnie's grandmother says it's a kinda punishment."

"Punishment? To who?"

"To us. White men mostly, I guess. For invadin' and chewin' up the land in ways he wadn't s'pposed to. Overfarming it. Burning it. Ain't much killin' of Indians anymore, starving 'em out of their land and such, but the people who done it is still here. Or at least their ancestors is."

"Oh, Christ, come on, Jimmy, you don't believe that." Arthur was truly angry now, and he was no longer worried about the volume of his voice or caving in the ditch. "I ain't got nothin' 'gainst no Indian girls and they grandmothers, but I also ain't gonna believe everything they say either. The 'sakamutchi?' You think they's the ones causin' the storms?"

Jimmy shook his head. "It ain't the Skadegamutc *caused* the storms. But...it's all one. The storms, the spirits, the curses, they're all back now." He began to choke up now, shaking his head. "I told you them stories was old. Old as Santa Fe.

And the one Lynnie told about them witches was goddamn scary, Artie. I can't remember it all, and I don't want to."

Arthur let Jimmy's story—his girlfriend's grandmother's story—settle in, but he wasn't yielding completely, despite what he believed. He frowned, "Shit, Jimmy, these storms been ravaging 'cross Oklahoma and Texas for years now. They's just now getting to New Mexico. You tellin' me it's a witch from two hundred years ago is responsible for all of it?"

"I ain't tellin' you nothin'! And you ain't listening!" Jimmy's temper was flaring now, as it was wont to do in situations where he was either challenged or accused of doing something he hadn't. "The storms is something else, somethin' bigger, and the ones been comin' through here brought back the Skadegamutc! Except...I think it was us!" He choked back tears now, desperation on his face. "I didn't want to think so, but...it was us that released 'em, Arthur. Ralph and Bucky and me."

Arthur put his hand up, trying to calm his brother. "Alright, Jimmy, just relax. Let's take a breath. I think this place has gotten you a little nutso. Let's get out of here 'fore that fire's gone for good and get some oxygen in our brains."

Jimmy didn't speak, but he led the way to the entrance and back to the stairway that led to the entrance of the hollow, and in less than a minute, they were back outside in the ditch, where the light of day felt like bleach, a cleanser for Arthur's mind.

Jimmy took in the air with a gulping breath and smiled uneasily. "Sorry, Arthur. I'm...not sure what happened in there."

"I don't think you and your friends should be coming back here," Arthur said. "You ain't s'possed to be here anyway, and you get caught again y'all gonna get tossed in the slammer." Arthur tried to smile, but it came off as a tired sneer.

Jimmy nodded, but his face looked anything but reassured. For the first time in as long as Arthur could remember, his brother looked scared. "We all took a stone, Arthur. Me, Bucky and Ralph. And now Ralph's aunt is dead. Right after the storm come."

"I thought the storms and those witches were different. You said the storms was somethin' else."

Jimmy closed his eyes and shook his head, as if for the first time coming to accept what he already knew in his heart to be true. "They come with the storm, Arthur. That's what Lynnie's grandmother always said. They come with the storm."

Chapter 15

"It's the stones," Chris said, a luster of discovery in his voice.

"The Orange Rocks," Arthur corrected, just as his brother had corrected him decades earlier.

"So, your brother thought that taking the stones—the Orange Rocks—it what? Awakened them? Disrupted some ancient sleep or something?"

There was no answer from Arthur, not immediately, and Chris suddenly saw the film of unconsciousness return to the man's face.

Chris frowned and sighed and then stared to the ceiling, exasperated. And in that hiatus, as Chris reflected on the pertinence of what Arthur had just told him about the altar, he suddenly felt encouraged. The words of Arthur Richland had been clear, specific, despite his story being almost seventy years old. It had to be true. At least in the general sense. And if it truly was the removal of the Orange Rocks that had released the Skadegamutc to the world, that it was the stones in the bottom of the altar that, once removed, had released from prison the bloodthirsty witches, then that arrangement could be recreated. Somehow. It was a longshot, of course, impossible maybe, and even if it could be accomplished (whatever 'it' was), there was no guarantee he would get Jaycee back. But there was hope. Something concrete to work with. What that work would entail exactly, he didn't yet know, but it was something. The altar. The Hollow. Those were places and things that might still exist today if they'd been left undisturbed. He needed only to get to the site and...and what? Dig? Hire an excavator? How much would that cost him? How long would it take? And even if he could find it, what of the stones themselves?

Suddenly the enormity of all that lay ahead, if he decided to pursue that route, was overwhelming. It *was* impossible. Even if Arthur could remember the exact location, certainly the excavations had been done by now, the ground as it was in 1939 upset beyond recognition. And if not, if the government never followed through with the dig, then certainly development had occurred over the decades. There was probably a strip mall or parking lot where the Sampson farm used to be.

Chris' thoughts were spiraling now, so he turned back to his interviewee and shook him by the arm. "Mr. Richland, did you hear me?"

"Huh?" Arthur was staring out the window toward the lawn, which was illuminated in a gorgeous green, the sun smiling down upon it, promising another warm day to come. The elderly man was still lost in his own story, not quite sure where he was in the world now that the segment with the altar and the Orange Rocks had ended.

"The Orange Rocks? Did taking them lead to Ruby's disappearance? And to the murder of that woman at the store?"

Arthur continued his vacant gaze, appearing to ignore the question. But after a pause, he looked over to Chris and said, "Tell me about your daughter."

Chris sighed and his shoulders slumped. He was so frustrated he wanted to cry. Instead, he took a long blink and reset his focus on Arthur, remembering his promise never to push too hard. He was getting closer, and he just needed to keep going, regardless of whether the direction was forward or sideways. There were different paths to every destination, he knew; he just had to be patient. He kept his tone even and unaggressive and replied, "I've told you, Mr. Richland, her name is Jaycee, she's six years—"

"I mean tell me about *her*. What she's like. I already know she's a beaut, but is she clever? Does she like Barbie dolls? Or dinosaurs? Dancing or football?"

Chris gave a sad grin as he let the question marinate. *Just follow the path, it's the only one in front of you.* "Smart?" he said. "Sometimes I think the hospital gave us the wrong baby she's so smart. Because trust me, neither me nor her mom were getting any calls from the navy to design their nuclear subs. I mean, we aren't imbeciles, don't get me wrong, but we're not Jaycee. She was gonna be...is gonna be something special." He cleared his throat, fighting the tears. "And like you saw, she's pretty like her mom, and she's a girl's girl, you know? Though..." Chris wiped a tear and laughed at a vague memory "...she does like to get dirty. Like *really* dirty. Like worms and bugs kind of dirty. But only if she's wearing a clean, white dress, of course." He could feel himself choking up again and paused, not wanting to get too far afield if he could avoid it. He sniffled, "What else do you want to know?"

Arthur's eyes suddenly turned steely, his expression forbidding as he sat up and stared into Chris' face. "She wasn't an artist by any chance?"

Chris' face flushed to white. "Are...are you asking me if she could draw?"

Arthur smiled. "Yes, exactly."

He scoffed. "Best drawer I ever saw. At least for her age."

Arthur nodded, as if this detail somehow slid another piece into place.

"What does that mean? Does Jaycee's being able to draw have something to do with the stones? The witches?"

"I'm not sure, not exactly, but I think in a way it does. In a way that'll help bring her back, I hope. Keep her alive for as long as...well, keep her alive."

"How...how could you know something like that?"

"The girl you described—smart, pretty, creative beyond her years—sounds like it coulda been Ruby you were just talking about."

"Ruby could draw too?"

"Might have been a Rembrandt you were looking at when you saw her drawings. Would have been hard to tell whose was whose?"

"What does this have to do with...I mean the drawing part...what...?" Chris didn't even know what word should come next in his question, and his head began to swim with confusion.

Arthur nodded. "I've thought a lot about that question over these years. And I've come to believe it's not exactly the drawing that matters, not per se, but more of whatever that thing in the brain is that allows a person to draw with such ease. Expert-like, without really trying. Like they were just born to do it. Could be the case with other things too, I suppose—music and painting and sculpting, I guess—I really don't know. But I think it's why someone like Glenn Flannery couldn't fight against it. Why most of us can't. And someone like Ruby—and I'm hoping Jaycee—could."

"So, it's just coincidence that they were about the same age?"

Arthur shook his head. "No, I don't think so. I think that's an important piece of it. The Skadegamutc, they came to protect at first. To protect the land and the people that lived on it. And then they came for revenge." He shuddered now. "I think the younger ones, it's their innocence that attracts the witches, and the ones like Ruby and Jaycee, it's their intelligence—and I think maybe their bravery too—that allows them to come back."

With this thought, Arthur turned to the window again as if considering this last part of his theory for the first time. Or perhaps the first time in many moons.

Chris listened to the story like Moses on Sinai, and though he felt like the theory was thin and a bit too speculative, he appreciated Arthur's faith. Chris couldn't quite bring himself to believe this theory entirely, not with all his heart, but it was a way to move forward on the path. "So, what do I have to do, Mr. Richland. What did you do when Ruby was taken? And how did you bring her back?"

Arthur looked over at Chris now, and the glaze of confusion had returned to his eyes. Too many questions had come at once and now the thread was split. Chris cursed himself, but he quickly changed the course of his inquiry, hoping to bring Arthur back online. The story. His story. That was the one he needed to tell. "Do you remember what you did to bring Ruby home," Chris asked.

Arthur shivered at the question, but he kept his eyes staring toward the landscape. "I spoke of innocence earlier. And I do believe it's one of the reasons she was spared. My Ruby. And I believe the same will be true of your daughter. But it's more than that. It's a story of sin as well. A story of redemption."

Finally, Arthur turned and faced Chris again, and the young visitor could feel the laser heat of the old man's stare upon his face.

"Let me tell you about someone not so innocent," Arthur said, "and then you'll begin to understand how she came back."

Chapter 16

"Jimmy, hurry up with that jack, will ya?"

Jimmy hauled the jack behind him like a suitcase through an airport and then parked it by the front passenger tire, next to where Randall Richland sat with a pressure gauge in hand. Jimmy and his father were alone inside the lone bay of Chester Sutton's garage, where the owner allowed his employees to use the space on off days, as well as during certain hours when the garage was closed. It was Sunday afternoon, so Sutton's, just like most of the rest of Clayton, was shuttered until Monday morning.

"Pressure's fine on the tire, so it's gotta be something else throwing the alignment. Hope it ain't the suspension."

"What if it *is* the suspension," Jimmy asked, nibbling at the edge of a fingernail.

"Well, then, it'll be more work than I got in me today. Doubt Chester's got the parts anyway. Might have to go to Santa Fe if it's a real problem."

"We'll still go to the fair though, right? Even if it is the suspension?"

Only a day had passed since Arthur's visit with Jimmy to the Ditches—and two days after Janet Flannery had been murdered at the front counter of Downes Grocery—but already the fair had made its way back to the forefront of his brain, just as it had in Arthur's. The prospects that the trip to Albuquerque would be canceled was almost too much for either boy to fathom.

"Can't say yes or no without seeing what we got. But the fair's a few days out still, so let's just figure out the problem first, then we'll get to worrying about what it means for other things." Randall flashed his son a soft smile now. "But I wouldn't worry too much. What's the point of having a pa that fixes cars for a livin' if he can't fix cars, eh?"

Jimmy grinned widely. "Yes sir."

Randall Richland jacked the car up and then grabbed the tire at either side, and then he began to shake it like it was a guy who owed him money. Next, he shifted his hands clockwise so they were on the top and bottom halves of the tire, and there he gave the rubber ring a similar motion. He turned to Jimmy. "Wheel's tight. Means the suspension's probably good."

Jimmy gave a quiet sigh and a genuine smile of relief. "Well, heck, that's as good a—"

"The hell is this pulling in here?"

"Huh?"

But Randall didn't reply to his son, as he was looking past Jimmy now with a narrow gaze and clenched jaws, staring toward the only proper road that ran through Clayton, New Mexico.

U.S. Route 87 entered New Mexico from the east, snaking northwest across the border at the juncture where the Oklahoma and Texas panhandles joined. The road then bisected Clayton like the part in a child's hairline, right down the middle until it meandered off to the north on its way toward Colorado. And the first place anyone saw when they entered Clayton on 87 was Chester Sutton's Garage and Service station. This was no incident of fortune, of course; Chester Sutton had planned this locale with precision, situating his shop strategically at just that spot. He had even taken several days erecting his own hand-painted signs miles outside of Clayton, assuring that any weary travelers would be "Fixed and Fueled at Sutton's!"; that is, if they could just trudge on for another hour or so. Of course, travelers and tourists didn't pass through with much frequency, not in the beginning anyway—most people in America still didn't own a car in the early '30s—but Sutton's was the last stop for petrol until Raton, and so any out-of-town customers who did come through almost always stopped and filled up.

And so, though Mr. Sutton wasn't exactly running Standard Oil in those days, with what he made from the residents of Clayton (who were investing in farm equipment and pickup trucks more and more with every month that passed), he did a good business and had become, almost certainly, the most financially successful man in town.

And then in 1935, Chester Sutton's outside customer base exploded as the heat and drought and storms arrived in Texas and Oklahoma, and the lack of food that followed began driving people west for a new start in California. Some men arrived alone or with their new brides, and this category of traveler, those without heavy burdens, though they were as poor as any, were normally young and healthy, and thus there was a hopefulness to their demeanor, knowing that sun and sea—and even the possibility of fortune and fame—awaited them in Los Angeles or San Francisco or wherever within the Golden State their hearts carried them.

But most who came through Clayton were not of this genre, and they entered the town's border as families of eight, nine and ten, in cars that had been loaded to impossible capacities, stuffed to the gills with bodies and luggage that were bursting with coats and rugs, dishes and broken toys. Or else they arrived in pickup trucks, the beds of which were stacked high with furniture and children, vehicles that coughed tubercular exhaust as they teetered to make the turn into Sutton's. Of course, they too had little money to spend, and Jimmy and Arthur, any time they were around the garage during these encounters, always marveled at how they'd gotten as far as they did without the tires exploding beneath them.

Jimmy turned to see the object of his father's stare, and as he did, he saw that the class of migrant approaching on that day was of the overstuffed-truck variety, rumbling toward them like a blind, old rhinoceros, hauling on its hitch a trailer made of wood and netting, the latter material somehow containing its cargo despite the bulge created on all sides.

The truck slowed and drifted to the left now as it approached Sutton's, the brakes and steering parts grinding in pain as it turned finally into Sutton's Garage.

"Will you look at this lot," Randall grumbled. "Goddamn Okies never stop comin.'" Jimmy's father snapped the dirty rag in his hand over his shoulder and stepped out of the garage into the sunshine of the day. He popped a toothpick between his lips and then marched slowly forward until he was standing in front of the pumps. There, he put his hands in his pockets and his chest up high. It looked to Jimmy like he was guarding the fuel, or else looking for a fight.

As the truck came to a stop, Jimmy could see three kids atop the truck, including a boy about his own age who was standing on what looked to be a broken schoolhouse chair. He was shirtless, and though he was a white kid, his face was as black as any African man he'd seen in National Geographic magazine, stained with grime and soot and who knew what else. Next to him was a girl about six, only slightly cleaner than her brother, and beside her was a teenager who couldn't have been more than seventeen, smoking a cigarette. They all had the expressions of men returning from war.

Inside the cabin of the truck were four people in all, two women and two men, and they each exited the car with haste, coughing and exhaling the stagnation and heat that had built up inside over God only knew how many miles. The driver settled his cough and gave a conciliatory smile as he stood just outside the truck, not making any move toward the stern-looking mechanic before him. Randall was outnumbered seven to one, and though the seven hardly looked like the type to rob a man for fuel, anyone who was that outmanned would be wary—should be wary—and not likely above taking a shot at a person if he thought him aggressive.

"How do?" the driver called.

Randall said nothing, giving only a slight click of his chin in response.

The man smiled and nodded, accepting Randall's quiet suspicion. "Was hopin' to get some fuel. That is if you got any."

To Jimmy, the driver appeared to be several years older than his father, though, in truth, he was probably a few years younger, late thirties maybe. The two women were also in that range, Jimmy guessed, while the other man was a generation older; Jimmy guessed him the father of the driver.

"We's closed," Randall answered. "The Lord's Day."

The man nodded in understanding. "Of course. Amen. I believe it was Him who brought us to you if I'm honest. Didn't think we'd see another town 'fore we ran dry. Ain't got enough to get to another, that's for sure. We was hoping to make it to Colorado by morning. My wife's got family there. Says we welcome to stay a day or two 'fore we get on west."

"California?"

The man sighed and then gave a wide smile and a nod, one that said he understood the cliché they were demonstrating. "That's it. Monterey area."

"Hmm. Well, suppose you shoulda planned your trip out a little better. Tough to get to California—or Colorado, for that matter—without gas."

The man fought back a grimace and nodded. "You are right about that," he said. "We had some trouble outside Enid; was no way to foresee it, I'm afraid."

"Injun ambush?" Randall guessed, mostly as a joke.

The man laughed. "No, no, 'fraid it wasn't nothin' as excitin' as all that. Radiator. Took half the day to find water to fill it."

"Mmhmm." Randall's eyes flashed to the girl sitting atop the truck. She met his eyes for a moment before looking away again, taking a drag on her cigarette as she stared blankly toward some place in the distance. Randall turned back to the driver. "Not sure what to tell you then. Like I said, we's closed, and this ain't my shop to be makin' decisions about openin' up. Specially on the Sabbath." He paused and added, "If I did though, gotta ask, you got the cash to pay for the fuel?"

Now it was the man who looked away, this time to the woman who was certainly his wife. She frowned and gave the faintest shake of her head. She was no doubt the bookkeeper of the group, and it was clear the books she was keeping now were blood red. He looked back to Randall. "Fraid that went dry a few miles back as well. The cash that is."

"So how was you thinkin' you'd pay exactly?" Randall was genuinely confused now.

"Was hopin' to work for it. Y'all got some tendin' to do around here, I'll bet. I'm pretty good with a wrench. And my boy up there can sweep and fetch and whatever you need." He clicked his head toward the garage. "I see you got a car on three wheels over there. Maybe I could help you out there. Know a thing about tires and—"

"That's work for me and my boy," Randall snapped.

Jimmy was still at the threshold of the garage, and having now been referenced, he walked onto the lot, revealing himself.

"And a good lookin' boy he is," the driver said, nodding toward Jimmy.

"Yeah." Randall glanced again to the trio on top of the truck. "Those your kids there?"

"That's them." He smiled proudly.

"Good lookin' as well." Randall Richland looked at the daughter now, the older one who was smoking. "That one in particular. Very pretty."

The driver gave a smile with his mouth only and nodded in agreement.

"So, then, see, I don't need no help fixin' cars; that's my occupation. But maybe you can do something to earn your way." He looked back to the teenager. "Or more specifically, maybe she can do somethin'."

"Now you look here—"

"I'm looking right at you!" Randall interjected.

"It's alright, Pa."

A silence fell across the lot of Sutton's as the feminine voice drifted down from above.

"Sher—"

"I said it's alright." The older daughter crushed out the last of her cigarette and stood, brushing off the front of her dress, dust falling everywhere like brown snow. "Ain't like it's the first time; sure it won't be the last."

"You listen here—" the older man started, the driver's father. He took a step forward, and Jimmy could see immediately that twenty years ago things might have gone quite differently. There was a toughness in the man's eyes that bled through, and if he'd had a gun, Jimmy had no doubt he would have shot them both—Jimmy included—and then spat on the ground behind him as he drove off. But as it was, he was past his prime, and unarmed, so the wife of the driver grabbed him by the arm and pushed him back inside the truck, crying as she entered in behind him.

The driver simply turned his back and walked away from the garage, gliding past his truck before stopping at the edge of 87. There he pulled out a cigarette and lit it, watching the empty road while his daughter descended the heap to the lot below.

As she came down, Randall turned to Jimmy, who's eyes were like damp marbles, the disappointment so palpable that Randall dropped his gaze a moment and looked back to the girl, as if reconsidering what he was about to do. But then he turned his head back toward Jimmy and clucked his head forward. "You get on home now, Jim. We'll fix the wheel tomorrow." He then smiled a grin so forced and fake Jimmy would never forget it, not for the rest of his twelve remaining years on earth. It would be the look that helped him forgive himself and Arthur for what they would do a few weeks later.

"Now that I know it ain't the suspension," Randall added, holding firm the terrible grin, "it won't take too much to get it done."

Jimmy didn't smile back, and instead he gave a slow, unconscious shake of his head, one last attempt to bring this moment to an end.

"Go on now. Tell your mother I'm working late."

Jimmy turned and began to walk, and before he turned the corner of the garage and began on the road home, he heard the girl speak again. It was only one word: "Where?"

Chapter 17

Chris remained quiet, sympathetic of the trauma Arthur's father's actions must have caused him and his brother. He was curious as to how he could tell the story with such detail, however, having not been there at the time, but the answer to that question came instantly.

"You're probably wondering how I come to know this story so well—the whole scene with my father at the garage—when I wasn't even there that day. What those migrants looked like. Who said what and when. That was Jimmy's story, eh? Jimmy's cross to bear?"

Chris didn't reply, but Arthur nodded back at him anyway, agreeing with whatever skepticism might have been running through the man's mind.

"Well, I suppose I filled in a few of the details, but not as many as you might think. Jimmy told me about every element of that incident a couple days later, from the second they walked into the garage until he was running home in tears. Of course, that was after two days of hiding in his room and walking around school like our dog had died. Knew something was wrong though, something other than what had gone down at the Ditches, just didn't know what until he let it all pour out. And when he finally did, the story hit me the same way, like an iron fist to my stomach. And then it stuck there. Lodged in like a kind of cancer. Or maybe a scar is a better comparison. A scar right down the middle of your chest. It doesn't kill you, you know? And you don't feel the pain after a while. But you never forget it. You can't. You see it every day in the mirror, so the reminder never goes away. And even when you don't see it, you still know it's there. It registers inside you." Arthur's face turned sour now, his eyes squinting as the dormant grief from his past finally resurfaced inside his heart. "That's how it was with my father. Each time I saw him after that day, Jimmy's story would begin to play in my mind like a kind of reel-to-reel movie. Happened so often it started to feel like I *had* been there myself." Arthur paused now, and his expression of pain bled to sadness. "After I did what I did though, what I believed I had to, the hatred I had for him seemed to transfer into me. For a long time after, the image of that migrant girl is the only thing that let me get to sleep at night."

Chris was still processing the story of Randall Richland and what had happened at Sutton's Garage, but with these last two sentences from Arthur, he was brought back to the present. "What do you mean by that? After you did what?"

Arthur stayed quiet, however, not ready to reveal that portion of the tale.

Chris let it go for the moment and said, "I don't understand, Arthur. What does any of this have to do with Ruby?"

"Ruby?" Arthur blinked frantically, a queer smile now replacing the bitterness on his face from seconds earlier.

Again, Chris' stacked questions had disorganized Arthur's thinking, or so it appeared, so he chose the one that concerned him most. "The story about the migrant girl and your father, what did that have to do with Ruby?"

"It isn't to do with Ruby," Arthur replied quickly, "it's about innocence." And then, as if to add more mystique to his response, he added, "Innocence and guilt."

Chris Boylin lifted the heels of his hands to his eyes and rubbed, and then he ran his fingers backward through his long mane of hair, trying to bring a physical resetting to his mind. He was feeling depleted now, physically and emotionally, and though he felt he was making progress, knew he was drawing closer to a mission, his skepticism was still flaring.

Chris pulled the chair closer until he was inches from Arthur and said, "Listen, Arthur, I believe you. Okay? Everything you've said about your sister and the killings and the...Skadegamutc, I believe it. I have every reason to and no reason not to. All you've told me so far rings of the truth. Like a gong in my belly it rings true."

Arthur smiled now, accepting the words as those of gratitude.

"But I don't come here just to listen to old stories. Not unless they can directly help me find Jaycee." Chris' voice was rising with each word, so he took a breath and put his hand up in apology. He stared past Arthur now to the window outside and readjusted his tone, making sure that each word from that point forward would be heard with crystal clarity. "And I do think you can help me, Arthur. That the story of Ruby's disappearance can help me find my daughter. And that means that each second that passes without me finding Jaycee is because of you."

Arthur's smile bent downward, and he turned toward Chris, his eyes shifty now, as if recognizing the presence of danger.

"I'm sorry for your memory, Mr. Richland, and I'm sorry you ended up here alone in this place. But if I never see Jaycee again, alive, I'll blame you for her death."

"I'm try—"

"I think you know where she is. Or...if not *where,* you know how I can get her back. It's in your mind, in your story, and you acting like your brain is a mold of Swiss cheese isn't going to be good enough for me." Chris' rage was bubbling now, though he kept his voice low and calm, hoping that the man would respond to his actual words without getting spooked by his tone. It was a risk, of course, he understood that, but demanding answers was a thing he'd yet to try. As was a direct threat, which he cast forward next. "So, I'll tell you this right now, Arthur: if you forget the rest of this story—or God forbid you die before you finish telling it—I'll hunt you down in hell and kill you again."

Arthur felt a storm collect inside him, a rush of adrenaline that he rarely felt anymore. But he was encouraged by the speech of Chris Boylin. The resolve and determination, as well as his willingness to believe the incredulous. And the promise to kill for what he loved. This was the kind of man who would do what was necessary to bring his daughter home, and perhaps to bury the Skadegamutc forever.

Despite these thoughts, however, Arthur remained quiet, and Chris' decision to intimidate suddenly felt like the wrong tactic. "I'm...I'm sorry, Mr. Richland," he said, a pang of distress and regret now replacing the rage in his gut. "I just—"

"And when he walked in the house later that night..." Arthur continued, picking up the story of Jimmy and his father from where he'd left it, just after Jimmy had heard the last word of the migrant girl. "...it was a half hour before supper."

Chris stayed quiet, realizing now that no matter his conviction or the danger he tried to impose, he couldn't overcome science or disease or the workings of Arthur Richland's mind. It was like screaming at a deaf man. All he could hope for was that the things he'd told the old man would register, at least on some entrenched level of his brain, and then would stick there like the scar Arthur had used as an analogy moments earlier.

"The look on his face that night was one I didn't quite understand at the time and wouldn't until a few days later when Jimmy finally told me what happened. There was pure unhappiness in his eyes, devastation. It was Glenn Flannery's face in the newspaper the day after he'd killed his wife and was headed to the courthouse. Looking at my father that night, I thought someone else in town had died, or that he had just come from Dr. Olesen and found out he had cancer or cirrhosis and had only weeks to live. But Randall Richland was no smoker, and not much of a drinker either. No sir. He was a man who had just sinned. A man who was culpable. And when Jimmy told me of his guilty act, I was ashamed of him from that day on."

He looked away again, as if searching his soul to find whether this sentiment still held true. He frowned and continued, not finding the answer.

"My mother saw it too, I think. Fumbled a dish right onto the kitchen floor. It didn't shatter, and I remember thinking at the time what an unsatisfying sound the plate had made, clunking like an iron pan on the wood, the dust cushioning it from breaking. It was a miracle, really." Arthur closed his eyes again and smiled, tilting his head to the ceiling, letting the memory wash over him, trying to capture that moment again in its fullness.

"Arthur?" Chris prodded, his voice soft and low, a hypnotherapist bringing a patient back from immersion.

"Except that wasn't the real miracle," Arthur continued, responding to the voice. "The real miracle was my father's sin. And the price he would have to pay for it." Arthur paused again and nodded, as if he'd forgotten this epiphany at some point in his life and had remembered it again just then. "It wasn't a small thing for my father to look so vulnerable," Arthur continued, "so devoid of confidence. Never saw that exact look ever again, nor did I see the same father. He was changed by what he did, and from the day Jimmy told me about the incident, the only question in my mind was why he had done it."

"Maybe he just wasn't a very decent person," Chris offered, somewhat aloofly. He was exhausted by the restraint and balance he was forcing himself to uphold, and his words came out slow and defeated. "I'm sure you've considered that possibility."

"That's just it, Mr. Boylin; he *was* a decent man. Not kind or friendly, perhaps, but he was honest and loyal. God-fearing. His life was my mother and his children, or at least Jimmy, if not his other two. And to display himself so...grotesquely in front of his favorite child, it was...unprecedented. He was no abuser, sexual or otherwise. What Jimmy described as happening at Chester Sutton's that day wasn't Randall Richland."

"Maybe you just misjudged him. You were a kid after all. Kids don't know the half of what's going on in their parents' lives most of the time."

"I'm not a child now, Mr. Boylin. And I know all about the naivete of children. I had a son of my own. And I still have a grandchild. And great-grandkids too. And I know you think I'm an old fool and that anything I say about my father will just be in defense of his character. But you're wrong. I was never a great fan of his. Even when I was very young, I never had that burning adoration I sometimes hear described from men about their fathers when they were boys. I suppose that was due to my jealousy, that of his affection toward Jimmy over me, I don't really know." Arthur opened his eyes wide now and cocked his head, a sign that what he was about to say shouldn't be ignored. "But whatever feeling or desire took control of my father that day, the one that made him use that girl in the way he did, it had to do with what was released from the Ditches."

Chris gave Arthur's words their due consideration, pausing not just to mollify the elderly man, but to truly reflect on his words in the context of the story. And then he shook his head and said, "But your father didn't kill anybody. The girl and those migrants weren't found murdered in the bay of Sutton's Garage. And he didn't die himself. From what you've told me, it seems like that would have been the more consistent result if the Skadegamutc had been there. Or if they were responsible. Besides, you didn't say anything about a storm that day. I thought the storm was...I don't know...necessary?" Chris was confused now, and his head hurt. And besides finding Jaycee, all he wanted to do was go back to his motel room and sleep.

Arthur smiled. "I'm pleased that you've been listening. But it wasn't the Skadegamutc that presented that scenario to me that day."

"Scenario?"

Arthur nodded. "It's one I thought on for many years. And when the time is right, I'll tell you what I've come to believe. But it's too early in the story for that!" Arthur's eyes blossomed. "But it is important, Mr. Boylin, so file it away for later. You'll need to make a similar choice to the one I made."

"Please, Mr. Richland, I—"

"But I know you will make it without hesitation. That was not me, however. Not even when I knew the truth of what I had to do. As you correctly noted, I was just a child; I didn't have all the confidence that you have now."

Chris leaned back in his chair now and stared at the man, intrigued in a new way by Arthur's words. They felt like the beginning of an answer.

"And maybe it's time then to get to the nub, eh? Everything else I've told you is relevant, rest assured, but now we should talk about the day Ruby disappeared." He readjusted the pillow behind his back and sat straight, and then, with a gleam that appeared like a firework in his eyes, he said, "Alright then: the fair."

Chapter 18

"We're next, Jimmy."

Arthur said the words conspiratorially as he licked his lips and wrung his hands, watching as the huge metal wheel started to turn again, lifting the bottom chair upwards, the gears at the hub of the machine grinding painfully as if this were the last hoist of its life before it finally died forever. Arthur prayed not; despite his bubbling anxiety at the thought of actually rising 90 feet into the air, his fear was no match for his excitement.

"How can you tell?" Jimmy asked, looking skeptically at the long queue of riders in front of them. "There's so many people ahead of us."

"I already counted 'em. I know it. I can see who all's together and who's riding alone, and we're gonna be next."

"Hey, it's Artie! Artie Richland!"

The call came from ahead, from one of the cars on the wheel, and Arthur looked up to see Sherman Caswell in the second car from the bottom. Arthur had noticed his classmate within the first twenty minutes of arriving at the fair, but he'd kept his distance until now, his eyes averted, hoping the boy wouldn't spot him in return. Next to Sherman was Tammy Yarlow, almost without debate the prettiest girl at Bronson Cutting Middle School. On a list of people Arthur would have wanted to run into from Clayton, Sherman Caswell would have been near the bottom. Arthur pretended not to hear him.

"Your date's a little small to ride this one, Artie!" Sherman called, referring to Arthur's sister Ruby. "Maybe she could sit on your lap!"

Arthur was embarrassed, but he could almost feel the boil of hate rise like thin lava inside Jimmy, and he knew if the taunting went a second longer, the queue would become a scene. Jimmy had learned how to control his anger over the years—from ages five to eight he was a molten volcano—but like a volcano, it stilled lived inside him, and it had begun to rumble louder over the last two weeks, ever since the incident with their father and the migrants at Sutton's Garage.

And once the volcano in Jimmy erupted, no one, not even their father, could control it. And though there weren't many things that activated Jimmy's temper, an attack upon his sister, verbal or otherwise, however indirect or innocuous the slight might be, was one of them.

Jimmy's eyes had grown narrow now, a cobra studying a curious ground squirrel, silently daring the boy to say another word.

"Alright, Jimmy, just cool it," Arthur said. "You know Sherman. The guy's a jerk."

"And don't forget to hold your boyfriend's hand either!" Sherman shouted, nodding toward Jimmy.

With that, Jimmy stepped from the line in a blind wrath, like a grizzly mother toward a foreign bear that's stumbled upon her territory. He pushed through a pair of teenage boys, splitting through their shoulders, the top of his head at the level of their chests as he passed. The boys said nothing in protest, seeming to note the danger of rage in the child, and they only watched in silence as Jimmy strode toward the fencing that separated the Ferris wheel from the queue. He reached the metal barrier, and, for just a moment, Arthur thought he was going to scale the fence and rush toward the wheel itself. What he would have done at that point, Arthur didn't know, since the car Sherman was riding in was a good twenty feet in the air; but he wouldn't have put it past his brother to start climbing.

Instead, Jimmy simply leaned over the fence, glared up at Sherman, and yelled, "Fuck you, you little prick! Come down here and say that to my face!"

Sherman gave a visible flinch to the threat, and Tammy Yarlow looked away in embarrassment as the calls of 'Hey!' and 'Watch it!' and 'There's kids here!' erupted from the adults both on the wheel and in line, aghast at the language spewing from this pre-teen child in front of them.

Finally, Sherman forced a projected laugh, throwing his head back in an exaggerated motion, trying to appear unfazed, though it was obvious to nearly everyone that had he not been in a metal cage two stories above the ground, his reaction would have been quite different. He looked past Jimmy to Arthur again. "Control your dog, Richland!" he yelled, and then he extended the middle finger on both of his hands, swirling them around in a figure eight motion, ensuring both Arthur and Jimmy felt the full effect of the gesture.

"You better hope this thing never stops!" Jimmy screamed, and with his threat cast, the cars began to turn again, with Sherman's gondola gliding slowly past Jimmy at eye level before it began its climb toward the sky. Jimmy stood and waited for the wheel to make one more full turn, eyeing Sherman's car as if his own life rested in the balance, careful not to lose sight of it as it made its revolution. And when the car finally passed in front of him again, he called, "Hey!" pointing toward the car with an accusatory finger. "Hey shitface! I'll be waiting for you! You hear me! I'll be waiting right here!'"

Neither Sherman nor Tammy looked Jimmy's way, as both pretended to be distracted by the amusement of the ride, though Sherman gave a nervous sideways glance just at the last moment before the car rose again.

Jimmy finally turned and walked back to his place in line, oblivious to the stares that followed him, most of which were accompanied by frowns of disappointment and disapproving shakes of the head. "I'm gonna knock his head off when that thing settles," he said, rejoining his siblings in line.

"No, you ain't either," Arthur replied. "You hear me? If you do that, you ain't gonna get to ride, and we're all three gonna get kicked out." Arthur scoffed. "Plus, Sherman's six inches taller'n you and thirty pounds heavier. Could be it's your head gets knocked off."

"Pssh. You don't think I can take that pussy?!"

"Jimmy, 'at's enough! You don't see Ruby right here?"

Jimmy looked side-eyed at his little sister and frowned, knowing it was she who was part of the reason for the dust up to begin with.

"And it don't matter if you can take him or not. You start fightin' in here, they gonna send us out of the fair entirely, and Ma's gonna wonder why we's in the parking lot and not the fairgrounds. And what do you think Pa's gonna say? All that racket about fixing the wheel so we could get to the fair, plus what he paid for the tickets, and then you're gonna blow it with a scrap at the Ferris wheel."

Arthur thought of the misaligned wheel on their pickup again, and then of Jimmy's story about the westbound fruit pickers at Sutton's. It was a memory that surfaced many times a day now, usually within minutes of Arthur waking in the morning, with Arthur sometimes believing it had been a dream, and that their father wasn't the ogre he now believed him to be. How could he have forced that family like that? The girl? For a gallon or two of gas? It was the act of a monster. Of a lunatic. Like Jack the Ripper or Lizzi Borden. It was possible Jimmy had misinterpreted the scene, of course, and that the family had in fact done real work for the fuel and then were on their way, no harm done to anyone. But each time Arthur considered this possibility, he thought of his father's expression that night when he arrived home, and any doubt was erased. He wondered if his mother knew. If she cared.

"Fine," Jimmy replied with a grumble. "I'll leave it for now. For y'all. But when I see that prick back home, he's got somethin' comin'."

Arthur sighed and rolled his eyes. "I'm sure he'll be in a fit of terror," he joked, but in a deeper part of his mind, he was glad not to be Sherman Caswell, the boy who was now in the crosshairs of Jimmy Richland. It wasn't so much that it mattered today or next week, but in four or five years, once Jimmy got his legs under him a bit and some flesh on his bones, the boy was gonna be a problem, and Arthur was glad to be on the same team as his brother.

Arthur looked down at Ruby for the first time since the confrontation between Sherman and Jimmy, and though her eyes were alert and bright, she seemed not the least bit disturbed by anything that had unfolded thus far. Arthur forced a smile. "You gonna be ready, Rube? We're getting on next?"

Ruby put her hands on her hips and lifted her chin high, staring up at the enormous metal contraption. "I am ready," she answered, enunciating each of the words.

Arthur snickered and shook his head, baffled by the overtly casual demeanor of his sister, who, to that point, had simply floated through the line with her older brothers, unconcerned with her surroundings, never asking about how it all worked once they sat down in the car and the wheel began to turn. Arthur, himself, (not yet fully versed on the concepts of the laws of gravity), also had plenty of questions about the physics of the ride, most of which had to do with why the cars didn't flip over once the wheel started coming back down the other side, no matter how many times he'd seen it happen. But he quietly attributed Ruby's passiveness to the idea that she didn't really understand that they were actually in line to *ride* the Ferris wheel and not simply to continue watching it from afar.

But Arthur knew that wasn't the reason. Not really. Ruby was smart, and the reason she didn't seem scared was because she wasn't.

"My legs are gettin' tired though," Ruby announced, and as the line had once again paused, Ruby plopped herself down at the feet of her brothers, the bottom of her yellow dress landing flush in the dirt. It was one of her older dresses, but Arthur knew he would get a crooked eye from their mother anyway once they regrouped for lunch, a look that would contain a tacit question as to why he let his little sister get so dirty. But they'd been waiting almost an hour, and he couldn't expect a five-year-old to stay on her feet much longer than that.

"Try not to get too dirty though, Rube, huh? Ma'll have mine if you come back lookin' like a orphaned alley cat."

Ruby smiled and nodded, and then, quietly, she began to trace a finger through the dirt, her tiny digit disappearing beneath a layer of dust that was two inches deep if it was a millimeter. Arthur followed his sister's finger like the swaying watch of a hypnotist, tilting his head a fraction, first to the left, then to the right, trying to identify the curves and lines that were searching for a cohesive form. Then, in a flash, materializing like a splashing rainbow in a dusky sky, the picture became obvious. It was of a cat, the shape appearing so suddenly to Arthur's eyes he released a quiet gasp and recoiled slightly. No doubt Ruby's decision to draw the cat had been subliminally prompted by Arthur's simile from moments earlier, as opposed to something she'd been planning during the time they were in line, and yet it emerged with such ease from the grime, as if she'd made the picture a hundred times before. And this was no cartoon cat that had surfaced from the dead soil below, nor was it just some two-dimensional face of a nondescript feline, where the ears and whiskers make it unmistakable to identify. Ruby had effortlessly outlined the whole of the animal, from serpentine tail to its shark-tooth-shaped nose, the contours and symmetry so perfect Arthur could find nothing out of place or inexact, even in the loose dust, a medium so unstable it seemed impossible that such an image could have been created.

Arthur swallowed and squeezed back the sting of a tear in his right eye. "That's...incredible, Ruby," he said without a hint of patronization.

Ruby cocked her head and studied the picture now, curiously, as if not quite seeing the majesty her brother was. "Thank you, Arthur," she replied.

"I mean, I always knew you was good at drawing, but—"

"We gotta get outta here!" a voice called from ahead. "Now! Let's go!"

Arthur looked up from Ruby's cat and toward the direction of the voice, and there he saw a family of five or six, the father flustered and searching as he grabbed his daughter by the arm, tugging her in the direction of the fair's entrance. The mother and other children followed in confusion, abandoning their place in line as if their names had just been announced to win a hundred dollars, but only if they could make it to the ticket counter in the next thirty seconds.

As if triggered by the movement, the queue behind Arthur and his siblings began to surge forward, and Arthur and Jimmy absently flowed with the wave, Arthur wincing as he saw the footfalls of the children immediately behind them land squarely on Ruby's cat, separating the body in two at the shoulders.

"Come on, Ruby," Jimmy called, unaware of the destruction of a masterpiece that had just occurred below him. "You're gonna get trampled."

Ruby stood and stumbled sideways, and Arthur reached for her hand, and as he did, he noticed several more people ahead of them begin to exit the line, each moving in the same direction like a school of fish, scrambling away from the Ferris wheel and toward the fair's lone exit.

Soon, a steady murmur began to bubble around the fair, arising at the start like the hum of crickets before building seconds later to the baritone of a cattle stampede.

"What's going on?" Arthur uttered, mostly to himself. He chuckled nervously. "Why's everyone chickenin' out."

Jimmy shrugged, unconcerned, and Arthur looked to Ruby now, searching for any clues she might have gleaned through her unique intuition. She didn't meet Arthur's eyes but rather his shoulder, and perhaps a spot in the air above it, gazing off to some place in the distance. And her face, which had been calm and playful to that point, suddenly bled to confusion.

And then fear.

Arthur tried to speak but the words stuck in his windpipe, so he cleared his throat and said, "You don't have to get on, Rube. I...I told you that, right? You can wait for us here at the bottom."

Ruby gave a long blink and her lips parted just barely, and then she shook her head, negating Arthur's words. She gave a second blink, this time keeping her eyes shut, as if trying to wish away some reality in front of her. When she opened her eyes, her face melted to a frown, and then Ruby gave a heavy swallow and lifted a finger—the same enchanted finger that had drawn the perfect cat a minute before—and pointed it over Arthur's right shoulder to the spot where she'd been staring.

Despite the direction of Ruby's aim— to his right—Arthur instinctively turned and looked over his left shoulder, toward the Ferris Wheel, where the sounds of laughter and delight that had scored the day to that point had since evaporated, having been transmuted into the rumbling mutter that now reverberated all around them. He followed the ring of metal upward to the top car where Sherman Caswell and Tammy Yarlow were positioned now, at the apex of the ride. Arthur could see only their shoulders and heads, but both appeared as motionless as mannequins. Tammy, however, had her arm raised, finger extended, holding a pointing pose that duplicated Ruby's almost exactly.

Arthur looked back to Ruby. "What's wrong, Rube?" he asked, rattled now.

"Look!" she shouted, her voice as loud as Arthur had ever heard from his sister, from any five-year-old, he figured.

Arthur finally turned to his right and looked up to the sky, and as his eyes focused on the horizon, searching for the danger, he heard Jimmy beside him say flatly, "Oh, shit."

It took a beat before Arthur found it, or perhaps 'labeled' it was the more precise description, as this pause in recognition was only because the outline above them was so large that it looked to be part of the landscape, like a mountain range had suddenly materialized before their eyes. But Albuquerque's mountains, though impressive by the standards of most ranges in the United States, weren't anywhere near on the scale of what Arthur was seeing, and they certainly weren't so close in proximity.

Within seconds, the low stampede of voices from the Ferris wheel and the fairgrounds turned to screams, and the

polite maneuvering of families through the crowd to the
only exit point of the fair turned to chaos. Young couples
pushed older ones to the side as they dashed to the entrance
and the presumed safety of their automobiles. Men and
women dragged their children behind them like suitcases,
knocking other stray children who were not their own to the
ground if they dared enter the path of their dashes.

"What is that, Arthur?" Jimmy asked, his attention now
rapt, his body as frozen as Arthur's, both boys taking in the
approaching doom like they were waiting for the Resurrec-
tion. "A hurricane?"

The absurdity of Jimmy's question snapped Arthur to attention, and he grabbed Ruby by the hand and snatched her
from what remained of the Ferris Wheel line, pulling her toward the row of carnival games that lined the center of the
fair. "Come on, Jimmy!" he called. "Ain't no hurricane, but
it'll kill you like one!"

Shelter inside the open setting of the New Mexico State
Fair was sparse, and what did exist was flimsy, not built to
withstand much more than a steady wind. But Arthur could
see the gate at the front of the fair was already beginning to
bottleneck, and being that they were kids, unaccompanied,
they would no doubt be shoved backward with each step of
progress they made toward the front. And even if they did
somehow make it to the gate, there was a good chance they'd
be trampled to death there as the clog of humanity grew, especially Ruby.

Arthur and Ruby barely dodged the flow of bodies that
now headed like a deluge toward the exit, crossing through
the human river like they would traffic on a busy street,

mostly in places like Chicago or New York, a detail Arthur knew about only from pictures in books and magazines. Miraculously, they cleared the swell unmaimed, landing outside the riot on the perimeter of the human surge. Arthur checked the exit once more, rethinking his decision now, considering whether an attempted escape was worth the risk. He wanted to get out of there as much as anyone, and if they waited too long to try, they would end up stuck inside until the storm passed. But there were too many people now, and he knew with Ruby on his hip they'd never even make it to the exit without being pushed to the ground, let alone through the gate to safety, at least not in time to avoid getting caught outside in the deadly cloud.

Arthur took a breath and gathered his thoughts, working out the skeleton of a plan, something to provide them at least the base of shelter. "You okay, Rube?"

Ruby nodded and then glanced one time in each direction. "Where's James?"

Arthur quickly looked around for his brother, and though he didn't immediately spot him, he wasn't worried. He knew Jimmy would be fine. "He'll catch up. We're not gonna try to leave just yet, okay. There's too many people trying to get out at once."

Ruby's eyes widened questioningly. "What about Ma and Pa? Won't they be trying to?"

Arthur dropped his eyes for a beat but returned them almost instantly to his sister. "They'll be okay. They're adults, and they know what to do. It'll be just for a few minutes until the storm passes. I promise."

Arthur raised his eyes back to the sky, which had the color and swirl of something born in hell, and then to the stream of bodies still flooding toward the exit. He continued to pull Ruby gently backward, widening their distance from the crowd, which had now assembled in a formation resembling ants fleeing a flooding hill. He took two more steps and then his back hit something hard, and he turned to see the counter of one of the carnival games. Behind the counter, a woman of about twenty-two stood with her arms crossed; her eyes were locked on the brown catastrophe approaching from above. Against the wall behind her was a stacked trio of milk bottles and a sign above them that read **Win the dog of your choice!** Beside the sign was a picture of a hot dog, and next to that picture was an actual dog, or a toy version, one that had been stuffed with sawdust and stitched sloppily together.

"Excuse me, ma'am," Arthur said. "Can we wait inside there with you?"

The woman ignored Arthur, never moving a muscle, not even a shift of her eyes.

"Ma'am?"

The woman blinked finally, a signal that she had heard Arthur. "No," she answered, still not eyeing the kids. "Get on outta here."

"Please, we—"

The girl finally broke from her spell and looked down at the intruding children, scowling. "Get on outta here, I said! Go find your mother!"

Years later, when Arthur would finally come to accept all that had happened to him and Jimmy—and Ruby—in the fall of 1939, he would come to believe the milk bottle girl had scrammed them so rudely in order to protect them, though he doubted she knew there was more in that shadowy brown cloud than just dust and stone.

Arthur huffed and pulled Ruby further into the carnival area of the fair where a dozen other booths lined the premises. He didn't need to waste time on the milk bottle game for shelter; within steps of that booth was the center of game row—the midway, Arthur had heard it called—the area of the carnival that ran the length of the spectacle right down the middle. The booths there looked no better than the milk bottle one, but at least now they had options. He glanced to his right and his eyes drifted down to the fair's entrance/exit again, and there Arthur could see that the crowd of anxious attendees had grown by double, and at the sight of the mob, a gurgling feeling arrived in him that madness would be descending there in moments.

And in a glimpse, Arthur saw it already had.

Amongst the panicked crowd, scattered throughout the rows of bottlenecked mayhem, he could see people lying on the ground, some covering their heads and necks as the feet above them stepped on and kicked at their backs and shoulders. Others lay helpless on the ground, and Arthur could see a head or limb occasionally flopping to one side or the other as it was struck absently with a boot. *Were they dead?* Arthur assumed not, just unconscious, but there was no way to know for sure. And with the idea of dead and dying bodies now fresh in his head, he thought of his parents. Randall and Dotty Richland were as fit as any of Arthur's friends' parents, but that didn't mean one of them couldn't have tripped during the flight to the exit or been pulled to the ground as they tried to help someone else who had become trapped beneath the swarm.

"No," he muttered, and then snapped his head to the opposite direction, away from the mass. He stared down to the far end of the midway now, where the carnival proper reached its furthest point, just before the grounds disappeared beyond the fences into the brown and red desolation of the New Mexico desert. And there, standing alone, was the pavilion of human oddities, a structure in the shape of a circus tent with a sign adorning the top that read: **FREAKS and Living Wonders! Open Wednesday – Sunday.**

Arthur knew the freak show tent was the main attraction for many who came to the fair, and it was also why his parents had chosen a Monday to visit. For his father, it meant lighter crowds and easier parking; for Dotty, it was her way to protest the exhibit, finding the exploitation of people less fortunate than she to be about as un-Christian a thing as one could imagine. "We don't revel in the misery of others," she always proclaimed, and Arthur figured paying money to see human deformities qualified as reveling.

And Arthur was now glad for the decision. He had noticed the tent first thing in the morning, just after the Ferris wheel, and everything about it had scared him. The design of the lettering on the signs; the pictures of hairy-faced women and elephant-nosed boys; the promise that someone named Madame Lilian would see into his future and reveal all things about his past. He knew most of it was a hoax (there was no way the elephant trunk that projected from the boy's face in the picture could have been real), but some of it had to be true, and it was that uncertainty—about what was real and what wasn't—that made him shudder.

Arthur turned from the oddities tent as if slapped by it, and he focused again on the other booths on the midway, quickly trying to decide which was best suited as a storm shelter, if, in fact, there were any at all which could serve that purpose. At first glance, they all appeared timeworn and rickety, seeming to have been slathered together with spit and mud a day or two earlier with boards that had been quarried from the remnants of Noah's Ark. Arthur's dad would have claimed the structures were the last type anyone would build to protect a person from a dust storm, a fact the milk bottle girl probably knew as well, though she had decided to accept whatever fate was arriving to her in the cloud.

But Arthur wasn't giving up quite that easily. Despite now feeling the front-end approach of the storm, the light wind and the descent of darkness, he calmed his mind for a moment and scrutinized each of the tiny pavilions with care, taking his time now, trying to find any advantage one might offer over the others. It took him an extra twenty seconds or so, but he soon found it. Or at least he thought so. One of the booths—*Balloon Darts!*—had a space which had been carved out beneath the countertop, unlike the others which had a flat piece of plywood for a façade. And this cavity seemed to run the width of the stand and all the way to the rear of the booth where the thrown darts were deposited. It was just a narrow slot, eighteen inches high or so beneath the thrower's stand, but it appeared tall enough for him to crawl beneath—and Jimmy whenever he arrived—and certainly tall enough for Ruby.

"There, Ruby," Arthur said calmly, pointing to the booth. "Where the balloons are. You see that gap at the bottom?"

Ruby nodded.

"That's where were going."

Arthur marched quickly to the balloon dart station and Ruby followed, and as they stepped to the counter, Arthur prepared his speech for the person manning the stand, praying he or she would be someone a bit more pleasant than milk-bottle girl. But the scenario was even better: the stand was empty. Whoever was charged with working that particular game had abandoned his post already and was no doubt now amongst the horde at the entrance trying to leave before the cloud of dust finally descended.

But before he and Ruby squeezed themselves beneath the flimsy stand, potentially trapping themselves if the booth collapsed atop them, Arthur decided he would first investigate the inside of the stall, to verify he wasn't missing some unidentified protection behind the counter. "Wait here," he said and then like a fox hopped the twenty inches of countertop and landed with a splat in a muddy puddle on the inside of the booth. He looked down to see the entire dirt floor was a mud pit, and then he realized it was from the popped water balloons, and that the gap in the front functioned as some type of collection area. As for further protection inside the booth, he saw nothing but thin walls and shaky tables, so Arthur bounced back over to the thrower's side, and as he landed, Jimmy was standing there, having materialized next to Ruby like an assistant in a magic show.

"Thanks for waiting!" Jimmy said. "Geez, Arthur, I was looking everywhere for you!"

"I had to get Ruby out," Arthur answered quickly. "She'd a got trodden if we just stood there. You said yourself." He paused and looked steadily at his younger brother. "And if you was anyone other'n you, Jimmy, I'da looked harder for you. But I knew you'd be fine."

Jimmy accepted the compliment—which was entirely sincere—with a smile that started as a begrudging grin and flared to a flash of teeth and dimples. "I know you knew that, Artie." He looked to the balloon dart booth and scanned it up and down. "What's the plan?"

Arthur explained about the hiding spot, and within moments, each of the siblings had contorted themselves into the wet pocket beneath the thrower's stand of the balloon dart game, with Ruby going first, followed by Jimmy and Arthur. They laid head to foot, with Ruby at the top of the chain and Arthur at the bottom, and though Arthur had to curl his knees to his chin and press the top of his head against the soles of his brother's filthy shoes, he could fit himself fully inside. Arthur doubted the flimsy covering above them would withstand a steady rain, let alone a dust storm the size of a forest, but they were at least enclosed now, partially protected from the wind above and the debris that would soon accompany it.

"Hey, Artie," Jimmy said, raising his voice now to contend with the gale and dust that was now steady and growing by the second.

"What?" Arthur barked back.

"What if this old stand buckles and buries us? They ain't never gonna find our bodies 'neath here."

"Shut it, Jimmy!" Arthur snapped, mainly to protect Ruby's worries, but, truthfully, his own as well. "It ain't gonna collapse and we ain't getting' buried. The worst is we gonna have to ride in the back of the truck for six hours in wet clothes." The soggy contents of destroyed balloons beneath Arthur had already seeped through his shirt and down the right side of his pants. But if that was the cost of his plan, it was a small price to pay.

There was a spell of silence and then Jimmy spoke again. "Hey, Arthur?"

"I said, 'Shut it,' Jim."

"It ain't about that though."

"What then?"

"Up there." Jimmy's arm was extended, his hand outside the cover of the stand, and he seemed to be pointing to a spot somewhere in the far distance. "Look at 'em up there, Artie."

"Look at who? I can't see what you're talking 'bout."

"Up there. On the wheel. They's as trapped as a duck in a well."

Arthur was tucked tightly in the back of the hiding space, and, as a result, his eyes were flat and focused, able to see only that which was on level ground in front of him, and not much beyond the width of the midway. But Jimmy's voice had a tone of fascination in it, and fear, so Arthur instantly maneuvered himself to the edge of the cavity to get a better view. And as he looked skyward in the direction of the Ferris wheel, he saw what his brother was seeing, and he felt the fear as well.

The wheel towered in front of them only fifty yards or so out from their impromptu hiding spot, and the cars on the wheel's outer edges now rocked steadily in the wind. Despite the enormity of the approaching dust cloud, there was still only a moderate gusting at that moment, but it was one which promised to be a full-on squall in a matter of minutes. Arthur moved his gaze down now, toward the base of the ride where the control booth sat, and he nearly shrieked at the sight. There was no one there. The machine had been left unattended, abandoned by the fair workers, leaving everyone on the ride stranded.

The riders on the top two thirds of the wheel were now hollering downward for help, though their cries were barely audible from where Arthur lay, lost in the sound of wind and the shrieks of grounded fairgoers who were still dashing for the exit or else trying to force their way through the front gate, having arrived there already.

Arthur lifted his attention from the booth to the cars positioned at the bottom of the wheel, all of which were empty now, the occupants of those gondolas having exited from their static positions in the revolution, likely jumping from a height of what Arthur estimated to be ten or twelve feet from foot to ground if they had hung from the edge of their cages and dropped straight down. A painful fall, perhaps, maybe a turned ankle or a buckled knee. But they'd live to tell the tale.

The cars above, however, those on the top two-thirds of the wheel, were too high for jumping. And though the occupants of those gondolas—none of whom had looked to be older than twenty-five, if Arthur remembered correctly—on a normal day could probably have climbed to the hub and then worked their way over to the lower spokes before navigating to the ground, they would have been fools to try such a trek now. The wind and dust were peppering the atmosphere with a steady spit, and the sway of the cars would have made any attempt to exit them treacherous at best, fatal at worst.

"I feel kinda bad for him now," Jimmy said distantly, a rare note of sympathy in his voice. "That asshole Sherman, I mean. And I sure as hell do for Tammy. She don't deserve to be stuck up there."

With the mention of Sherman, Arthur guided his eyes up to the top of the wheel where one car rocked like a chapel bell at the apex. It was Sherman and Tammy's car. He expected the boy to be cowering there, screaming even, the way most bullies reacted in times of crisis and panic. But there was no cringing in his seat or clutching to the sides of the car. Instead, Sherman stood tall, his chest forward, shoulders confidently back like a soldier during an inspection at boot camp. He appeared to be staring straight ahead, in the direction of the approaching cloud, though Arthur could no longer see the mass of gas from his vantage beneath the kiosk. Arthur fixated on the figure of Sherman, and though he could see neither his eyes nor the details of his face, something in his posture frightened Arthur. The stillness of his body, the quietude of his poised figure. There was too much composure there, Arthur thought, especially in contrast to the chaos erupting all around him, including from the riders in the cars below him. It was as if the boy were in the middle of a dream, or a nightmare, one that he knew he was currently having and thus had no fear of experiencing, knowing that he was safe from any true harm in the end.

Tammy was only a foot or two behind Sherman, still seated on the metal bench of the novel ride, but her body language was a negative image of Sherman's, tense and crouching, tucked into a defensive coil. And her hands were plastered to the sides of her face in a pose of terror and confusion. Arthur couldn't distinguish her voice from the rest of the noisy chaos ringing in the atmosphere, but it was clear she was screaming, bearing down with each shriek, her posture reminding Arthur of a stranded hiker shouting down a mountain ridge.

Sherman seemed not to notice her, however; his attention was on the sky.

"How are they gonna get down?" Ruby asked, the crackle of her tiny voice sending a tingle through Arthur's body, popping his attention back into place like a dislocated kneecap.

Arthur closed his eyes and took a deep breath. To his shame, he quietly thanked Jesus that it was Sherman and Tammy at the top of the wheel and not he and Jimmy and Ruby. Had it been their misfortune playing out currently, it would have been Arthur's responsibility to get his siblings down, to keep them calm and reassured as they climbed their way from the deadly heights. Would they have followed him if he insisted? Did he have that kind of leadership and resolve to keep his own terror at bay while leading others? Or would he have been more like Tammy, thick with panic?

Arthur had never been that high in the air, not even in a building, so he had no way of knowing for sure, but either way, he knew if it were him and Jimmy and Ruby up there, he would have wanted someone on the ground to notice their desperation, and to help them in any way they could. Well, Arthur *had* noticed, and though he couldn't imagine a way to help them directly—he was just a kid, after all, barely able to lift Ruby off the ground—he could at least find someone who was capable. There had been a police car at the front entrance when they arrived that morning, and he thought he'd even seen a fire truck parked in a side lot just beyond the row of barns.

But the swell of the crowd was overwhelming now, panicked and desperate, and Arthur knew there was no way he would ever get close to a cop, let alone pull one away from the mayhem and toward the Ferris Wheel. Not with the storm gaining strength and the flood of people continuing to surge.

"Arthur?" Ruby repeated.

"What, Rube?" Arthur retorted with an irritated snap.

"How do they get down?"

"I don't know!" Arthur shouted and then instantly lowered his voice, adding, "I don't, Rube, I'm sorry. But...but they'll be okay."

"How?"

"Cause these fair machines is safe," Jimmy offered, seeming to recognize that Arthur had reached the end of his rope, at least as far as an explanation or words of reassurance for Ruby were concerned. "The Ferris wheel was 'vented in Chicago—that's what I heard, anyways—and Chicago's 'bout the windiest place in America. The Windy City they call it. This little New Mexico gust ain't enough to bring them cars down."

This seemed to assuage Ruby for the moment, at least based on the silence that followed. Then, after the pause she asked, "What about Ma and Pa? You really think they're okay, Arthur?"

With the mention of his parents again and knowing the fear his mother would have felt if it were her children stranded on the Ferris wheel, Arthur suddenly felt bolstered with determination, with responsibility. "We'll find 'em, Rube. After the storm passes. They'll be scared for us, I know it, but we'll be fine and so will they. I promise."

"Not the people on the Ferris wheel though," Ruby reminded. "They're gonna die up there, right? All of them."

"No, they ain't either! Geez, Rube! What Jimmy said's true. Take a lot more'n a dust storm to knock that big wheel down. They'll be dirty, for sure, but they ain't gonna die."

"I never wanted him to die," Jimmy said now, defensively, clearly ruing his earlier confrontation with Sherman. "I was just mad is all. And Jesus, Tammy is Bucky's cousin. She can't die."

It took a few seconds for his brother's words to tally, but when they did, Arthur nearly vomited at the revelation. He knew that Tammy Yarlow and Bucky Mason were cousins, but it took Jimmy's words of regret to remind him of the fact.

Cousins.

And Janet Flannery had been Ralph Brater's aunt. Bucky and Ralph were Jimmy's best friends, his only friends really. One had recently heard news that his mother's oldest sister had been murdered in cold blood, and the other had a cousin whose life was also now in danger. It was coincidence, of course, no connection to be made; what had happened at Downes was a once-in-a-lifetime tragedy, a memory he could slowly forget over time, gradually, until he was old enough that he wouldn't remember it at all or would recall it as nothing more than a nightmare he once had as a boy.

But *two* tragedies of that magnitude would surely stay tattooed on his mind for eternity, unerasable, so if he wanted to live a life without that kind of scar tissue, he had to help. Or at least try.

Arthur believed what Jimmy had told Ruby was true—that the wheel was solid enough to withstand the storm—but he couldn't know for sure. The storms that had come through over the past few weeks had been different than those in previous years—at least that's what everyone in Clayton said—and Arthur supposed at some point, if they continued to strengthen, the wind *would* become strong enough to knock things even as big as Ferris wheels to the ground. He couldn't imagine seeing such a thing happen on that day, but he supposed it wasn't impossible.

Arthur looked back to the wheel and studied it now, carefully, just as he'd done with the carnival games, focusing on the design of the frame and the jutting spokes, the symmetry from each car to the center of the ride. It had plenty of areas to climb from and to, level slabs of metal and wood on which to step, but only for someone who was already on the ride. There was nothing Arthur could do to help the riders from the ground. They would have to climb down on their own.

Or?

The operator's stand!

The thought jumped into his mind like a hare from a fire pit. The cockpit. Or control station. Whatever it was called. Arthur might not have a ladder to send up or be able to climb up on his own, but surely he could figure out the controls of the wheel and start it up again. How hard could it be? It wasn't flying an airplane or manning a submarine. There were probably two buttons on the thing. One to start it and the other to bring it to a stop.

Without another pause, Arthur scurried from beneath the low porch of the dart stand and quickly got to his feet, instantly feeling the sting of the dust and debris in the wind on his face and legs and arms.

"Arthur!" Jimmy yelled. "What the hell are you doin'?!"

"I gotta help them," Arthur replied calmly, ducking down to see his siblings lying in the mud, looking like escaped fugitives trying to keep clear of a pack of bloodhounds. "I gotta at least try. I'm gonna go try to start the wheel up again."

"What? Start the...you don't know how to do that."

"It can't be nothing to it. You just...I don't know...press a button probably. And—"

Arthur stopped when he saw Jimmy's eyes flicker to his right once and then back to him, and then again to the right. And this time they locked there and blossomed, growing to what must have been twice their normal size. His brother opened his mouth to speak but couldn't, so instead he gave an unconscious flick of his head skyward, directing Arthur to follow his gaze which was now aimed toward a spot across the horizon. It was the same expression Ruby had shown only minutes earlier, Arthur thought, and he knew there was nothing good to be found in it.

"Oh my god," Jimmy mouthed, barely making a sound.

Arthur turned quickly this time, instinctively raising his hand to shield his eyes from the wind which was now interspersed with tiny bits of trash and pebbles. And as he craned his neck upward, casting his stare on the car of Sherman and Tammy, he saw the cause of his brother's fear.

The two young teens were both still inside the car, stranded like the rest of the high riders; but above them—maybe six feet, maybe twenty, Arthur couldn't quite tell from his distance—was a hole of pure blackness, like a scoop of the sky had been removed with a large spoon, leaving behind only the darkest of voids. And within this new void was a thick scribble of light, the color of which was as bright and orange as the clearest of sunsets, the shape so stark against the blackness it looked to have been seared there, branded as if by some cosmic cowhand.

Arthur's thoughts spun wildly as he witnessed the phenomenon, first summoning the storefront of Downes' Grocery, then of Janet Flannery, a rusty screwdriver entering through the left side of her skull until the flathead came sticking out the right. And then he thought of the garage of Chester Sutton's, where Arthur's father was pumping gas into a tin lizzie, honoring his end of the deal while a family sat shattered inside.

And then his thoughts spread wider across Clayton, to the farm of Ty Sampson and the craters unearthed by Jimmy and his friends. From there his mind went beneath the surface, underground to the altar and the room where a series of primitive pictures had been etched into a wall centuries earlier.

And then his brain cast aside all of it. The murder of Janet Flannery, the sin of his father, the wretched pictures of torture and sacrifice and violence upon the altars.

But not all the pictures.

In Arthur's mind's eye, illuminating there like the images of the boardwalk at Coney Island, black and white in the newspaper but which he'd colorized in his imagination, he saw the Skadegamutc, the crude, craggy outlines which had smoldered above the radiance of the torch like a ring of fire. It was the same glow he witnessed now above the Ferris wheel.

Whether it was the same ancient creature Arthur was seeing now he couldn't have sworn by; the lights were simply too far away and there was nothing—other than their color—which he could latch onto for certainty. But then the light began to shift, not as one beam, however, but in separate rays, jerking spastically, latching together at hard angles to start and then bending and curving into softer shapes. The light rays moved at varying speeds, like tiny bolts of lightning smashing into one another, creating a brightness Arthur only imagined existed in the center of stars.

It was electric chaos for ten seconds or less, and then what appeared to be random light shapes began to take form, beginning from the top with a single scraggle of hair and then quickly bending into an arc, rounding into the shape of a head. Arthur stood breathless as he watched the next set of features appear, that of the eyes, the same type he'd seen depicted in the cave below Clayton, large circles like miniature suns glowing in their sockets, forming like puddles of magma on the top half of the black face. And then a new characteristic appeared, one that hadn't been painted in any of the images in the Hollow. A bright line of light appeared, forming what could only be described as a mouth, stretching the length of the face before parting, opening wide and gruesomely. The head's orange features on the black background of the atmosphere now gave it the appearance of some deranged reverse jack-o-lantern.

Arthur felt dizzy as he watched the image take form, nauseous, staring in disbelief as the light rays snapped together, now bending down to form jagged shoulders and arms, then a torso, which was featureless but for the overall shape, twisting at just the right slants in the waist and hip sections to present a figure that was obliquely female.

And then the fiery outline of the witch was fully formed, and it continued to hover above the Ferris wheel car like some burning hummingbird, or perhaps an angry deity that had descended from the heavens to administer its punishment, beginning with Sherman Caswell and Tammy Yarlow.

It was all true, Arthur thought. All that he'd prayed—and later even suspected—was a myth over the past two weeks, since the day after Janet Flannery's death when Jimmy had led him to an altar in the bowels of Clayton, was, in fact, real. What he'd seen inside Downes' had been no mirage, no hallucination, but rather a distorted version of the thing he was eyeing now, something wicked and ancient that had been released from its prison with the removal of the stones.

Arthur had mostly buried those two days in the corners of his mind, as he had tried so hard to do with the story of his father and the migrant girl, chalking the events up as dark blips in the lives of the Richlands, of the town of Clayton at large, periods which all towns and families must endure at some point and then return stronger for having done so.

But now it was all resurfacing in a moment. On the edge of the wind in the heart of a storm. Lynnie Radich's grandmother had been right. The Skadegamutc, the ancient Native American witches that had for centuries lived as pictures on a wall in a vault beneath Clayton, were real, incarnate, and though Arthur had relegated the memory of them from weeks earlier to that of a dream, he had seen the uprooted evil once before, just a glimpse of it, through the window of Downes', just moments after the murder of Janet Flannery.

Arthur tried to move, to go forward to the Ferris wheel, to start the ride and rescue the stranded fairgoers as he'd set out to do when he abandoned his hiding space a minute earlier. But he was simply frozen now, locked onto the monster hovering above him. And though there was nothing precise he could point to that was malevolent or sinister about the shape in the sky, he knew the figure was ruinous, evil, something sent from the Devil himself. It was there for the purpose of destruction, to upset the order of things in Albuquerque and Clayton and New Mexico at large. And perhaps all of the western United States. The world beyond.

The shape continued to flicker in the sky like tiny fulgurations, and then, as if released from some throbbing prison, the figure of the irradiated witch doubled in an instant, spawning an identical twin of itself, this one wearing the same deranged expression on its face, ogrish and horrible.

And then, seconds after the duplication, the figures dissipated, blasting quietly into a dozen smaller beads of light, each of which remained visible for only a flash, like the tailing remnant of a firework disappearing into a July night. The duration of the scene was only seconds, but in that brief moment, Arthur was consumed by the light, hypnotized by the witch-figure and the clone she had produced. And as the reproduced figures sizzled into the ether, disintegrating like the seedhead of a dandelion, a sleepiness engulfed him, something akin to a draining of his senses.

And then Arthur was back to the world, his eyes dipping from the hovering space of the fire witches down to the car of the Ferris wheel where Sherman had since turned his body and was facing his date, looming over her with the same rigid stance he'd assumed only minutes earlier when he was still staring rapt toward the storm. But there was something more present about him now, a purposefulness to his posture that had not been apparent earlier. The positioning of his head and shoulders were high and stiff, the telltale pose of danger and aggression, and instead of his arms hanging dead against his sides as they had been minutes ago, he now held his hands at chest level, palms facing the sky as if offering his date some invisible body which he now carried with him, a form seen by his eyes alone. And though Arthur had no way to know for sure, if he had to guess, he would have said Sherman was smiling.

Tammy remained in the same defensive position from earlier, with her back pressed hard against the rear of the car. But her desperate shrieks toward the ground had now ceased, and though Arthur could make out only the top half of her face from his vantage, he could see she was shaking her head frantically, quivering it in the pleading signal one gives to keep someone away, an attempt to hold back whatever peril was being promised.

But Sherman wouldn't stay away. Instead, he moved steadily forward, and as he did, he turned his hands inward, closing the gap between them as he clutched his fingers into talons, reaching out for his young date, no doubt to grab her by the throat.

With this final move of violence, Tammy's hex was broken, and she began to scream again, this time hysterically, the dire shrieks of survival. She then pushed her body up until she was sitting on the back ledge of the car, stepping onto the seat to seize the high ground on her aggressor. She looked desperately over her shoulder and down at the descent behind her. There was no escape in that direction; a fall from that height would be fatal. The only chance she had was forward, so Tammy braced her hands on the seat back at either side of her hips, and then she thrust a foot forward toward Sherman, bringing her toe up at just the right moment, squaring it with Sherman's chin. But she had little leverage, and the kick, despite its perfect aim, had nothing behind it. Sherman was through the next kick in a second, and the slaps and scratches that followed were like cotton candy against his head and chest. Tammy turned now as if to jump from the seat back, no doubt to attempt a leap toward the inner frame of the Ferris wheel. It was the only play at that point, and despite the risk, it was worth it. If she landed the jump, she would be safe from Sherman, and if she could find a spot in the ride's skeleton to wedge her body tight, she could wait out the storm until help arrived. And if that wasn't feasible, she could at least make a try for the ground below. All she had to do was land the jump.

But it was too late for any of that. Sherman shot his right hand out and grabbed hold of Tammy's wrist, snatching her arm backward and her body into his own. He quickly wrapped his arms around her torso, locking his hands and forearms at her breasts, trapping her arms against her sides. He leaned into the girl now as if he were trying to crush her, and then he jerked his body in a spinning motion, fighting off the desperate flails of the young girl, her dire cries now penetrating the sound of the storm, reaching Arthur's ears like a cold sword.

Tammy was now against the front of the car with Sherman pressing his body behind her, crushing her against the wood and metal of the car's front. And then, with a motion that was as violent and purposeful as Arthur had ever seen—would ever see over the course of his long life, he imagined—Sherman snatched his body tall and stiff, as if he'd been struck by a bolt of lightning, and then he rotated his shoulders and torso a quarter turn, slowly at first, and then with a whipping motion back toward the front of the car, sending his date over the edge.

Perhaps the worst part of the image—one which Arthur would later think of as surreal, though he didn't know the meaning of the word at the time—was the sight of Tammy's tiny hands in the distance, and the desperation with which they grasped for the car, her twig-like fingers pleading crookedly in the empty space as she plunged toward the ground, frantic to find anything to touch, to grab. But even if a ladder had suddenly sprung up beside her, she would never have been able to overcome the force of gravity sucking her downward. And in what was certainly less than three seconds, her body smacked against the dirt at the base of the wheel.

There was a pause of silence, stillness in the air, and Arthur could only hear a whooshing emptiness in his brain. And then Jimmy's voice.

"Oh Christ! Arthur!" he shouted. "Arthur, what...what just happened!"

Arthur's feet were still frozen in place, but his head and body began to quiver as if gripped by some sudden chill. He didn't blink as he stared at the area where Tammy's body had hit the ground, and though he couldn't see her corpse, which now lay somewhere below the base of the ride, in his mind he could see her mangled body, the crushed bones of her skeleton, unable now to support the flesh and muscle and skin above it, and her eyeballs, which had likely launched from her face to a point yards from the rest of her dead body.

Tears now streaked Arthur's face through wide, brown canals of dust, but he ignored them, as he did the dry heaves that had begun to rupture from his gut. Instead, he simply coughed in spasms, letting the bile-filled spittle drip from his chin like a vegetative lunatic.

Tammy Yarlow. Bucky Mason. Janet Flannery. Ralph Brater.

"Arthur?"

The voice was faint, breezy, as if a memory had spoken aloud. He let it go.

"Arthur?"

Ruby.

The sound of his sister's voice brought Arthur just inside the perimeter of his mental fog, close enough to recognize that not only was there danger still afoot, but also responsibilities to which tending was needed, the most important of which was to keep his siblings safe, especially his sister.

"Ruby, don't look," he uttered, but his words were barely loud enough for him to hear, let alone Ruby, who was still crouching beneath the dart stand somewhere behind him. It was as loud as he could manage in the moment though. His vocal cords, like the rest of his bodily functions, had virtually seized, as if not to deny the resources from his brain, which was still trying to deduce what had just occurred at the top of the Ferris wheel. Arthur closed his eyes now, squeezing out the newly formed droplets that had forged there, and he concentrated on the tasks ahead of him, trying to vanquish the vision of the glowing witch and the second figure that had been born from her. And of Tammy's plunging body, an image that was now eternally etched into the folds of his brain.

He paused a second more and slowed his breathing, and then Arthur opened his eyes and cleared his throat to speak. "Ruby, don't look at it," he said barking, loudly and with some effort. "Don't look at the Ferris wheel. You got that? You close your eyes, or you look at Jimmy. Not at the wheel."

Arthur hadn't yet been able to turn himself from the crime scene, but he was aware of his surroundings again, and he waited for confirmation from his sister.

"Ruby, you hear me?"

Arthur turned and looked back toward the dart stand, searching the gap beneath it. Jimmy was still there, but Ruby was gone.

Chapter 19

Chris listened to the story without breathing, or at least it felt that way, and when Arthur reached the point of Ruby's disappearance, he felt like crying. He knew how Arthur had felt in that moment, the despair and guilt that surely landed in his belly that first second he noticed Ruby was gone. And since Chris already knew the rest of the story, or at least the spoiler, that she wasn't found that day or in the weeks that followed, he could sympathize wholly with the sickness that must have plagued Arthur over the next many days.

"I'm sorry," Chris said, softly, sincerely.

Arthur gave a sad smile and nodded. "I knew it the minute I didn't see her there. I don't think I acted in that way, not at first, but deep down I knew she was gone, and that we weren't going to find her. Not that day."

Chris grabbed the back of his own neck and stared toward the floor, nodding. He had had the same feeling. "I know."

Arthur paused and then asked, "Does her mother hate you now? Blame you for what happened?"

Chris gave the question real consideration, wanting to give an honest answer to what would seem obvious. "Right now, I don't know if she's let that part enter her mind yet. She's still in work mode. Rescue mode. Using every resource and ounce of energy she has to find Jaycee. She's probably somewhere in Nebraska with a team of troopers right now canvassing every house along the interstate. But I know this, if she doesn't hate me now, she will one day. If I don't bring Jaycee home safe to her, she'll damn me to hell." He paused now, giving the second part of the question consideration. "The thing is, she doesn't blame me for the accident, or even for losing her; she knows me, knows I would do anything to protect Jaycee, and that I really was trying to help those people in the Mercedes. But she does blame me for what I'm doing now. For coming to see you instead of working the same dead-end leads over and over again. And I guess I can understand that."

Arthur nodded, not needing an explanation.

Chris plucked a tear from the corner of his eye. "But what good would that do, you know? To drive up and down the interstate for the hundredth time. She was gone. *Is* gone. And the only clue I could really work with, the only lead I could follow that no one else was interested in were the figures of light I saw in the storm." He sat straight and took a heavy breath, clearing his lungs. "And I was right to do it. Thank you, Arthur." He wiped his eyes now without shame. "Even if I don't see her again, I know I was right to pursue this."

"You'll see her," Arthur said.

Chris didn't smile or nod at this, and instead he measured Arthur's face like a poker player, looking for the honesty there, the lucidity, eyes that were at once cogent and decent, promising something real, something other than consolation or the vapid stare of a dying man. And though he couldn't be sure exactly what was in the man's eyes, there was enough life in them, enough softness and honesty, for Chris to remain hopeful. "Okay," he said. "Okay."

"And when you do, my advice is not to ask too many questions. Not from her. You'll want to, I know. You're going to want to know everything about every minute she was gone. Where she went..." he paused, approaching this next part delicately "...whether anything bad happened to her. But she isn't going to answer you. Not with any satisfaction. It will be frustrating, tortuous even. You'll just have to accept that she's alive, that you got her back."

Chris listened and measured Arthur's words, and then he asked, "How can you be so sure? You can't know this will happen."

"You just need to have faith. And when the time comes, to do what you must."

Chris shook his head slightly, rolling his eyes and frowning at the insufficient answer. And for a reason he didn't know, he asked, "Why did you never leave here, Arthur?"

"Here?"

Chris shrugged and looked around the tiny room. "New Mexico, I mean. This...this nightmare that happened when you were a kid. I think for most people that would have been enough to send them running for the border in either direction. You're not in Clayton anymore, I get it, but you aren't far from there either. Why?"

Arthur shrugged and pursed his lips. "Wouldn't have mattered where I went. Didn't matter to Jimmy?"

Chris champed at the bit to pursue the question of what happened to Arthur's brother, but he waited instead to see if the man would continue down the path on his own. He didn't, so Chris kept with his original line of questioning. "But still, just to leave the bad memories behind. A lot of people would have left for that reason alone."

"When you leave behind the bad memories, Mr. Boylin, you leave the good ones behind too. And I never wanted to forget those. Whatever the price." He paused and nodded gently to Chris. "And maybe there were reasons I stayed that I never even realized."

Chris appreciated the wisdom of the man's words in a way he had yet to recognize. He would never leave Jaycee behind either, no matter the torture it caused over the rest of his life. "If you're ready to tell me what happened to Ruby, I'm ready to listen. Go at your own pace."

Arthur looked up at Chris and frowned. "I'm ready."

Chapter 20

"Ruby?" Arthur had heard her voice only seconds earlier, sounding as if it had come from the place he'd seen her last, in the cove beneath the dart stand. She couldn't have gone far, he thought, but the entire run of the stand was now empty. Arthur felt the blood rush from his face; his stomach retched. "Jimmy?" he whimpered. "Where is Ruby?"

"What?" Jimmy replied, his tone dreamy, his voice unhealed from the sight of the Tammy Yarlow slamming toward the earth.

"Ruby! Where did she go!"

Jimmy finally turned his gaze from the Ferris wheel and looked to the space just above his head, where Ruby had been tucked less than a minute ago. "I...what? I don't know." Jimmy was panicked now. "She was here. She was just right here!"

"Well, she ain't now!"

The dread sprouted quickly inside Arthur, and his breathing, which had all but ceased for what seemed like a full minute while he watched the events of Tammy and Sherman unfold, was now deep and quick, and the tears of sadness that had flowed for a murdered girl had been transmuted to those of fear and desperation. He spun his body in a tight circle, rotating in slow quarter turns, searching the grounds for any sign of his sister. But the wind was whipping now, with pockets of dust filling the air, and despite the craving for a clear view, he couldn't keep his eyes open for more than a few beats.

Arthur managed to maintain a squint however, a narrow slit of vision, but even with his eyes slightly open, he could barely make out the shape of the Ferris wheel any longer; and he couldn't see the milk bottle stand at all, which was only a few yards away.

"Ruby!" he screamed and then closed his eyes as he waited for a reply. He kept his chin high, and his ears exposed, but the wind had grown so deafening it consumed even the loudest screams of the patrons now. Arthur imagined the panicked escapees were in a full-on riot by now, battering and clawing at one another as they attempted to squeeze through the narrow gate to the ostensible safety of the parking lot.

Had Ruby gone there? he considered. *Searching for their parents?*

Arthur turned and took several steps in the direction of the entrance, hoping by some miracle that he could get close enough to at least see the throng, and if he could accomplish that much, that through the masses he would spot Ruby somewhere low in the crowd, turning with hopeless confusion as she tried to locate her mother and father.

But within seconds, Arthur realized his own journey was pointless. The wind was blowing from the east, from the direction of the entrance, and the sting of the microscopic bits of sand and pebbles was unbearable against his face. He ducked and turned his back to the gust involuntarily, relieved to have the bite of the storm on the back of his neck now and not his face. But the desperation to find his sister still burned, the adrenaline flowing like an angry river. And Arthur felt slightly encouraged now, knowing that if *he* couldn't stand the force of the storm against the front of his body, then Ruby wouldn't have been able to either.

He lifted his head and stared in the opposite direction of the gate, down to the far end of the midway where the tent of oddities sat, and then he braced his back against the wind and took a few small steps, careful not to go too fast for fear of being knocked forward to the ground. There was no guarantee Ruby had gone that way, of course, but Arthur sensed that she had, seeking shelter from the storm that had increased to a demonic force in only a matter of minutes.

It took Arthur a few strides, two or three clumsy footfalls, but he found traction quickly, and within seconds, the details of the oddities tent came into full view, including the monstrous artwork he'd seen earlier, the posters now hazy and shrouded, giving them a more ominous view than they presented already. Arthur stopped and inhaled a quiet breath as he took in the images once more, noting new graphics now, placards he hadn't seen upon first glance, including that of a dark woman with an elongated neck, hailing from a land Arthur had never heard of and was sure he would never visit. Below that picture was another poster, this one showing a pair of twin ladies, beautiful in the face and body, smiling dizzily despite being joined together at the neck, or perhaps it was the head, it was difficult to distinguish based on the growing cloud gusts and the somewhat clumsy drawing.

Arthur kept moving forward until he was within a yard or so of the tent entrance, and there, painted across the flaps of the tent, was a large hand with the words *Madame Lilian* printed in the middle of the palm. KNOW THE FUTURE! was the tagline below the seer's name, and a small pair of eyes peered from two of the fingers on the hand.

Yet, despite the horror the signage hoped to invoke, the tent and the grounds around it appeared relatively peaceful, especially in the context of the disorder of the day. But that peace was not to last. A thin cloud of dust was already forming above the apex of the tarp, hovering there, promising to devour the tent below at any moment.

"Ruby?" Arthur called, leaning forward, trying to project his voice inside the tent without having to physically touch it. But the flaps looked heavy, and with the blowing wind, if his sister were inside, she wouldn't have heard him.

"Is she in there?"

Arthur screeched at the words of his brother, who was now standing beside him, his penchant for slinking unnoticed on display once more. Arthur shook his head. "I...I don't know."

Jimmy looked suspiciously at the tent. "I guess we should find out."

Arthur nodded, happy to have his brother with him. "Yeah." The boys took a step forward when Arthur stopped suddenly and asked, "Did you see it, Jimmy?"

Jimmy stopped, his nose almost to the tent. He didn't turn, but he lowered his head, a move of shame and regret. "I saw it," he answered, and then he finally turned toward his brother. "Did we do that? Did me and Ralph and Bucky kill

Tammy Yarlow?" And then, as if the weight of the question had been crushing down on him for weeks, he added, "And Mrs. Flannery?"

Jimmy had seen the same images Arthur had, the ghastly light witches that were unmistakably the drawings from the Hollow. Arthur wanted to say the name aloud, to acknowledge that the Skadegamutc were indeed there with them, to punish and kill the ones who had released them. But doing so felt like an admission of sorts. A line that once crossed could never be spanned back over again. He felt a shiver of terror pierce the back of his neck, a distant awareness that if Bucky and Ralph had been targeted—which Arthur had no doubt they had been—then Jimmy was next, and someone close to him would be killed.

"You didn't kill anyone, Jim," Arthur said, somewhat unconvincingly, "but we gotta find Ruby before—"

Jimmy was crying now, beginning to lose it. "I didn't mean to do this! It was a mistake! Why didn't they just close the Ditches off like they said they was goin' too!" He looked at Arthur now. "What are we gonna say we saw?"

Arthur had played this last part out in his mind already—several times by now—but each time he did, he could never reconcile the part of Skadegamutc. No one would believe them. It was why he never mentioned the lights to Sheriff Brickell, and why he knew Ruby hadn't either. There was no point. They were kids, so what they said was already taken with a grain of salt, and when you added in villains from fairy tales as the reasons for things going south, you were all but dismissed.

Unless someone else had seen it too, he thought. *Someone other than he and Jimmy.*

Or Sherman.

Arthur thought of Sherman now and it scared him as much as the appearance of the Skadegamutc. Everything about his posture, the animal rigidness and determination, the predatory focus, was Glenn Flannery on the day he'd murdered his wife. And though Arthur hadn't been close enough to see Sherman's eyes for comparison, he was sure the same blank gaze was there the moment Tammy went over the rail.

"Arthur!"

"What!" Arthur snapped, shaken back to the moment.

Jimmy had pulled himself together, but he was still distraught and confused. "Why did he do that?" he moaned. "Why did he throw her over like that?"

Arthur shook his head. "I don't know, Jimmy. Same as I don't know why Glenn Flannery done what he did. But it ain't your fault. We just gotta find Ruby and get out of here before—"

A stifled scream came from deep inside the tent, and that noise was followed first by the sounds of erratic slapping, and then by the sounds of choking, gurgling, a resonance that was both tight and liquid, echoes of desperation and spittle. But the wind by the tent was howling now and the noises were barely audible, so Arthur moved in closer until he was only inches from the palm that fronted the tent flaps. He stared slack jawed at the open hand, a look of anticipation upon his face, as if waiting for it to turn suddenly and wave him through, or even to part at the crease between the middle and ring fingers, to open on their own, the mystic Lilian offering passage into the genie's cave.

But there was only stillness from the canvas flaps, their thick construction continuing to shroud whatever assault was unfolding inside, so, without another thought, Arthur grabbed his brother by the arm and pulled him forward, bringing him along into the tent beside him, knowing neither would have had the courage to go it alone.

As the boys exited the crescendoing of the storm and passed into the coolness of the tent, the canvas brushed across Arthur's face, and the musty smell reminded him of the crusty, bound mummies of Egypt, of the pharaoh Tutankhamun, the boy king who'd been discovered two decades earlier and about whom Arthur had taken a great deal of interest when he was younger. But the space inside, though sprawling and spacious, was far from suitable for a king. The air was still and foul, the lighting dim and lonely, generated by various candles which seemed to burn in all corners of the large, partitioned space. Arthur was thankful for them, of course, as they offered not only guidance within the tent, but also a semblance of relief from the smell.

"I don't want to be in here, Arthur," Jimmy muttered. "I can barely see anything anyway."

"Well, were in here now and we ain't leavin' until we've looked everywhere for Ruby."

Jimmy didn't argue, and instead he looked warily around the tent. "What happened to those noises?"

The tent was crowded with draperies that hung like sheets from a clothesline. They weren't hung to dry, however, but rather to create separation, distinct rooms, no doubt forming the individual quarters of the oddities who traveled with the fair. And Jimmy was right: the sound of the struggles had fallen silent, and though on the one hand it was a relief, it also signaled that a trail had gone cold.

Arthur pulled back the first curtain to his left and stood firm, his chest out, willing to accept whatever sprang from the station. But there was only silence that emerged, and though the room was nothing more than a dark abyss for several beats, as Arthur's eyes adjusted, the shape of something large began to form in the darkness, blossoming as a long wide shadow in front of him. He guessed it to be an animal, at first, and his heart began to pound, imagining that he had awakened a bear or tiger, and that he and Jimmy would be mauled to death any second when the beast finally awakened.

But as Arthur studied the form closer, he could see it was no animal, but rather a woman, lying on the floor flat on her back and sleeping as quietly as a baby. She was enormous, the size of a large walrus, and Arthur matched her with Miss Minnie the Fat Lady on the poster outside. Both boys stopped breathing at the sight of the woman, fascinated and terrified at once, but Arthur took the opportunity to search the area around the woman, looking for Ruby. But there was no sign that his sister had been there, so he closed the drape quietly and motioned for Jimmy to follow him further into the tent.

They crossed through the center of the large space, entering the main area where the customers assembled and waited their turn to circle the pavilion, walking slowly in the queue, no doubt with cocked heads and queer smiles as they ogled the peculiarities of nature. When Arthur and Jimmy reached the rearmost section of the pavilion, they stopped in front of a row of seven or eight separately hung draperies which created partitions along the entire back of the tent. And there, they stopped and listened. They could hear a voice now, garbled and feminine, speaking words which sounded like some ancient form of English, with syllables and syntax that, though it wasn't quite intelligible, sounded close to correct. It was coming from the curtain straight ahead of them, and this time Arthur motioned for Jimmy to pull the shade back. Arthur had brought them this far, he rationalized; it was his brother's turn now.

Jimmy shook his head with a frantic pleading of *No!*

"Go on!" Arthur whispered, nodding toward the room. "It's Ruby at stake!"

Jimmy gritted his teeth in frustration and then studied the drape suspiciously. And then, summoning that characteristic that had sent him marching toward the Ferris wheel to threaten Sherman Caswell's life, he reached forward and yanked the cloth barrier to his left.

And then he screamed.

Behind the drape, sitting next to each other on the floor of the dust-covered room, was a pair of thick girls, women, mirror images of one another, almost literally, leaning against each other shoulder to shoulder. Behind them several candles burned, and as the flames flickered wildly at different speeds and angles, they created an even more terrifying element to what was already a scene of horror.

Jimmy had reached his breaking point, and without another word, he turned and shouldered past his brother and then ran back to the front of the tent and through it, back into the storm.

But Arthur remained standing in place, staring at the conjoined twins below him—'Siamese twins' as they were advertised on the poster—just as he would have done had they come to the fair on the weekend and bought tickets for the attraction. But these weren't the sisters from the picture on the outside of the tent, young and lovely and happy with their lot in life. These women were short and heavy, with deformities that seemed beyond that of their adjoining birth defect. Their arms were too short. Their legs as well. With large heads that appeared ill-suited for the necks upon which they rested, one of which was now flopped back and to the right, the woman's tongue hanging like a slab of pink meat from her mouth, her eyes tossed somewhere into the back of her head.

Arthur wanted to scream, to follow Jimmy and flee the tent in terror, but he couldn't take his eyes off the twins, and he could see now that it was indeed their shoulders that were attached, and likely their chests as well, though they were somehow clothed, and he couldn't see exactly how the rest of their anatomy unfolded. But they had a pair of legs and one arm each, and the girl to Arthur's right had her sole hand clutched around the neck of her sister, squeezing with thick fingers at her sister's windpipe, pinching the life from her lungs as her tiny fingers dug into the skin at her throat. The murdering sister was leaning back slightly to get the leverage she needed to commit the act, and the shortness of her arm made it possible. And what was likely a rather beautiful smile on most days was charged now with hate and ferocity, homicide.

The victim twin was flailing her one arm wildly, trying to grip her sister's arm in desperation, or her hair, anything she could reach that would stop the killing that was about to occur. But she was losing energy now, and in her eyes a glaze of absence was rising.

Another minute or two and she would be dead, and as Arthur continued to watch in frozen cowardice, irrelevant questions began to arise in his mind as to what would happen to the other twin if one died. Would she die soon after? Were their organs connected in a way that they both needed to live for either of them to? And in this case, if the twin was killed by her sister, what of the crime itself? If she could survive alone, would she go to jail if found guilty? And how would that work exactly with a corpse attached to her?

Arthur stared another few seconds and then slowly took a step backward, then another, before finally turning and sprinting across the pavilion and out of the tent.

As he exited into the dust storm, which was now raging like a twister, sending clusters of dirt and debris into Arthur's eyes and hair, he felt the sensation of muted joy. He stopped for only a moment while he got his bearings, but the air around him was thick and blinding, so he took several steps in every direction, searching for Jimmy and Ruby again.

And there, standing at the very edge of the fair's perimeter, his chest against the chain fence which cordoned off the fairgrounds from the desert, was Jimmy. He stood with his back to Arthur, staring toward the sky and into the distance.

And Arthur knew in that moment that the Skadegamutc had been there a moment ago and was now gone.

And that Ruby was with them.

Chapter 21

"How did you know?"

Chris asked the question softly, sensing the pain now coming from Arthur. He felt relief to have finally reached this point in the story, as if his own life had caught up with Arthur's previous one, and that from this point forward he would get answers on how to get Jaycee back.

Arthur rubbed his forehead and closed his eyes gently, reflectively. The memory of that final moment had mostly receded over time, or at least had the pain that accompanied it. But now that he'd told the story aloud, revealed it in his own words for the first time in sixty-seven years, it filled him like water in an aquarium. He opened his eyes and looked again at the stranger seated by his bed, eyeing Chris as if seeing him for the first time ever. "Hmm?"

"How did you know they took Ruby? That she was gone? With them?"

Arthur shook his head now, perplexed by the question. "I could hear them. I could hear what Ruby had described weeks earlier. The name on the wind."

Chris remembered again the story of Downes' Grocery, of Ruby's proclamation that she had heard the name of Glenn Flannery before he'd murdered his wife. "You heard Ruby's name?" He asked skeptically.

Arthur wasn't good with strings of questions, mostly because they made him nervous, like he was being interrogated, and it didn't take long to throw his thinking out of balance. But he felt cogent now, in control of his own thread, better than he'd been even a minute earlier. And he also detected doubt in his visitor's voice, that he believed Arthur was projecting his sister's ability onto himself.

"It's been over six decades since that day at the New Mexico State Fair, Mr. Boylin," he said, "so if you don't trust in my memory, I can't say I would blame you for that. I'm not sure *I* even believe the whole account of it myself." Arthur leaned in now, his eyes as wide and sincere as they'd looked throughout any point in the tale. "But I heard the voice as clearly as you're hearing mine now. I don't know if the sound came in through my ears or was somehow planted in my mind, but I heard it. Heard them say my sister's name. I didn't know how or why, and by the end of the night, I'd decided it hadn't happened at all, that I had, as you no doubt suspect, invented it to match Ruby's claim. But I *did* hear it, and the next time I saw those twins, I knew exactly what I had to do to get my sister back."

Chris remained quiet, letting the magnitude of the revelation stand. This was the crux of what he'd been waiting for. The beginning of an answer he'd sought since the first sentence of the tale. But he didn't want to disrupt the linear nature of the story. Even with Arthur telling the saga so willingly and clearly, Chris knew there was still the proper path to follow, the tempo as dictated by Arthur Richland. So, he measured his words and asked, "What happened then?"

Arthur nodded, as if that were the proper question, and then he replied, "I ran to the fence, to where Jimmy was standing, and by the time I was beside him, a matter of a minute or two after I'd exited the oddities tent, the storm had ended. Just stopped on a mouse's button. It was like some invisible hand had suddenly reached out and shut a giant window above, the one letting in the massive draft of dust and dirt. Grime and stones began to fall from the sky like rain, spiders and scorpions and birds too, creatures light enough to be swept up by the wind but which were no longer being carried along on the gale. It was just like Downes': ferocious and then over in the snap of a finger."

Chris recalled this detail from his own experience, how quickly the storm had ended on the interstate the day of the accident, though it hadn't quite registered until a day or two later, after he'd replayed the incident in his mind a hundred times.

"Jimmy was there," he said slowly, deliberately, resetting Arthur's place in the story. "Did he see what happened? Did he see Ruby get taken?"

At the harshness of the final word's consonants—*TĀ-kin*—Arthur closed his eyes and turned away, the term piercing his abdomen like a gallstone.

"Arthur?"

"No," Arthur replied now, slightly irritated at the persistence. "He never saw her. Never saw what happened." He paused. "That's what he continued to tell me."

"But you didn't believe him?"

Arthur glared at Chris now, a light string of spittle dripping from his bottom lip, which now hung low with disdain.

His eyes weren't quite blank, but they were cloudy, as if searching for the direction to go next. Chris wanted to urge the elderly man on more, but instead he waited.

Finally, Arthur asked, "Do you wonder what happened to the boy on the Ferris wheel?"

"With Sherman Caswell?" Chris clarified. "I do wonder that."

Arthur nodded and the tightness in his stare released slightly. He appreciated that the man had been paying attention to the details of the story, the names of the perpetrators and victims. It was important to him, to not let the evils of his own history escape or the innocents to go unremembered. He smiled and said, "Glenn Flannery was a grown man when he killed his wife, and they had no problem convicting and sending him to the chair within a year. But Sherman Caswell was a different matter altogether. He was just a kid. A teenager, yes, but not old enough to cast a vote or go to war. The thought of sending someone that young to the electric chair was more than most in the state could stomach. Especially the women." He cocked his head and frowned. "Still, though, once the story of exactly what happened to Tammy Yarlow was printed on the front page of the newspapers, including in the Albuquerque Journal, and after Sherman admitted to the crime—which many hinted he was coerced into doing—there were still plenty who wanted him dead. And, after a bit of debate in the public square, the prosecutor seemed headed in that direction. But then the advocates from Albuquerque got organized, and then liberals from all around the country did too once the story spread wider. There was even rumor that Clarence Darrow had a bead on the case and was making plans to show up in New Mexico with a legal entourage. Next thing you know, the prosecutor decided to charge him as a minor, and Sherman was sent to a detention center for kids somewhere in Las Cruces."

"I guess that was the right thing," Chris replied. "Especially if it really was something else that made him do it."

Arthur shot a look at Chris now, one that showed bewilderment, confusion that there was any questioning of the story, even now after all he'd been told. "*If* it was something else? It *was*. It *was* 'something else.'"

"Of course," Chris said nodding, sorry to have implied any doubt.

Arthur took the pillow now from behind his back and placed it at the headboard, and then he reclined slowly, resting his head on the cushion and staring straight to the ceiling. He was quiet for several beats and then his eyes began to shutter. "I'm sorry, Mr. Boylin. I'm afraid I can't go on any longer today."

Chris felt his heart begin to race, the adrenaline fire through his veins. But as he opened his mouth to protest, he could see the absence in the man's face. Age and sleep were a formidable opponent, and the truth was, Chris was exhausted too.

And as Chris stood to leave for the night, Arthur softened any lingering concerns.

"One more day won't matter, Mr. Boylin. I can promise you that. Come back tomorrow, and we'll get to the end."

Chris sighed and nodded reluctantly, not truly wanting to concede the story for the evening, and he considered again whether to attempt a rally, to incite in Arthur an idea or suggestion that would spark some deep memory to the surface of his mind. And then, if he could recall that buried detail, it might trigger him back to consciousness, inspire him to tell the rest of the story before visiting hours ended.

But Chris could see such a play was pointless. Arthur's eyes—which had yet to close for good but were sinking quickly—were glazed and distant, with nothing more in them to reveal for the evening. Chris could only pray he would make it through the night and give him the answers the next day.

Chris stood and walked to the door, and as he turned the handle to leave, something inside told him to ask, "The website said your father died during the time Ruby was missing. Is that part true?"

Arthur remained still, his breathing labored as the air flowed in and out through his open mouth, and then, as Chris began to open the door, Arthur replied, "Just be prepared, Mr. Boylin. It will be your only chance to save her."

Chris opened his mouth to question the remark, but a feeling told him those were the last words of the night, which they were.

And when he returned the following day, all hell had broken loose.

Chapter 22

Arthur opened his eyes to sheer blackness and the sound of silence, the latter of which he could never remember experiencing quite so vividly. The quiet was so dense he thought for a moment he'd died, or was on the cusp of death, and the stillness around him was the failing of his senses, a preparation for whatever awaited him beyond the world. Would the light he'd always heard about arrive soon? The wispy span of an angel's wings to embrace and guide him toward it? Or was darkness to be in his eternal future? The inevitable punishment of a crime for which he could never atone, no matter how many more days he had on earth.

But then he saw a green glow just a few feet in front of him, and as he lifted his head several inches off the pillow, his eyesight rose above the billowing sheets that were blocking his view and landed on the alarm clock atop his bedside table.

2:08.

Arthur took a gaping breath and lay quietly for several moments, first making a mental check of his bodily functions, and then of the events from the previous day. This latter accounting was a practice he'd made a habit of doing each morning (though it was normally several hours later), believing it was helpful in preventing a full mental decline.

The visitor.

Chris Boylin.

Arthur couldn't quite recall where in the story he'd left off with him, but he knew he was getting close to the end. To when Ruby returned. To his own atrocity, the telling of which, he prayed, would allow Chris to get his own daughter back.

Arthur's eyes finally adjusted to the darkness as the ambient light from outside began to fill the room. But the quiet there continued, and intuition forced Arthur to rise from the mattress and swing his legs over the side of the bed, touching his toes to the cool floor. He rarely woke during the night anymore—unlike so many of the insomniac somnambulists who populated Stratford Manor—and even when he did, it was only for a moment or two, nothing that forced him to leave his bed, usually to clear the remnants of his recurring dream before picking it up again only minutes later when he fell back to sleep.

But Arthur was up now, fully awake, and he rose from the mattress and stood motionless at the side of the bed. He took inventory of his bladder again, but all seemed stable there, so he walked carefully to the door, stopping for a beat after each step, listening for any sounds coming from the hallway. But as he reached the door, there was still only quiet, and so he waited there, his ear only an inch or two from the barrier as he stared toward the dark wall beside him. Where was the shuffle and chatter of the nurses? Or the beep of some heart machine, rolling down the hall toward some brewing cardiac emergency?

But there was nothing but silence, so Arthur smoothed his hand across the wall, tapping his fingers like the legs of a tarantula until he found the light switch. And when he flipped the switch up, he was met with a cold click and no light.

"Damn hovel!" Arthur grunted and then shuffled back to the nightstand on the side of the bed where he slept. There he picked up the TV remote and pressed the large red button at the top. Nothing. The power was out for sure; his alarm clock only worked because of the battery backup.

Arthur scanned the room, which, despite the lack of electricity, had now come into grainy focus, though it was still in a fog of shadow. Then, despite his first instinct, which was to exit the room and find a nurse or orderly, a move that, under the circumstances, made the most sense, Arthur stepped away from the door and walked slowly to the window, drawn to it as if by some smell or texture on his tongue, or else some other, less-obvious sensation. There was a dryness to the room's air, a staleness that was suddenly repressive, and the desire to gasp the refreshing oxygen just beyond the windowpane was nearly irresistible. He strode quickly to the window now, grazing his hip against the dresser as he passed but ignoring the near injury. He was desperate for the glass, to open it, to shatter it if necessary, and once at the window, he gripped the nylon cord of the blinds.

And then he paused.

Arthur swallowed and looked at the covered window now, an expression of pain suddenly filling his eyes. He was still gripping the cord, and the force of his grasp bleached his knuckles to white. He said a quiet prayer now, something he hadn't done in forty years or more, and then he held his breath and pulled downward on the nylon cable, slowly to start, gathering the first two or three slats with gentle, clattering clicks, revealing just the jamb of the window.

And then quickly he snatched the drawstring down with his full weight, exposing the window to the fullness of the room.

The Skadegamutc—just one of the beings—flared on the outside of Stratford Manor like a bed of deranged eels, the maniacal shape sparking and flashing in chaotic electricity, orange and popping like a bonfire in the wind. And though the witch's shape held, bonding together by some impossible, magnetic force, it sparked and danced wildly, erratically, as if on the verge of bursting. Behind and beside the Skadegamutc, in the ambient light of its own making, Arthur could see the debris of sticks and leaves that had recently been strewn about the grounds, pieces of shingles and shutters that had been cast like driftwood from the structure of the nursing home to the lawn below. And Arthur instantly realized there had been a storm that night, and with all of the excitement, the break to his routine, he had slept right through it. It was only the aftermath of silence that had awakened him. Or perhaps it was more. Perhaps it was the presence of the evil avenger outside, beckoning for him to awaken and come to it.

Arthur closed his eyes and pled silently for the swaying vision outside to be only that, a hallucination, the overripe manifestation of a decrepit brain. Or even that he was still dreaming—that would have been even better—though this last wish was beyond hope. He knew his dreams now better than he did his actual life, and what he was seeing now was not the creation of his unconscious.

Arthur opened his eyes again with one last appeal that he had imagined the demon sighting, but the Skadegamutc remained, its hair like electric currents flailing in the darkness, as if caught in some magnetic storm which attempted to pull it to the heavens. And then, right before Arthur's eyes, the image began to change, slowly at first with a silent crackling, and then like a raging fire as the witch's shape bled sideways, the borders of the orange body opening on one side, creating a second devil on its right flank, becoming a pair of witches, standing side-by-side like two of the Wayward Sisters of Macbeth. Their circular eyes were blank and dead yet taunting, their open mouths pleading for sustenance.

Arthur backed away from the window, though he was unable to look away, and then the sizzle of crackling glass burned into the room and was followed seconds later by the window's explosion. Arthur finally turned and plodded like Jack's giant toward the door of his room, stumbling once over the claw of the bed and smashing a rib into his dresser. But he caught himself from falling completely, and he was out the door seconds later.

"Help me!" Arthur called, the rattling words like a cough, erupting from his mouth before his body was fully into the hallway. And as he shuffled down the corridor to the nurse's stand, the frustration of age gnawing subtly in the back of his mind as he hunched forward in clumsy strides, he noted within moments that something was very wrong in Stratford Manor, beyond that which was no doubt entering his room behind him, seeping in from the lawn at that very moment. He downshifted until he was moving at barely a stroll, and seconds later he crossed from the quarters wing into the middle of the common area.

At first glance, the room was empty, which, in and of itself, was unsettling. Even at this hour, the common room was normally occupied by at least a few of the residents, the aforementioned insomniacs who came for the Tonight Show and stayed for the infomercials, or else the staff who took their middle-of-the-night lunch breaks there, relishing the calm that only came at that time of day.

But tonight, there was no one on the couch or in any of the club chairs positioned in front of the television. Nor was there anyone at the checkers table or staring out the window into the blackness of the night. Or under the table lamp in the reading area, thumbing through a six-month-old People magazine, staring at the beautiful people dressed in colors that must have seemed like they'd come from a fantasy world.

And then Arthur saw the outline of a profile in the shadows, of a man, his stiff figure staring to the front door of the center like a victim of Medusa.

As Arthur had suspected several days prior, when the last storm arrived, the center was indeed fitted with auxiliary lights, and one shone from the ceiling of the common area, just off-center, a few feet in front of the sole occupant of the room. It was the one spot in the room where Arthur could see clearly now, and though he couldn't know for sure, since whoever it was standing there was turned away from him, at first glance, based on the man's height and posture, it appeared to be Roger Desormeaux.

Arthur was wary, of course; with the odd placement of Roger in the room and the image of the Skadegamutc still fresh in his mind, he knew there was a connection, though what it was specifically he couldn't have said. But Arthur strode forward anyway, obligatorily, knowing he had to warn anyone who would listen about the threat around them.

"Roger!" he whispered, now moving as fast as his legs would take him down the hallway, a pace that was little more than a shuffling trot. "Roger, you have to...there's something dangerous outside. Go back to—" But before Arthur could finish his warning, he saw what he'd already known in his heart to be true: that Roger had been taken by the Skadegamutc, and that he had been a vehicle to kill, just as it had tried to use Lois Hernandez. Arthur was only four or five yards from Roger now, with the sofa that framed one side of the common area partitioning the two men. And as the lifeless body appeared to Arthur over the back of the couch, lying on the floor at Roger's slippers, Arthur shuffled his pace to a halt, his bare feet sticking to the linoleum like a rat on a glue trap. The sudden move sent him flailing forward into the sofa back, and had the couch not been there to brace him, Arthur would have fallen at Roger's feet, the difference between his life and death.

Arthur knew instantly it was Betty's corpse on the floor, and as he regained his footing and stood tall again, he could see her throat had been slit from her left collar bone to her right, reminding him of the image from the wall of the altar room when he was a child, the memory of which he'd spoken aloud to Chris Boylin for the first time in his life.

The rug of the common room, which was maroon in its original state, had turned a darker shade of red around Betty, the blood from the nurse's body having soaked through the area around her head, forming a halo of sorts around the upper half of her corpse.

Arthur opened his mouth to speak when he saw movement to his left, motion from the floor that was slow and languid. Arthur took a stumbled step in the direction of the movement, which was coming six or eight feet to Roger's right, and there his eyes fell on a second body. This victim was a man, and though he couldn't identify him, he was clearly injured, in danger of dying.

"Roger?" Arthur hacked out, his voice resounding through the center as if he'd screamed the name.

Roger turned his head quickly toward Arthur, a normal reaction to hearing one's name, though it was unlike what Arthur knew about those under the immediate spell of the Skadegamutc. He expected a trance from Roger. Or even eyes of regret and confusion, suddenly shocked by his actions from moments earlier of which he'd had no control.

But Roger didn't hesitate as he ran toward Arthur, a straight razor in his hand, the kind used to shave the male residents on the days the barber visited Stratford Manor. Arthur couldn't imagine how Roger had acquired the weapon, or how Betty had become his victim, but it was the Skadegamutc that was responsible, about that he was sure. And Roger was still in its grasp.

"Roger, no!" Arthur said, trying to turn as he shouted his plea. But his formerly weakened legs gave out, and he fell to the ground, where he sat now with his arms braced behind him, watching as his Stratford Manor enemy approached with a look of psychopathy in both his eyes and smile.

Roger kept coming, now running at a speed that was impossible for a man of his age and condition to reach, his lips pulled back from his gums as his imposter teeth shone large in his mouth, the razor blade held high by his face.

And then his eyes flashed even wider, and instantly they curled into a look of pain and fear as he stopped on a penny and shook his head in disbelief. Roger's eyes were no longer focused on Arthur, but rather on some point behind him.

Arthur turned in the direction of Roger's stare, and there, in the corridor just outside of his room, was the Skadegamutc.

The pair of electric witches wavered in place, seeming to have been born from the floor below them, a torch of fire and flame rising from the earth. Somehow, Arthur managed to stand, adrenaline bringing him to his feet, and he took a step backward, in the direction of Roger. He was trapped between the two evil forces, one the source, the other the prisoner.

"Roger!" Arthur barked, "Roger, run!"

But Roger couldn't take his eyes from the glowing figures, which now had moved forward, though they had done so seamlessly. And now their full shapes were on display as they stood tall in the corridor, the ferocity of their open mouths, the indifference of their solid orange eyes. And their femininity was evident as well, the curve or their shoulders and hips, the thinness of their faces and long glowing hair, as well as the suggestion of breasts and sex organs, though there was nothing of detail that could have been described with any accuracy.

"Roger!"

Finally, Roger blinked, awakened, and he looked at Arthur and raised the blade higher, up by his left eye, as if to slash it across Arthur's face. Instead, he placed the razor against his own neck, and then, with the delicacy of a chocolatier, he drew the blade across his throat, releasing a deluge of gore down the front of his gown.

"No!" Arthur screamed, and then he covered his face and slid down along the wall until he was on the floor once more. He buried his head in his hands, his mind flurrying with dismay, knowing that Roger's death was his fault, that he couldn't blame Jimmy anymore. What happened with the Skadegamutc, now and forever forward, was his fault fully.

Despite his guilt, however, his instinct for self-preservation reactivated quickly, and he moved his hands away and looked to the corridor warily, to the place where the ancient Tompiros monsters had been shimmering seconds earlier.

But the angels of Hell had done their destruction for the evening, and now, without a remnant of proof (aside from the broken window, Arthur thought absently), they were gone.

Chapter 23

By 8 am the same morning, the officers who had first arrived on the scene at Stratford Manor Rehab and Nursing Center had tripled in size. Amongst them were dour-faced detectives in blue Oxford shirts and steady blazers, guns on display at their hips, pads and pens up front, employed. Arthur had given his statement already, a blabbering mix of details that included the name Roger Desormeaux, but also that of Mrs. Mulrooney, his fourth-grade teacher whom he continued to describe as 'big-bosomed' to the detectives, causing one of them to roll his eyes, the other to blush. He could have gone with the story of the Skadegamutc, of course, and though it would have received the same reaction from the officers as that of Mrs. Mulrooney, he figured it unwise to tempt fate.

Arthur claimed to have no recollection of the broken window, and it was determined the shattered pane was a result of debris from the storm, just as it would have been had he blamed ancient Indian fire witches.

He was released from questioning within minutes, and once free, Arthur immediately began his preparations, which included loading a small bag with the only few items that still concerned him in life: four photos of his son at various stages in his life, another dozen pictures of his granddaughter and great-grandkids, and a letter from Jimmy just before he died.

And two round stones that had been taken from a hole in the ground on the outskirts of New Mexico sixty-seven years earlier.

These last items he hadn't touched since the day he'd moved into Stratford Manor, and though the cursed items felt as cold and horrifying as the day he'd collected them from Jimmy's place in Spokane, there was promise in them as well, the solid belief that they held the answer to returning Jaycee Boylin to her father.

Arthur sat by the window closest to the center's entrance, staring into the parking lot, which was swirling with emergency lights. And when Chris finally walked through the main doors just a few minutes after nine, Arthur was ready for his performance.

"Chris!" he yelled with a wave, struggling to his feet with a push of the chair's arm before staggering forward like an old panhandler. "Thank god, Chris. Get me out of here!"

Chris knew from the commotion of police cars and ambulances out front that there was ado inside, but he assumed it was to do with the sudden death of a resident. But as his eyes fell on the scene in front of him, the milling of police, the taped off section of the common area, he knew it was more.

The bodies of Betty and Roger had been removed, of course, the initial assessment of murder-suicide obvious. It wasn't wrong, of course, the evaluation, just lacking detail.

The other body on the floor was of an intern who'd started only a week earlier, and as far as Arthur could gather, he was seriously injured but would live.

"Arthur?" Chris started, "What...what happened?"

An officer stepped to the front and blocked Chris from entering. "Who are you here to see?" he asked.

"That's my son!" Arthur shouted. "Let him through!"

The desk clerk and a couple of the nurses gave half-interested looks about this revelation, but none of them knew Arthur's declaration to be untrue. Only Betty knew the truth, and she was dead.

"Is that your father, sir?" the officer asked.

Chris swallowed and nodded.

The officer frowned. "I'm afraid there's been an incident here. Happened late last night. Your father seems to have been caught in the middle of it. We think he might have seen it, but we can't get much out of him. He's been calling for you all morning."

Chris felt the burn of fraud arise in his chest, but he caught on quickly. "Can I speak to him?"

The officer frowned again and looked askance. "We were hoping actually—we're asking this of anyone with relatives who live close by—if you could maybe take him for a bit. A couple days even. I'm sure you're aware there was an attack by one of the residents a week or so ago, and now, well...would that be possible? To take him?"

"Chris! Get me out of here!" Arthur called again, inciting irritated stares from his fellow residents, most of whom seemed unaware that anything had happened while they slept, let alone that two of their Stratford comrades had died.

"I saw it all," Jacob Warner said absently from the edge of the common room sofa, nodding as he stared around the area at a sea of disinterested faces.

"Sir?" the cop repeated to Chris. "Will that be possible?"

Chris caught Arthur's stare now, and the elderly patient, whose dementia he knew was real to a certain degree—though, as Chris had suspected and now believed to be true, was sometimes used to his advantage, to avoid or distract—gave him the slightest of nods.

Chris looked up at the officer and nodded. "Yes, um, of course."

The officer gave an appreciative smile. "That's great. You're really helping us out here. Your dad says his bags are already packed, so if there's any paperwork or anything you need to sign, please do that, and, again, we're sorry about the inconvenience."

Arthur was already marching toward the front entrance before Chris and the officer finished the formalities, and before Chris knew what was happening, after a verbal assurance that he was, in fact, Arthur's son, he had signed a forty-eight-hour release form to check his 'father' out of Stratford Manor. He assumed the process for taking a cognitively impaired patient from a nursing home was more organized on a typical day, but the clerk who released Arthur had five or six phone lines on hold and another one ringing, and the cops were trying to clear the home as quickly as possible, so she was doing her best.

Arthur didn't say a word as he walked with Chris to the parking lot, fighting the draw to look back, fearing doing so might arouse suspicion, though from whom he didn't know.

Stratford Manor was in the throes of chaos at the moment, and one less patient to deal with would be a small blessing.

Chris opened the door to his latest pickup truck, a rented Nissan Frontier, clearing the passenger seat for Arthur before moving to the opposite side of the car to help the elderly man inside. But Arthur had already navigated the maneuver and was strapping the seat belt over his chest by the time Chris arrived.

Chris stood in the open doorway. "What's the plan, Arthur?"

"I have one or two ideas."

"Unless they're about how to get Jaycee back—soon—I'm not interested. I'll bring you right back inside and confess that I'm not your father. I need to know. Now."

Arthur looked at the man beside him, the grieving father, and he saw the pain again, that of his mother in 1939. "Of course it's to do with your daughter," he said, and for the first time since Chris Boylin had arrived at Stratford Manor, Arthur *felt* the man's pain as well. "Everything I've said is to do with her." He cleared his throat and added, "But we won't get her back with me in there. We need to drive. I'll tell you the rest of the story on the way."

Chris didn't argue, and something about the man's words, the sincerity of the pitch, buoyed him. He sensed not only compassion, but action, something they could do physically that might lead to Jaycee's return. He went to close the door, but before he did, he asked, "What happened in there, just now with the police, was it to do with the...the things that took Jaycee?"

Arthur was looking forward now, in the posture of someone waiting to be driven to his destination. Without turning, he said, "Of course, it does, Mr. Boylin. They're back. They have been for some time."

Chris closed the door and hurried to the driver's side of the truck. He entered and started the ignition and then focused back on Arthur and asked, "Are you okay?"

Arthur was touched by the question, that Chris had concern for him in a time of his own distress. He turned and smiled. "I feel...good." And then, as if not wanting to ruin the clarity that now swirled inside him, even if it lasted for only for an hour or two longer, he added, "They let me live. They could have killed me, or allowed Roger to kill me, but instead they let me live."

"They were there? The Skadegamutc?"

Arthur nodded.

"Why didn't they?"

Arthur had a shine in his eyes Chris had never seen before, one he suspected hadn't been there in years. "I think it wanted me to notice them, not to kill me."

Not yet, he thought, but he kept that addition to himself.

"And they want to return. They have no purpose here anymore. The Tompiros and their land, it's lost. Forever. And..." Arthur paused and cleared his eyes with several long blinks. "...they've taken their revenge already. On the ones responsible for their awakening." Again, this wasn't the whole of the truth. Jimmy and his friends had awakened the Skadegamutc initially, but Arthur was the one who had kept them from their slumber.

The one who possessed the stones still.

Arthur's words sounded profound, but Chris had one concern alone. "So why did it take Jaycee?"

Arthur rubbed his forehead, feeling that so many of the answers were colliding inside him at once. He wasn't losing the thread, thank goodness, but the exercise was exhausting, nevertheless. "Let's go, Mr. Boylin. At some point they'll know I shouldn't have left. Though..." he looked back to Stratford Manor, realizing it was the last time he would ever see his current home. "...I suppose that won't be for a while. In any case, we should leave. Drive east."

Chris shifted the car to drive and eased from the parking lot of Stratford Manor onto the highway, and within ten minutes or so, they were back on the interstate. He kept his eyes focused on the road ahead, unwavering with his gaze. Chris never took his eyes from the landscape anymore, especially when on the interstate, not even to adjust the radio or peek at his phone. It was difficult to maintain the discipline; after all, every ping on his phone could have been news about Jaycee, that she had been found, dead or alive. If he was desperate to find out, he would pull to the side and park, and then make the call back or check the text or voice message.

But he never looked away. The desolate land stretched for miles in every direction on the Southwest freeways, and he prayed—knew almost—that one day he'd see his daughter sitting by the roadside, shoulders slumped, bored, waiting to be picked up by her father, the father who'd abandoned her in the desert after crashing their truck into a guardrail on Interstate 412. It was irrational, this fantasy, but it was the only way he could bear the hours he spent driving alone.

"Why did it take her?" Chris repeated.

For this latest question, Arthur had the answer, or at least he believed so, but he kept the details to himself for now. "Because of what I told you, Mr. Boylin, it wants to return."

"What does—"

"Let me finish, Mr. Boylin." Arthur turned to Chris now, his expression pleading. "I'll never speak to a priest about this, and whether you absolve me or not, I'll likely go to Hell when my life is over. But let me finish, tell you about my sin, and then, I pray, you'll have the fortitude to do what you must to see your daughter again."

Chapter 24

"James!"

Arthur heard the call of his brother's name drift over the crowd as if it had been sent forth upon a flying carpet. The voice was that of his mother's, and for the first time since Ruby disappeared, he began to cry.

It had been over an hour since Ruby had gone missing, and Arthur and Jimmy had searched the grounds of the fair from end to end, at first in dire madness, and then catatonically, when it was clear they wouldn't find her. For the last fifteen minutes of the search, all Arthur could think about was the reaction his mother would have when she realized her daughter was missing.

Gone.

In seconds, Dotty was standing in front of her sons, first squeezing Jimmy by the upper arms, staring back and forth into both of her children's eyes, smiling at the wonder of their faces. "Where have you been?" she cried, her voice slipping on the final word, the first sign that tears were on their way. Neither boy could speak; an affliction brought on by parched mouths and shame.

And then Dotty's eyes drifted behind the boys, searching, and with each eternal second, her smile faded to confusion, then to a plastered grimace. She met Arthur's eyes again, and when she saw the hopelessness pooling inside them, she began to shudder.

"Ruby?" Dotty said quietly, now flashing her stare in every direction, as if she'd simply missed her on the first scan. And when it was clear her daughter wasn't with her older brothers, she shouted to the open space, "Ruby!" screaming the girl's name as if she had just spotted her on the precipice of some bottomless canyon. She looked backed to her oldest son and squinted. "Where is she, Arthur?" she quipped, her voice cracking on the 'she.' "Where is Ruby?" She spoke as if they'd reached the conclusion of some prank gone wrong and it was now time to confess.

Arthur shifted his eyes to Jimmy, the unconscious move of a coward, tacitly casting blame while also redirecting the question to his brother. He felt justified, however, since it was Jimmy who had seen Ruby last, or must have, despite his claims to the contrary.

"James?" His mother turned to her middle child, her eyes now frozen in astonishment, shock that she still didn't have an answer. "James, what happened? Where is your sister?"

Jimmy swallowed and then pouted like a toddler, his bottom lip dropping nearly to his chest. "We watched Sherman...and then she wandered off. I...I don't know where she went, Ma. Arthur thought she went to the freak tent, but when we got there...I don't know. She wasn't..."

Jimmy finally broke down into an all-out bawl, and Arthur was quietly impressed that he had held on that long.

Their mother, who normally would have taken at least a beat to console her son, even if she were still sore with him about some rule he'd broken or order he'd disobeyed, ignored the blubbering entirely and pushed past them both without another word. She headed in the direction of the tent of oddities, and at about the halfway point between the boys and the tent, Arthur watched his mother's quick march turn into a labored jog, and he wished more than anything in the world he could take her pain and make it his own.

"Boys!" It was Arthur's father now, entering the scene like an actor in a stage play, arriving in the wake of his co-star exiting stage right. "Where you boys been? Y'all look like you just got off an Okie caravan."

The caravan reference reminded Arthur of Jimmy's story, of a bartered teenage girl lying filthy beneath Arthur's father; and that image, combined with fear and hunger and exhaustion, was too much to bear in the moment. He bent over violently and vomited.

"Jesus Christ, Arthur!" Randall barked. "What in the hell's wrong with you? You eat somethin' you shouldn't have?"

Arthur rose and stared at his father, wiping his mouth. Tears of sickness and sadness converged in a gloss across his eyes.

"You okay, boy?"

Arthur could only shake his head. He wasn't.

Randall Richland noted something more profound in his son than just a little fair illness. "What's wrong?"

Jimmy answered. "We lost...we lost Ruby?"

Randall's brow curled, his eyes tapering to something reptilian. "Lost her? The hell's that mean?"

Jimmy was bawled out by then, and he answered soberly, honestly. "She was with us when the storm came, and then she ran off. We didn't notice until it was too late."

Their father clenched his teeth, and for a moment, Arthur thought they would shatter behind his lips like glass. "Goddamn five-year-old girl in the middle of the storm and you couldn't care to watch her?" He looked back to Arthur, the culprit for the crime. "Neither of you?"

The boys stayed silent.

"Tell me what happened. All of it from the start."

Jimmy explained the events again, and as he did, Arthur listened closely, wondering if he would mention the lights at the top of the Ferris wheel or the Skadegamutc. But Jimmy skipped that part entirely, focusing instead on the moment they noticed Ruby was gone, and then how they had followed her to the freak show tent. As he listened, Arthur tried to extract his own clues from the story, anything he might have missed, or changes to the narrative that would suggest Jimmy was lying about what he'd seen at the end. But Jimmy's description was still the vague retelling Arthur had heard four times by then, that Ruby was gone by the time he reached the fence on the opposite side of the freak tent.

That might have been true, Arthur thought, *but you know something*.

"What about you, Arthur?" his father asked. "You see anything different?"

Arthur's mind wanted off Ruby for the moment, so he shook his head quickly and switched to the topic of Sherman, the source of the half dozen ambulances and police cars that had convened at the base of the Ferris wheel. "Is Tammy Yarlow dead?" he asked.

Arthur's father gave a twitch of confusion, and then he glanced back toward the Ferris wheel. "Is that who that was fell out of there?"

Fell was hardly the word, but Arthur nodded anyway.

Randall bowed his head. "Jesus Christ. Clayton girl? Dies all the way out here? The hell are the odds of that?"

Maybe not as long as you might think, Arthur considered.

Randall looked back to his son. "How the hell do you know that anyway?"

Arthur swallowed. "Because I saw it. I saw her fall. Except it—"

"Randy, I can't find her!" Dotty Richland was running in a stiff trot toward her family, one hand over her mouth, on the verge of hysterics. She stopped six feet short of the group. "And no one will help me!" she screamed, turning in a semicircle, searching for the help that wasn't there. "They're all at the Ferris whe—" she covered her face and collapsed in a heap, the dust and dirt below her covering her dress like water. Arthur's father rushed to his wife's side, bending down and wrapping his arms around her stiffly. Arthur rarely saw affection like that from either of his parents, and certainly not from his father; despite the circumstances, it brought a sliver of hope to the moment.

"We'll find her, Dot," Randall said. "I promise we'll find her."

Dotty cried in her bundle for several moments, releasing the first of many bouts of sadness that would be arriving over the two weeks, and then she stood again, her sights now locked on Arthur once more. It was a look that anyone observing from the outside would have labeled as hate. She walked toward both of her boys and stood before them, smoothing out her blouse and clearing the dust that had collected there. She took a deep breath and asked steadily, "What did you boys see?"

Jimmy was quiet now. He'd told his story already, and he wasn't going back on the details. And their mother was looking at Arthur for answers now, her eyes on him alone.

"I swear it, Ma," Arthur said, as calmly as he could muster, "the one minute she was underneath the dart stand, and the next she was gone. Wasn't even a minute." He paused. "But..."

"What is it, Arthur?"

"Right before. I was just tellin' Pa. Up in the Ferris wheel, I saw—"

"I don't care about the Ferris wheel!" Dotty's voice boomed across the fairgrounds, and most in the vicinity turned to look at her, many of them scowling at the insensitivity of the woman. "I care about my Ruby! Your sister!"

Dotty's face boiled with more to say on the matter, but on a dime, she turned and strode like a general toward the Ferris wheel. Arthur, Jimmy, and Randall watched in silence as she approached an officer at the base of the ride, rotating with him at every turn of his shoulders as he tried to clear her from his view and focus on the scene in front of him. But Dotty persisted, standing her ground, never backing off an inch, and finally, after several minutes, the officer acquiesced, tossing his hands in the air indignantly. He walked her over to a space away from the rest of the crowd and pulled out a pad of paper, listening and writing as Dotty narrated. With-in twenty minutes, three more officers had joined the posse, and then they made their way to the rest of the family, where statements were taken from Arthur and Jimmy. Within the hour, the search for Ruby was on.

The fair closed at eight o'clock normally, but with the Ferris wheel accident and the dozen or so people who were injured in the rush to take shelter from the storm—and then the disappearance of Ruby—by two o'clock the carnival was shut down for the day, and the property was clear of fairgoers an hour later. Except for the Richlands, who worked side by side with the officers, searching the grounds and the sur-rounding areas for Ruby.

A few hours later, nightfall arrived, and two hours after that, the search was called for the evening with the promise that it would resume at dawn. But it was obvious the officers believed Ruby had been snatched, kidnapped in the chaos of the storm by some wicked opportunist, taken to a place only Heaven knew about. There was no evidence to support this theory, of course, only guesswork and experience, but af-ter interviews with several of the fair workers, including the milk bottle girl and a few of the other midway attendants, there was little else to go on. Arthur hadn't heard whether the Siamese twins had been questioned, but he assumed not, especially since one may have been dead by then.

As for Arthur and Jimmy, they had told the officers all they were going to say on the matter, which included seeing Sherman Caswell murdering Tammy Yarlow, as well as the fracas amongst the twins in the oddities tent.

The Skadegamutc, however, didn't come up.

The brothers were huddled now in the narrow space behind the seats of the truck. Jimmy was sleeping, his head against the metal frame of the cabin, while Arthur sat up straight with his eyes closed, unable to drift. Finally, the sound of the car door opening sprang Arthur to awareness, and his mother and father entered almost simultaneously. Without a word, the truck started, and they headed for home.

For the first twenty miles or so, Arthur listened with a sickness in his belly to the words of his mother. She didn't talk to anyone directly, but she did speak, mostly about the neglect she'd shown by allowing a girl as young as Ruby to go off with her careless brothers. That was perhaps true, Arthur thought, it *was* careless of her, and thus he was absolved of blame, if only in a backhanded sort of way.

When they arrived back in Clayton the sun was just cresting above the skyline. Thankfully, Arthur had slept most of the way home, waking in unison with the car bending left onto the dirt drive where it cruised to the front of the house and parked. For just the meagerest of moments, he thought all that had happened the night before was a dream. That the fair itself hadn't happened at all, and, even better, the glorious day still awaited him—him and Jimmy and Ruby—waiting on the horizon like the gift it had been for almost a month.

But reality returned to Arthur with the opening of the passenger door, and he watched in silence as his mother stumbled from the truck and toward the house, leaving the door swung wide behind her. Arthur then watched his father and Jimmy follow seconds behind, and once they were inside the house, Arthur finally joined them.

Inside, to Arthur's surprise, his mother hadn't gone straight to her bedroom. Instead, Dotty Richland sat at the kitchen table, head in her hands, crying, each sob causing her head to bob as if a jolt of electricity were being sent through her body in stagnated waves. It was a rare state in which to see his mother, and Arthur couldn't help but cry as well, first silently, as tears streamed quietly down his face, and then audibly, mimicking his mother's magnitude.

"I'm sorry, Ma," he said, his words delicate, dripping with apology. He stood well back from his mother now, feeling the severity of her hurt burn from her like lava. He wanted to go to her, but he dared not. "I'm so sorry."

Dotty's crying came to an abrupt pause, but she kept her head buried in her sprawled fingers. Finally, she lifted her head slowly and looked at Arthur, her jaw clenched like a chained dog, taut with aggression. She scoffed and shifted her eyes in disgust, and then she stood and walked to her room, never looking back as she closed the door behind her with a slam.

Arthur looked to his father, but Randall Richland dropped his eyes almost instantly. "She's tired, Arthur," he said, no sympathy in his voice, just a point of fact. He slid his own chair out and stood. "We all are. Longest night any of us have had in...well, maybe ever. I'm gonna get some sleep; you boys need to also. We'll figure out the rest of it after." He nodded toward the back wall of the kitchen. "There's potato salad in the icebox. Your mom made it 'fore we left." He walked to the bedroom door and opened it without another word.

"Are they gonna find her, Pa?" It was Jimmy now, desperate to be parented, needing to hear that everything would be okay, even if it was he, Jimmy, who was responsible for most of their current trouble.

Their father pursed his lips and nodded. "Yeah, James, they're gonna find her. *We're* gonna find her. Now go on and get some food, and we'll work on it tomorrow."

Randall entered the bedroom and closed the door quietly behind him, while the boys lingered in their respective standing positions, quietly, waiting for the argument to ensue. But there was only silence from the room, a feature both interpreted negatively.

After a minute or two of listening, Arthur walked to the kitchen's lone shelf beside the basin and grabbed two bowls, and then he used a towel to wipe the dust from inside, a move that was as automatic by now as blinking. He retrieved the container of potato salad from the icebox and slapped heaping portions into the bowls, and then he brought them to the table, rattling one down in front of Jimmy and the other before the chair beside him. Arthur was starving, and he knew Jimmy was too. They hadn't eaten since breakfast that morning, and with that idea now front of mind, along with the growl of his stomach, he thought of Ruby and how hungry she must have been in the moment. Wherever she was.

The brothers ate in silence, and though they wanted to finish what remained of the potato salad, they knew to leave enough for their parents; though, Arthur figured, they wouldn't be up again until morning, and what remained of the potato salad would have to be dumped by then.

The boys sat in front of their empty bowls and listened for any conversation that might erupt from their parent's room, and when none came, Jimmy finally looked up at Jimmy and said, "You can't talk about it, Arthur. Not ever."

Arthur knew what his brother meant and had agreed with him implicitly, a point that was obvious based on his silence during their interviews with the police. Neither boy had spoken a word about the Skadegamutc, or about the lights that had appeared in the sky just before Tammy Yarlow's murder. These were one in the same, of course, something the police wouldn't have known, and as Arthur reflected on the point now, he considered whether Arthur and Jimmy should have just said what they saw above the Ferris wheel—not necessarily what they already *knew*—and then allowed the police to take the information and do with it what they wished.

But the brothers didn't give a word of detail, not of the Skadegamutc or the lights that had materialized suddenly in the storm, and certainly not of the Hollow or the stones that had been removed from the altar. And as Arthur sat with his brother in the dark house, he wondered if perhaps the reason they hadn't was because they feared when one piece of the truth was told, the rest would flow behind it. Of course, it was doubtful anyone would have believed the tale, but Arthur and Jimmy feared the consequences anyway, and thus they'd hid what they knew. Arthur understood it was wrong. Sinful.

Arthur put his fork down and stared back at his brother, and then he replied, "Ruby's gone, Jimmy." He lowered his voice slightly and leaned in, peeking toward his parent's room. "And we know why. We might have caused the whole goddamn thing." He sighed and closed his eyes, praying this last part wasn't true, which, technically, it wasn't. *They* hadn't caused anything. It was Jimmy and his friends who had caused it, or at least that's where the clues were pointing.

But it didn't matter now. All that mattered was getting their sister back.

"We can show them to the Hollow," Arthur continued. "Ma and Pa, at least. And then they can decide whether to pass it on to the cops. Then...I don't know...maybe the police can find a clue there or somethin', somethin' that'll tell where she went."

Jimmy shook his head at the suggestion. "No, Arthur! It's nothing they can do. I..." He paused.

"What is it?" And then, "Do you know where she is, Jimmy."

"No!" Jimmy snapped, and Arthur immediately shushed him. Jimmy lowered his voice and added, "I don't, Arthur." Tears streamed down his face now, though his voice remained clear. "I know it's my fault, but I don't know where she went. You can't tell though. Sheriff already warned me about going there, and...I don't want to go to jail, Arthur. That's what's gonna happen to Sherman, and I...I can't go."

Jimmy began to sob quietly now, and Arthur let him carry on. Even if their parents could hear him, they would assume it was over Ruby, which, for the most part, it was. Arthur considered the whole scenario again, gazing past his brother as he replayed the details of the day and the weeks prior. Of Ruby and Sherman, but also about the Flannery incident and his father's actions with the migrant girl at Chester Sutton's. Finally, Jimmy's sobbing waned, and Arthur mused aloud, "Why did they take her, Jimmy? Why did they *take* Ruby and no one else? Everyone else either got killed or did the killin'."

Jimmy looked up at Arthur, hope in his face. "What if it *wasn't* them? What if it was just a coincidence? What we saw—the lights—and Ruby's vanishin'? That could be it, right? Maybe they did have somethin' to do with Tammy Yarlow, but someone else took Ruby?"

Arthur wanted to roll his eyes, to mock the suggestion, but instead he glared at his brother and said, "No, Jimmy. That ain't right. You know it's not." Then he added, "Not sure how that would be better anyway. Now tell me again, and don't you lie to me: you didn't see *anything* after you ran out the tent?"

Unlike the half dozen other times Arthur had asked the same question, this time Jimmy hesitated, averting his eyes.

"Jimmy!"

Jimmy whipped his head up and met his brother's stare. "I'm tellin' you that, yeah. I didn't see nothin'. But..."

"But what?"

"I *heard* something. A voice, I guess. Up in the wind or something, drifting away, like they was leavin' the fair and headin' off to...hell, I don't know where."

Arthur had stopped breathing as he waited for his brother to finish. He had heard them too, of course, saying Ruby's name, but he suspected what Jimmy had heard was something different. More important.

"What did you hear? What exactly?"

Jimmy shook his head. "It was just one word."

Arthur swallowed.

"Sacrifice."

Chapter 25

"Sacrifice?" Chris asked.

Arthur nodded.

"What did that mean? What was the sacrifice?"

Arthur put a hand up now, a signal to Chris to slow the inquiry, knowing that the combination of questions might throw him off, and he no longer wanted the option to bow out of the story. It was beginning to shine brightly in his brain now, the details of an incident from 1939, items that had lived in a cloud of dust for so long he'd almost forgotten the story entirely. But it was coming back, first in pieces, and now like a landslide. He wondered if somehow it was this re-firing of his memory that had brought the Skadegamutc to him the previous night. That it had resurfaced on its own, and now with every word Arthur told to Chris Boylin, he drew it closer to him. It was a theory he'd never quite explored before, and it wasn't one he was prepared to now.

"You probably wonder what happened to Jimmy, huh?" Arthur said, a non-sequitur of sorts, as if a neuron had involuntarily fired off in his brain in search of some unresolved thought from days or hours earlier. But he'd asked the question with full lucidity, needing this part of the tale to be told as well.

And Chris *had* wondered about the fate of Arthur's younger brother. Not as much as he did Ruby and her return, but it was Jimmy who had unearthed the Ditches, the one who, along with his friends, had found the fissure in the side of the earth and the passage down to the altar. And the Orange Rocks, of course, the disruption of which had released an eternal evil back upon the earth. Arthur hadn't said this last part explicitly, but it was the implication of the story thus far.

"Yes," Arthur answered, "I have wondered. Is he...alive?"

Arthur shook his head. "He died a long time ago," he answered solemnly.

"I'm sorry."

Arthur barely shrugged a shoulder and closed his eyes ruefully. "No one knew why he did it. Not for sure. Just received a call one morning. A stranger telling me he was dead."

Arthur never said, but Chris guessed on his own. "He killed himself?"

Arthur took a breath and nodded, and then he put his hand to his chest. It was a move he hadn't made for decades, though the habit clearly still existed inside him. He closed his eyes and steadied his breathing now, and when the oxygen was flowing properly again, he added, "Hanged himself in a jail cell."

"Jail?" Chris hadn't seen that part coming—Jimmy dying in jail—but now that he knew, it made sense, at least the part about taking his life. Suicide amongst inmates wasn't uncommon, so that didn't make for a great mystery. He didn't surmise the thought aloud, of course, but perhaps it was obvious on his face.

"I know what you're thinking," Arthur said, as if reading Chris' thoughts, "he killed himself because he was locked up is what you think. And, I guess to an extent, that was true. But only indirectly so."

"What do you mean by that?"

"Something changed in Jimmy after that fall. After Ruby, and all that preceded and followed her disappearance." He scoffed. "I know, you're saying, 'Of course he changed. Who wouldn't after all that?' And that's right. That's true. God knows I changed. Ma and Ruby too. All of us. Of course." Arthur gave a curious cock of his head. "But with the rest of us, the scars faded eventually. Even with Ma. Even after my father...died." Arthur paused and turned toward the window, reflecting on his father. "But not with Jimmy," he continued. "He couldn't shed it. Couldn't ever outrun it. Though that's what he tried to do."

"What do you mean by that?"

"Jimmy moved out to Spokane when he was nineteen. 1947. Wanted to get to the wettest, furthest place from New Mexico he could imagine. After what we knew of the Skadegamutc, and what we thought we knew about the desert and the dust storms. He figured that was the sensible move. Things had settled after Ruby came back, but we could still feel the darkness in the town."

Chris was becoming frustrated by the narrative, Arthur speaking of Ruby after she had returned without knowing how or when it happened. But he'd promised himself to let Arthur go on his own path, at his own pace, and the pace was quick now, fluid and purposeful.

"Jimmy and his friends had all been punished for their mischief, but for my brother, even with Ruby's return, it didn't feel over. Not for him." He paused a beat. "And now we know it wasn't."

Arthur broke off the story again and closed his eyes in a lengthy blink, and Chris thought he was drifting to sleep. But he popped them open after a few seconds and continued.

"Of course, there are much further places than Washington he could have moved off to, though not many wetter, I suppose. And that was the key for him, I think, to get clear of the dust and grit, away from the dry and the brown, to some place that couldn't sustain cacti and scorpions and vengeful Indian witches." Arthur hesitated now, musing. "Always used to wonder how things would have been different if we'd been born a few years earlier and were of age to go to war. I almost made it, but by the time I turned eighteen, war was just about over. We'd a gone off to France or Italy or Okinawa, maybe died in one of those places, somewhere far off from Clayton, leaving this...curse...to just shrivel on the vine." He shrugged, as if the theory didn't quite hold water. "Then again, if we'd been born in a different time, all this might not have happened at all. But I still wonder." He shook off the fantasy and continued. "Anyway, Jimmy opened a garage up there within six months of arriving, and with his skills, he was able to do alright for himself. At least that's how it seemed from afar. He talked about bringing Ma and Ruby up there as soon as he saved enough, but I don't think he ever really intended it. She used to call me sometimes and complain about Jimmy's false promises, about how he didn't really want to be near her, and that she was the reason he moved away to begin with. But of course, that wasn't it. Jimmy didn't want our mother close to him because of *him*. He didn't want anyone close. It was why he never had a steady girl or ever talked about starting a family. He always thought if he kept moving, they would never be able to find him, never be able to pin him down. And that maybe one day he'd find a spot in the world where he felt safe." He sighed again and shook his head. "I always prayed he'd find that spot. Just to give him some peace from the torture of his life."

Chris cleared his throat, as if to bring the story back to the facts alone. "*Did* they find him there? In Spokane? Is that why he killed himself?"

Arthur shrugged. "Hard to say. I didn't talk to Jimmy much by then. I stayed in New Mexico, got married, had my own things going on. Steady job, family in the pipeline. I tried a few times to get Ma and Ruby to come live with me, but my mother would have lived on the street before she allowed me to take her in. She said married couples should be left to themselves and all that. But, well..." he paused.

"What is it?"

"It wasn't about my marriage. My mother never liked me much at the end of all of it. Or maybe didn't trust me is the better way to say it. Not after Ruby. And less so after Pa's death."

Chris didn't know how exactly, but he knew this final point was important to the overall story.

"Anyway, Jimmy had his garage going for work, but as far as I could gather from a handful of letters and a couple of phone calls, he was living a kind of tent life. In the woods, on campgrounds and farms, anywhere he wouldn't be confined, somewhere he could flee on a moment's notice."

"But he never said for sure that he'd seen them?" Chris asked.

Arthur shook his head. "And I never asked. But even if he hadn't, he was definitely seeing shadows. I've no doubt on that. And whether he was fifteen miles from Clayton or fifteen-hundred, he was never gonna be at ease again." Arthur shrugged. "Jimmy had his theories about them. Obsessed over them after Ruby came back."

Ruby. She was the chapter of the story Chris needed to get to, but Arthur shifted back to Jimmy immediately.

"He broke into a pawn shop one night and tore the place apart, although the only real damage the police said was to the neon lights on the front of the store. Jimmy'd been drinking, and I think the lights reminded him of them."

"That's why he was in jail?"

Arthur nodded.

"Not exactly the crime of the century. It couldn't have been more than a fine for something like that. Maybe community service."

"You're probably right, but it never got to that. He couldn't take it. Couldn't take being locked up for even the shortest of times."

"I'm sorry," Chris said again, sincerely. And then he added, "When did it happen? His...death?"

"1951. Four years after he left Clayton."

"Oh geez," Chris said. "I didn't realize he was—"

"So young?"

Chris nodded.

"I never did figure Jimmy long for this world; but I also never thought he would go at twenty-two."

"Were there any storms in the area at the time."

Arthur shot a glance to Chris, and for the first time since Jaycee went missing, Chris returned the stare. It was just for a moment, but long enough to have the impact he'd intended with the question.

"Why did you ask me that?" Arthur replied.

The question came forcefully, as an accusation, but Chris kept his calm. "Maybe being locked up *is* what killed him, but not the way you think. Maybe they did find him, and his hanging was the result of not being able to escape."

Arthur had never considered this possibility, and now that the theory was spoken aloud, he felt foolish for not having done so. He nodded, enchanted by the hypothesis. "Yes," he whispered. "Maybe."

They were still more than two hours from Clayton, and Chris and Arthur rode silently for the next few minutes; for a moment, Chris feared Arthur had dozed off. But when he glanced quickly to his right, he saw the man sitting wide-eyed, alert, staring straight ahead with the look of someone gathering his thoughts, putting a string of pieces into their proper order. Then, without a word, the man picked up the lone bag he'd brought with him and reached inside, and then he brought out the rocks he'd held in secret for over fifty years.

For a moment, Chris felt as if he were looking down on the car from some floating vantage above, disbelieving. "Are those...?"

Arthur nodded and stared at the rocks the way one would a photograph of a long-deceased loved one.

"Why do you have those?"

Chapter 26

Jimmy and Arthur went to Lynnie Radich's house the next day, deciding that if anyone had a suggestion on what they could do to get Ruby back, it would be Lynnie. They arrived before the sun had risen, before news of Ruby or Tammy Yarlow or the riot at the fair had reached Clayton. And there they waited for a half hour on her front porch, and when her father came out a few minutes past dawn, he stopped and stared at the boys, not with anger but curiosity.

Arthur looked away shamefully, but Jimmy stood and approached the man. "Hi, Mr. Radich?"

"Jimmy."

"Is Lynnie home?"

"Is she home? It's ten minutes past six. She's got school today. Where else would she be?"

"Yes sir. I'm sorry, sir. Can we...speak with her?"

Lynnie's father frowned. "Hold on," he said and then turned back inside. He came out a minute later and nodded his head. "Go on. She's in the kitchen."

The boys nodded their thank yous and entered the house, and there they found Lynnie alone at her kitchen table eating breakfast.

"What are you boys doing here?" Lynnie asked, barely glancing up, unfazed by the presence of the Richland brothers in her kitchen at dawn.

Arthur and Jimmy each gave the other a sideways glance, and then Jimmy immediately broke into the story of the previous day and night. He described every detail, including the lights that had appeared over the Ferris wheel and the forms that they became. Arthur chimed in where necessary, whenever a point of importance was skipped or forgotten, as well as to tell the section of the tale that included the Siamese twins.

Lynnie listened without taking a bite of her food, the spoon hovering by her mouth, seemingly without blinking, and within a few minutes, she was fully informed. "Tammy is really dead?" she asked.

Jimmy nodded.

Lynnie bowed her head and reflected on the fact. "She was Bucky's cousin."

"Yeah."

"Does he know yet?"

Jimmy shrugged. "I don't know. Maybe by now."

There was a pause of silence, and finally Arthur interjected. "Lynnie, what about Ruby? Have you...heard of this before? Of the...witches and...?" He didn't quite know how to phrase the question, and while he was searching for the words, a voice that sounded as if it had rung through the walls chimed from the back of the house, from an area that was only a few steps behind them.

"Do you have the stones?"

Arthur flinched and turned to see an old woman at the threshold of the doorway. Lynnie's grandmother, he presumed.

"Nani," Lynnie uttered, confirming Arthur's assumption.

Nani took a step forward, entering the light of the room for the first time. The woman was elderly, the wrinkles in her face advertised that fact instantly, but she had a brightness to her that Arthur wasn't used to seeing in old people, and a posture that was as straight as a pole. "Do you?" she repeated, and this time her words were singed with anger.

Jimmy opened his mouth to speak, but his jaw hung silently. He nodded however, answering the question.

"What stones?" Lynnie asked.

"The Orange Rocks," Arthur said.

"Orange Rocks?"

"Return them," Nani said. "Immediately. They should never have been taken."

Arthur swallowed and his eyes narrowed. He shook his head and said softly, "No. Not Jimmy's. Not until we find Ruby."

Nani dropped her eyes a moment and then returned her stare. "She is gone."

"No!" Arthur said. "Not as long as the Skadegamutc are free. We can get her back. A sacrifice. Jimmy heard them. We can get her back. He felt it. And I know it in my heart."

The old woman looked at Jimmy now, her eyes curious. But they soon turned sad. "Return the stones. Cover them. Wherever you found them. Cover them where they will never be moved again."

Arthur stood now, a single tear streaming down either side of his face. He shook his head. "I'm not covering anything," he spat. "Not until Ruby comes back."

"What stones?!" Lynnie called.

Nani nodded, as if accepting of Arthur's reply. "Then more will die," she said.

Arthur paused a moment, as if ready to acquiesce, and then, without looking at Lynnie he said, "Sorry 'bout ruining your breakfast, Lynnie. Come on, Jimmy. Let's go."

Chapter 27

"**A**rtie, you're coming with me today."

Randall Richland walked past his son without looking in his direction. He had a medium-sized bag strapped across his shoulder, and he strode like a drill sergeant toward the pickup truck parked in the driveway.

Arthur was sitting on the front porch reading an article in Reader's Digest, one he'd read a dozen times before, about manners in school, lessons he'd not quite incorporated into his daily scholastic routine. But he was just skimming the words really. It was barely 7 am, and his plan was to kill the whole of the day until sunset. It was Halloween, and though the fall holiday had yet to take hold the way it would decades later, with costumes and candy, Arthur and Jimmy were keenly aware of the date this year and the spirits that supposedly came to life. The Skadegamutc was something real in their lives now, something damning and ruinous, and after almost a week since their day at the fair, with Ruby still missing and by now presumed dead (at least by the police if not Dotty Richland), it felt like the hauntings of the holiday in that year had come to life. And with their mother's near daylong stretches of catatonia, every day felt like a cursed one.

And though neither Arthur nor Jimmy had given up on Ruby's return, they were at a dead end as far as next steps, tacitly waiting for another storm to arrive, one that might bring their sister home to them. There was no real reason to believe such a thought, but it was something to hold on to as hope.

On that day, however, they were looking forward to getting off their property a soon as night fell, to forgetting about the catastrophe of their family for a few hours while they went into town with some of the other kids from Clayton, including Ralph Brater. Jimmy's friend had been spooked when his aunt was killed—spooked enough that he'd returned his stone to the altar two days after the murder—but he had rallied from the effects of the crime quickly, returning to school by the end of that week.

Bucky Mason, however, had taken the death of his cousin poorly, and he hadn't been seen in town since. His mother had told Jimmy he was going to be away for a time while he dealt with the grief. Arthur didn't know what that meant exactly, but it sounded an awful lot like a mental institution to him.

"Coming with you?" Arthur asked his father, already dreading the answer to his next question. "Where?"

"Oklahoma City?"

"What?"

"You heard me." Randall Richland tossed the bag from his shoulder into the back of the truck and then kicked the rear tire. He then opened the door and slid into the driver's seat, closing the door behind him with a purpose.

Arthur stood staring at the truck in disbelief. The thought of riding ten hours or more to Oklahoma, alone with his father, the man who had treated Arthur (and Jimmy too, to be fair) like a cactus in the yard since Ruby had vanished, was nearly unbearable. He would have rather walked to Oklahoma by himself than ride with his dad.

Randall reached over and rolled down the passenger window with three aggressive cranks. "You hear me?" he barked.

Arthur stepped from the porch and walked to the open passenger window, standing well back from the pickup, as if avoiding some poison gas that was leaking from the truck. He looked inside and asked, "Why?"

Randall turned to his son and frowned, debating whether to honor the request for an explanation or simply snap the command again like a drill sergeant. He decided on the former. "Because that's where the fair is now," he replied. "And the police have run out of ideas for finding Ruby. I promised your mother they would find her. And that if they didn't, that I would."

This didn't answer Arthur's question, and he wanted to reply with *Then why don't you go by yourself*. Instead, he asked, "So, what'll us going to the fair do? How's that going to find her?"

"These fair people travel from one town to the next. One state to the next. Folks who worked the Oklahoma fair'll be the same ones worked the New Mexico one. At least the ones we're going to talk to."

"Who's that?"

Randall sighed, tired of the delay. "Ruby disappeared from the freak show tent, least that's what you told the police."

"I never saw her there though. Just said I thought—"

"So that's who we're going to see. Maybe you'll recognize something there."

"Recognize something? I...that doesn't make sense, Pa. I told you every—"

"Get in the goddamn car, Arthur! We got a long way to go and we're wasting time!"

Arthur nearly choked on the lump that arrived in his throat, but he held back the tears.

"Your mother has barely spoken a word since Ruby went missing!" Randall's teeth were clenched, and he was pointing his finger downward with sharp stabbing motions on every word.

Arthur knew his father was scared and angry, had maybe even accepted that Ruby was gone forever. But all Arthur could see was the venom of a predator in his father now, an abuser of a wayward Okie girl.

"I ain't seen her eat a crumb in a week! You want her to starve to death! Cuz that's what she'll do if we don't get Ruby home!"

Arthur expected his father to break down now, to start crying after the outburst, but he only kept his fuming gaze on Arthur, who finally lowered his eyes and bowed his head. And without another word, he opened the door of the truck and sat inside. And within ten minutes, after a stop at Chester's to fill up, they were en route to Oklahoma, Arthur quietly choking back tears as he turned his face toward the window.

The hours passed quickly. Arthur remembered stopping a few times along the way to fill up—once with the gas can in the back, another time at a filling station—and another time or two to pee on the side of the road. But aside from that, it was one continuous spell of sleep and silence and stagnant thoughts until they arrived at the fairgrounds late Friday afternoon.

"We ain't here for fun, Artie. You got that?" It was the first complete sentence his father had spoken directly to Arthur since Clayton.

Arthur followed his father to the gate, where they paid their admission and entered the fairgrounds. And as Arthur passed through the large metal entrance, he saw in an instant that the Oklahoma State Fair was something quite different from the one in New Mexico. There were three times as many rides, sprawling like weeds in every direction, and ten times as many tents, as far as the eye could see, each containing animals or food or games, the prizes of which no doubt shamed those to be won in Albuquerque. There was even a stadium with a track, where cars of the like Arthur had never seen (that assessment based on the posters on the outer wall of the arena) raced inside. Arthur couldn't witness any of the race from the common grounds, but he could hear the motors and the cheers of the crowd, and his heart pounded at the images that flashed in his mind.

And when night fell an hour later, there were so many electric lights it was as if it was high noon all the time, a setting as bright and fantastic as Arthur had ever seen. Of course, on the day his family had been at the New Mexico State Fair, the whole place was shuttered before nightfall, but Arthur knew even if it hadn't been, it wouldn't have compared to what he was seeing now.

And the crowds. There was a sea of people shoulder to shoulder in every direction, of all ages and shapes and heights, many of them with skin colors Arthur had never seen before, some wearing clothes he'd only viewed in magazines. Of course, the large number of fairgoers made for longer lines at the rides and exhibits, but, as Arthur had been crudely reminded in the parking lot, they weren't there for the fun.

Besides, other than waiting for their dinner at the hot dog cart, there was only one line they were getting in that day: the one leading into the tent of oddities.

"That's where we're goin' now," Randall said flatly. "To see them twins, specifically."

"What?"

Randall nodded his head slowly, with conviction. "That's right. I told you that 'fore we left why we were coming."

Arthur figured it was to visit the oddities tent, but not to talk to the Siamese twins. "They're still doing the...show. Even after what happened." Arthur knew 'show' wasn't quite the right word, but whatever the term was, he didn't have it in his vocabulary.

"They are."

"But the attack? The sister? She didn't get in trouble for that?"

Randall shrugged. "In trouble with who? The police? Not that they didn't believe what you told them. I think they believed you full on. Believed every word you said about what the one was doin' to the other. Hell, they could see the markings all over that girl's throat. And she couldn't even talk when they tried to interview her. And the one who did the attacking, of course she said she couldn't remember any of it. The first one coulda pressed charges, I suppose, but not sure how that would have worked exactly." Randall pondered for a moment the same question Arthur had the day of the incident: what became of one Siamese twin when the other was charged with a crime. "Probably why she didn't," he added.

"But what are *we* doing here, Pa? I don't understand."

"Don't understand what?" Randall stood tall and still, facing forward in the direction of the tent. And when he spoke, his voice was low, his tone ever so condescending, and Arthur could sense impatience brewing in his father.

"I don't understand why we're here." Arthur said the words softly, not whining, not wanting to unbalance the man beside him.

Randall grinned ironically and gave a quick jerk of his head, still not meeting his son's eyes, a warning that this was the last lap he was prepared to go around on the subject before the conversation turned sour. "Because I think they saw something, Arthur. I think they know—at least one of them does—something about Ruby's disappearance. And you're gonna talk to them to find out what that is."

"Me?"

Randall nodded. "See if either of them remembers you. Remembers Ruby. Or saw her before she..." Randall shook off the remainder of the sentence. "Tammy Yarlow was killed that day," he said, "so whatever *she* saw she ain't in a position to say. But if she could talk, I think she'd have some interesting things to tell, huh? Things about why Sherman did what he did." He shook his head now, exasperated. "I know that boy's a goon, but he ain't no killer. And this...this Siamese twin who almost died, I'm guessing her sister ain't no killer either. She saw something. She had to have."

It was obvious now that Arthur's father suspected there was more to Ruby's disappearance than just what had been propositioned by the police, which was that she'd been snatched, either by a fair-going vagrant or some paroled carnie, and then whisked out of town before they could catch up with him. But Arthur's father was beyond that theory now, clearly, had just brought up the subject of Tammy Yarlow. Why would he have mentioned her with Ruby if he didn't think there was a connection? Just because both incidences happened on the same day? Suddenly Arthur felt a burning need to tell his father everything. About the Hollow and the altar, about the Orange Rocks Jimmy and his friends had taken, and how he was sure they were the cause of Janet Flannery and Tammy Yarlow's death. And Ruby's disappearance.

But it was too late for that. At least in that moment. They had driven all day, three-hundred-and-fifty miles, and it had been almost a week since Ruby went missing. How could Arthur decide then to tell the full story? If he confessed to what he knew now his father might beat him right there in the line. So, instead, Arthur simply nodded.

Arthur mimicked the pose of his father now, quiet and patient, facing the open palm of the tent of oddities some twenty yards ahead of them. And as he stared into the black gap between the tent flaps, a peculiar feeling entered his gut, one that he could only vaguely identify. He was nervous yes, anxious about seeing the conjoined sisters again and being emotionally thrust back to that day in Albuquerque. He was still scarred by it, obviously, all of what had happened that day. The disappearance of his sister. The taking of her by a pair of ancient demons whose existence he still hadn't wrapped his mind around. And seeing the Skadegamutc in the sky just seconds before watching Tammy Yarlow drop to her death. For the first few days, he'd been haunted by it all, debilitated, but now that a week had passed, even with Ruby still missing, he'd managed to block most of the evil visions from his mind, gradually, minute by minute, relegating the events to the periphery of his brain as a misinterpretation of what his eyes had seen, something randomly tragic and unconnected to the Ditches or the Hollow or the altar.

But now that he was back at the fair (albeit a different one than in Albuquerque, but a fair nonetheless), the smells and sounds and chatter of the crowds were excruciating. His stomach tumbled and grinded in a way that was beyond just nerves or anxiety. It was a sensation closer to sickness, the kind that arises sometimes during automobile rides, when the truck passes through a ditch or over rougher sections of the roadways. Only Arthur couldn't close his eyes and ride this feeling out. It was too complex, an amalgamation of fear and worry and guilt, as well as one that threatened punishment for all he'd withheld from his family and the police. Like his father, Arthur too knew the twins had a story, at least a portion of one, even if they now doubted it as much as he did. Arthur had kept the story of the Hollow and the Skadegamutc secret, to honor the oath he'd made with Jimmy, but also to protect them both from jail or whoopings or even the ghost witches themselves. And in the moment, when his father had insisted on this trip to Oklahoma, he had kept his silence still, assuming that, though it might be a day or two of discomfort, it would all end in a wild goose chase and they would be back in Clayton having tried their best to find Ruby.

And then Ruby would appear. Any day now. Arthur held that belief close to his heart, even if he didn't know how exactly.

But now that they had arrived in Oklahoma, it suddenly felt as if the trip was productive, important, that they were close to something. Close to Ruby. If not physically then spiritually.

"Why didn't they interview her?" Arthur asked finally. "The police? When she could talk again?"

"Pshaw! Come on, Arthur. You think they care that much? By the time she was speaking clear again, the fair had moved on. And the cops wasn't about to chase some freak across state lines. For what? Even if she was guilty of somethin', or had somethin' important to say, wasn't like they coulda taken her into custody or anything."

"So..." Arthur was about to continue with the questions, but the line began to move, and he took it as a sign to call off his stalling. Nothing he said was going to change Randall Richland's mind anyway.

They walked through the palmed tent entrance, and Arthur felt his stomach sink as the smell of the fabric transported him back to the day in Albuquerque, and as he began the loop around the pavilion, he barely noted any of the other oddities, including Miss Minnie the Fat Lady, the first stall of the attraction and the only other oddity he'd seen that day.

He put his hand to his chest, gauging the race of his heart, and what normally was a way to relax himself, today made him more anxious, as he could feel the pounding as if it were a hammer coming through the opposite side. But he kept his feet moving, and finally they were in the back of the pavilion standing in front of a banner that read: "Borghild and Inger - the Siamese Twins of Norway!"

The sisters were smiling and waving, the deformities of their bodies somehow overshadowed by the glean in their eyes and the brightness of their smiles. They waved in unison, following each of the spectators as they passed with flirty bats of their eyes, sometimes blowing kisses to the boys, who blushed and hurried along, and then began to laugh once they were past them.

And when Arthur reached the center of the attraction and the eyes of the sisters turned toward him, the sister to his right continued the show with a wink and wiggle of the fingers on her lone hand, but the sister to his left, the one who had been nearly strangled by her twin a week earlier, put her hand to her mouth in shock.

"It's...it's you," she said, speaking with an accent Arthur would have guessed more Nebraska than Norway. "Why are...what do you want here?" She was staring at Arthur as if he were a ghost, as if she recognized him from a nightmare she'd had as a child but had never been able to shake.

The family in front of Arthur and his father turned and stared back at him, their expressions confused, impressed even, that he, Arthur, with his presence, had somehow freaked out the stars of the freak show. But they continued shuffling forward toward the stall of the elephant boy, leaving Randall and his son alone with the Siamese Twins of Norway.

"What did you see?" Randall asked now. He took a step forward, moving past the line of tape on the floor that divided the oddities from the spectators, an area off limits to customers.

On cue, a burly man in a tight suit walked quickly over to Randall and loomed over him, forming a human barrier between himself and the twins. "That'll do right about there, sir," he said, his voice chipper, though dripping with danger. "The signs are posted for a reason, assuming you can read." He pointed to one of a half-dozen placards around the pavilion warning not to enter the stalls, this one directly over that of the Siamese Twins of Norway.

Randall felt the burn of aggression, and his first notion was to fight through the man, to take the left twin by the collar and shake whatever she knew to the floor. But he thought better of it. He was outmanned by the bouncer by fifty pounds, and, even if he wasn't, he knew reinforcements would arrive soon after, and he'd be in the back of a paddy wagon within the hour. He shook his arms out, popping his sleeves down, and then he said, "I *will* need to talk to her though. Right now."

"Well, she's workin' right now, as you can clearly see. And even if she weren't, you're not talking to anyone that doesn't want to talk to you back."

Randall glared at the beefy security man, and Arthur could feel the steam building inside him again. Randall Richland was a hothead, and though he wasn't known to get into physical fights in Clayton, that was mainly due to the fact that no one there wanted to scrap with him. It scared Arthur to see his father this way, and again he thought of the migrant girl.

"It's alright, Rusty," the left twin said—the one called Borghild, Arthur knew now—and she looked back to Arthur as she rubbed the side of her face.

Her sister—Inger—looked away from Arthur and Randall now, toward the portion of the line that had already passed, and Arthur knew it was a stare of shame, about what she'd done that day in Albuquerque, though she likely didn't remember any of it.

"He's right though," Borghild continued, "we are working, but the tent is only open for another hour. And then we're done for the night. If you...you want to talk about it, you can come back then. I'll tell you what I saw. What I know. I think it's something you'll want to hear."

Randall sighed and nodded, "Alright. Alright, yes, thank you. That's what we'll do then."

"Just him." This time it was Inger who spoke as she nodded toward Arthur. She then cocked her head toward Randall. "I don't like the way this one speaks to us."

Borghild gave a curious sideways glance to her sister, but in an instant, she backed her play. "Just him then," she confirmed.

"Now listen here, this is my son and I'll be damned if I'm leaving him here alone with the—"

"Then you'll be damned, I suppose," Borghild snapped. "We'll talk to your son alone, or we won't be talking to anybody at all." She then unleashed the brightest of show smiles. "Good day, gentlemen."

The security guard crossed his arms and raised his chest, a sign that the woman had made her wishes known, and now it was time to leave.

"It's okay, Pa," Arthur said finally, breaking his scared silence. "Maybe...if she knows something, then—"

"Hey! Let's move it along!" The shout came from a place in line by the tent's entrance, where the queue had bottlenecked, thanks in large part to the encounter at the Siamese twins stall.

Borghild's smile waned and she added, sincerely, "Meet us back here at 8:30, handsome. I'll tell you what I know. I'll tell you what I saw happen to your sister."

"What did you see!" Randall barked, and then he moved again across the line to perimeter of the stall.

The burly man moved in to detain him, quickly now, his chest and arms bulging with bad intentions; but Arthur stepped in front of him, turning toward his father as he did, pressing his chest into his dad's belly and wrapping his arms at his waist.

The guard stopped just short of plowing into Arthur's back, and he pointed at Randall over Arthur's head, a wicked smile on his face. "You don't come back in here! You got that! You do, I'll have you tied up and carried out!"

"Come on, Pa," Arthur said, still enveloping his dad as he backed him from the twins' stall toward the front of the tent, praying he would reach the exit before Randall lost control and got them both kicked out. He thought of Jimmy as he pushed his father backward, the one who had inherited Randall Richland's temper.

For the next fifty-two minutes, Arthur sat on a bench outside the racetrack, while his father paced back and forth in front of him, asking every few minutes some passerby if he had the time. Arthur played a game with himself each time the strangers spoke, trying to guess correctly what the watch would read. He was right about fifty percent of the time, as it was never more than five minutes later than the time before.

Finally, at 8:30, Randall nodded toward his son that it was time, and they returned to the tent of oddities, Arthur walking sullenly behind his father who rushed him forward.

"You find out what happened to her," Randall pressured. "You got that?"

Arthur nodded and then pushed through the tent, which was empty of customers, just as it had been on that Monday when the attraction was closed. Rusty appeared again, and by now he had dropped the friendly demeanor, no doubt still stewing from the confrontation with Arthur's father. But he escorted Arthur anyway, back to the partitioned area of Borghild and Inger.

Inger looked at Arthur now, staring at him the way most people stared at her, with a sort of awe and pity. But she wasn't the sister Arthur was interested in. She had been in the state of Glenn Flannery when Ruby had vanished; what she knew, he guessed, she knew only from her sister.

Arthur looked at Borghild and said, "Hello, ma'am. Thank you for talking to me."

Borghild smiled the same gentle one she had given Arthur just before he'd left an hour earlier, and he could see a genuine kindness in the woman.

"You know already, don't you?" she asked.

"What?"

"I see more different faces in a day than most people do in a year. Especially in these parts. And unlike with most people, with me, people don't try to hide their feelings. They can be mean, yes—often, in fact—but they also tend to be open when they see us. And I can see you have something on your mind more than just a question about your sister. You want to see if what you already know is true."

Arthur felt as if his brain was being peeled back, and that this rotund mistake of nature was peering down inside it. He felt naked, alone. But she was right, so he nodded.

"I appreciate your honesty, so I'm going to reciprocate."

Arthur scrunched his face, not liking the sound of the word.

"It means I'm going to be honest with you too. I don't know if what I'm going to tell you is true, because I don't know if what I saw was *real*. For all I know, me and Maggie was drugged somehow by a guest passing through, and that's why she acted crazy, and I saw what I did."

"Who's Maggie?"

Inger raised her hand, and Borghild smiled. "I'm Jane, if you can believe it. Those names on the banner are for the show. Anyway, I won't take offense if you don't believe me, and I don't want your father coming back in here with a problem. Rusty wasn't kidding about what he said he'd do to him."

Arthur nodded.

"Okay, then. Your sister, she was the little girl with the pretty face who ran in here like there was a litter of new puppies waiting for her. The one that went missing a short time later. Am I right on that?"

"Yes, ma'am."

"It was only us and Mary in here at the time." The twin nodded toward the area where the Fat Lady's stall was, the woman he and Jimmy had seen sleeping on the day of the disaster. "And then..." She paused, swallowing, a signal that she was preparing to reach the nub of the tale. "Something followed in behind her." Jane's eyes watered almost instantly as the memory returned. "It was glowing. *She* was glowing. Like some kind of electrified woman." She laughed at this, a coughing, terrified laugh, knowing the words must have sounded ludicrous, though they were the exact ones she'd meant to speak.

Arthur's face flushed to white, and his jaw opened slowly until it hovered halfway agape.

Jane nodded, the look on the boy's face validating what she'd seen. It relaxed her slightly, to know she hadn't gone mad. "I tried to scream at the girl—your sister—because I knew whatever was coming up on her was something terrible. Something evil. And that was when Maggie grabbed me by the throat."

Maggie was crying now, weeping softly with her head cocked away from her sister.

"Your poor sister, I don't know why she came in here at all, but when she saw Maggie grab me, the look on her face, she was so concerned. I've never seen that kind of compassion in a child. Especially one as young as she is." She paused now and looked away from Arthur for the first time. "She must have at least felt there was something behind her, but she never turned, never saw the thing that snatched her."

If Arthur weren't frozen in terror, he would have been crying too, but instead, he stood silently, listening.

"It gripped her like a...like a serpent. A dragon. And though I was in the throes of my own terror, I felt...lucky. Lucky that it wasn't me in the grips of it. It had covered her so completely I couldn't make out any sign of her at all. Not a sliver of skin or clothes or...nothing."

Arthur's face burned now, imagining the fear his sister must have known in that moment. He nodded sharply now, to let the woman know he was listening, and that what she had seen had indeed been real.

"What is it?" she asked Arthur, tears in her eyes now. "How could that have happened?"

Arthur shrugged. "I...I don't know really." And with that, a tear fell from his own eye, so that all three in the group were now crying.

Jane got herself together. "It's okay hun," she said. "She's going to be okay."

Jane's words suddenly sobered Arthur, and he stared at the woman, his look scornful and bewildered. "*Okay?*"

Jane took a breath and nodded, preparing to finish the story. "The way it...ended, I guess...I thought at first was the result of no air to my brain. A hallucination caused by a lack of oxygen. And over the last few days, I've considered that *all* of it was due to that. Hell, I don't think even Maggie's believed me until now."

Maggie neither confirmed nor denied this, which, to some extent, confirmed it.

"But your sister...and the light witch...they started to fade away. It was like steam into the air. They just began to get fainter and fainter until it was like they disappeared entirely, waned into the background of the world. Again, I thought it was a trick of my dying brain, a delirium, death squeezing the last juices of reality from me." She looked at her sister. "Maggie, she was so strong but...look at her." Jane waited for Arthur to glance toward Maggie. "It's impossible for her to be that strong." She paused. "And I would have just let go, I suppose, accepted that Death had arrived, but...I had seen it! It wasn't a mirage. I just...on some level I knew it wasn't." She paused again. "And then..."

"Then what?"

Jane shrugged. "She spoke to me. She was gone already, but I could hear like she was whispering directly into my ear."

"Who did?"

"Your sister."

"What?" Arthur had asked the previous question as a formality, assuming the voice had been that of the Skadegamutc. That it was Ruby who had spoken was a revelation. "Ruby?"

Jane nodded. "If that was her name."

"How did you know it was her?"

Jane cocked her head and smiled, staring past Arthur now as she reflected again on the day, the moment. "Because her voice was sweet, comforting even. And there was a certain confidence in it the way she spoke. I just knew it belonged to the face I had seen a few moments before."

Arthur felt shaky now, afraid that he would ask the wrong question next and somehow disrupt the interview. But he trudged forward and asked, "What did she say?"

"She told me to fight, that it wasn't her fault—meaning Maggie's—and then she said 'you can't hurt me.' This last part she said, it was directed to the thing. The thing that took her. I don't know how I know, but I do. She didn't sound scared either. It was like she knew it couldn't hurt her."

Arthur was breathing heavily now, but he managed to follow up with, "Was there anything else?"

"If there was, I didn't hear it. I don't remember anything more."

Arthur stood in silence as he stared at the woman, tacitly imploring her to try to find more, somewhere in the recesses. But Jane only looked back and said, "Sorry, hun."

"What should I do?" Arthur asked. "It was a question for his father really, or even the police, but he didn't trust either of them more than he trusted Jane, a.k.a. Borghild, one half of the Siamese Twins of Norway."

"If everything I said really happened—and based on the look on your face, I know now that it did—I haven't the foggiest idea, hun. Who's gonna believe me? And even if they do, where would they start to bring your sister back?"

"At the fairground," Maggie said suddenly.

Jane turned her thick neck toward her sister, who was looking directly at Arthur now. Her eyes were wide and alert, having shifted from the stare of shame she'd shown earlier to one of determination, purpose.

"What?" Jane asked. "What do you know, Maggie?"

"You can bring her back. You can bring back Ruby. But it won't be for free."

"What are you talking about Magg—"

"I heard her."

"You heard Ruby, too," Arthur asked.

Maggie gave a single shake of her head, which was bent at an odd angle compared to her twin, making the move a labored one. "Not your sister. The thing. The witch."

"What?" It was Jane again, flabbergasted to be hearing this for the first time. "You told me...I said about the girl and you—"

"I know. But I...I didn't want us to get involved with this."

"What?"

"How was that going to work, Jane? They would have taken us off the show. They almost did anyway. Or they might have let us go entirely, not wanting to deal with the headache. And after the girl from the Ferris wheel, I was afraid if they knew the oddities were involved with the missing girl, they might close the fair down for good. At least for this year. So...I thought it best to just move on. Besides, like you said, who was going to believe us? And what were they going to do about it even if they did?"

"You could have told *me* at least," Jane muttered, clearly hurt.

Maggie frowned and nodded. "But you're better than me, Jane. If I'd confirmed what you saw, you would have told. Insisted on the police." Jane didn't argue this point, and Maggie turned back to Arthur now. "I'm sorry for not speaking up. But I'm glad you came here now."

Arthur didn't care either way about the apology, he just wanted to hear the rest of what happened to his sister. "What did the Skadegamutc say?"

Maggie didn't clarify the name she'd just heard, but she shuddered at the sound of it, and then she said, "*A sacrifice.*" She nodded now, confirming her memory. It said, *A sacrifice*, and then...for just a moment, the light of her glow flashed inside the tent."

It was the same word Jimmy had heard, and Arthur simply shook his head, the detail too much to take in at once.

"And that it's there, on that ground, where the sacrifice needs to happen."

"What?" Arthur sputtered. "What ground?"

"Listen to me, Arthur!" Maggie spit the words now, almost growling as she leaned her round body forward. "Listen to every word I say if you want to see your sister again!"

"Maggie—" Jane started, but she was overwhelmed by her sister's vehemence.

"You have to make the sacrifice," Maggie continued, this time without exclamation, but with the same resolve and clarity as before, "on the ground where your sister was taken. That is where it has to occur."

"Here?" Arthur asked, looking around the tent bewildered.

Maggie shook her head now, the action slow and leaden, like the grind of rusty gears. "No. On the *land* where it occurred. The place of the tent in Albuquerque."

"But...how can you know this?"

"I heard it all in my mind. The viciousness. The cruelty of revenge. But..." Maggie hesitated and closed her eyes, searching for the precision of the memory. She opened her eyes and said, "With that came the answer. Your sister was...fine...or at least she wasn't being harmed. Not then and I don't think ever. It won't punish her. Ruby, she's too...innocent or clever or...creative." Maggie paused on this final adjective and then nodded, as if she had finally figured the solution to a week-old puzzle. "Its malice came onto me, and I couldn't resist it. It's why I tried to kill Jane. I don't remember it, the strangling, but I remember the malice." She took a breath of relief, and a tear formed in the corner of each eye.

"What sacrifice?" Arthur asked again, the only question that mattered.

Maggie flashed her eyes past Arthur to the front of the tent, and Arthur knew in an instant if there had been no tarpaulin blocking her view, her eyes would have landed on his father standing just outside. She looked back at Arthur. "That will be your dilemma, Arthur."

And with that, Maggie looked away, as did Jane, both indicating they had told their stories and it was all they had to give to the boy.

Almost.

As Arthur turned to leave, Maggie finally spoke again. "Randall Richland," she said.

Arthur was rendered motionless for a moment at the sound of his father's name, but he quickly turned back to the conjoined sisters. He was surprised, of course, but perhaps not as completely as he should have been. "What?"

"That's your father's name, yes?"

Arthur nodded.

"It was the last thing I heard it say."

Chapter 28

C hris didn't quite know where the story had headed, but he felt queasy now, and he could almost feel a heat coming from the Orange Rocks still in Arthur's hands. They were as black as the old man had described, perfectly round like the metal orbs used in shotput competitions. They appeared as cannonballs the size of oranges, their weight evident by sight alone, appearing rough to the touch, grating like the skin of an avocado.

Arthur looked to Chris, as if waiting for him to incite the continuation of the story. But with every few seconds that passed, Chris could only stare down to the stones.

Finally, Arthur said, "'Why did I keep them?' That's your question, I suppose."

Chris swallowed and nodded his head, still astonished at what he was seeing. He looked at Arthur, "If you had...just returned them. They would have...they wouldn't have taken Jaycee. Or killed anyone else. Why didn't you?"

"Jimmy lied to me. When we were kids. He told me he had returned them. That he had gone to Bucky's house, gotten his rock from his bedroom, and then returned them to the Hollow the day after Ruby came back. And I believed him. I had no reason not to." He paused. "But later, as I looked back on it, I should have known."

"Should have known why? Why didn't he return them?"

"Because he knew. He knew that even if he returned them, it wouldn't have mattered."

"But...Ralph returned his. That's what you told me. And if the Skadegamutc had been...imprisoned by the stones, like Lynnie's grandmother said, then Jimmy and Bucky's were the last two to be replaced."

"Maybe that was true. But Jimmy never trusted it. He always knew it was only a matter of time until the Ditches got unearthed. Until the archaeologists came and dug the holes up fully, turning every piece of dirt over inch by inch. And they would obviously find the Hollow. And once they did, they would just undo whatever he tried to do make things right again."

"But if he never returned them at all, how would that help anything?"

Arthur shrugged. "I think it *was* his intention to return them. One day. After the government and the universities had investigated the site in full and then lost interest, setting up some monument there with tourists and plaques and a part time security guard. It's in the middle of nowhere, the Sampson farm, it was never going to become some great popular attraction. He just needed to wait it out. So, he kept them—hidden away, buried somewhere, I guess—and the minute he was able to, he left Clayton with them."

"So that's what we need to do? Return the stones? To get Jaycee back?"

Arthur hesitated and then said, "Not exactly."

"What? I...I don't understand."

Arthur sat silently for several minutes, and then he turned quickly back to Chris and said, "What I'm going to tell you now, this part of the story, is something I need you to listen to very closely. Without judgement or preconception. Not because I need your forgiveness or approval, but because of the instructive nature of it." He hesitated. "The sacrifice. You can't forget that part of the tale."

Chris swallowed, feeling a burn of fear in his chest. He didn't like the sound of the word *sacrifice* in that context, or the way Arthur had said it, and 'the instructive nature' part was ominous as well. He nodded anyway and said, "Okay, Arthur. I'm listening."

Chapter 29

Arthur and Jimmy were up first, waiting by the truck until their father arrived. Two days after Arthur and Randall's trip to Oklahoma, they were leaving for Albuquerque first thing.

Randall finally exited the house looking haggard and weary, but he moved with resolve, a suitcase in his hand that was almost certainly empty. "Joining us today, Jimmy?" he said, flashing a quick glance to his favorite child.

"Yes sir," Jimmy said flatly. "Hopin' I can help."

Their father stopped and stared at Jimmy, as if studying him. "Arthur told you what those twins told him? 'Bout Ruby?"

Jimmy nodded, and Randall gave a single nod back, a signal that he knew it was all a long shot—the prospects of finding Ruby in Albuquerque at the spot where she was taken—but that he was prepared to go through with it anyway. Arthur wouldn't have lied to him, after all, not about something as important as finding his sister, and he could only pray that what his son had been told by the Siamese twins in Oklahoma had been the truth.

And Arthur *hadn't* lied to him, at least not about the importance of going to Albuquerque.

The details, however, were something different.

Jimmy told his father a vague story of abduction, that Jane and Maggie had heard about Ruby's disappearance through the fair grapevine, and that, according to the gossip, she had been kidnapped by one of the wayward workers and was being held hostage. And if her family wanted to see her again, they would need to appear at the site of the pavilion at sundown. They came every day, he told his father, this according to the twins, hoping the family of the girl would get word of the demands and show with the money. And, of course, no police.

Arthur had concocted the story in his mind during his exit from the tent in Oklahoma City, and, considering the circumstances and the little time he'd had to conjure it, he didn't think it half bad. Whether his father believed in the details behind their journey on that day, Arthur didn't know, but he did believe the part about when and where they were to meet, and that's all that mattered.

And by 4 pm, after a drive of relative silence despite the three male members of the Richland family sitting shoulder to shoulder on the bench seat of the truck, they were at the site of the Albuquerque State Fair.

What was a bounty of sounds and colors and smells only days earlier was now an open parcel of desert, a landscape as bleak as the moon, with no indication anyone had ever stepped foot on the land, let alone to attend the state's annual fair.

But they were in the right place, as evidenced by the site's sole marker of civilization, the large billboard advertising the fair, right where the entrance had been. Whether the sign stayed up year-round, Arthur didn't know, but he was thankful for it, figuring that with Jimmy's help, he could use it to get his bearings, a signpost to find exactly where the tent of oddities had been erected on the day in question.

But, as it turned out, he didn't need to.

Randall Richland was unique in his directional awareness, never one to look at maps or ask for directions on the rare occasions when they traveled beyond the Clayton boundaries; and by the time Arthur was identifying what he believed was the spot of the front gate, his father already had the freakshow pavilion in his crosshairs.

"The Ferris wheel was there," he said, pointing to a spot just to their right. He then moved the same finger a quarter-turn of the clock and stopped. "Which means the tent was situated somewhere there." He looked back to the sign once to calibrate a more precise mark, and then he shifted the finger another few centimeters and nodded, and then he began to stride forward, leaving his sons in his wake.

Jimmy and Arthur stood in place as they watched their father walk toward the spot of the pavilion. The tension between them was obvious. "He can't really believe it, right?" Jimmy asked. "About the crooks and the money? How could he?"

Arthur shook his head. "I don't think he believes that part, no. But...I think he believes something...some version of what we saw."

"About the...Skadegamutc?"

Arthur could only shrug.

"But...how? How could he know anything about that?"

"Pa's lived in Clayton his whole life. Might know more than we think." Arthur had considered this idea for the first time back in Oklahoma City, the possibility that Randall Richland believed there was more to life than just what came from the dust.

"Boys!" Randall turned and called for his sons, who instantly began to walk toward him.

"When is it gonna happen?" Jimmy asked as they arrived next to their father.

Arthur sighed and searched the area. "They said sundown, but who's to know? Not sure they'll come at all. The twins said to leave the stones, that they'll see 'em from afar, and that'll be the sign that we are who we say we are."

Their father watched the boys as they conversed, and Arthur could feel the burn of suspicion on his face, as if his father knew he was lying but also telling part of the truth, perhaps the part that mattered most. The part where Ruby came home.

"This is about right, eh?" Randall said. "The games ran along there." He turned and nodded his head backward, indicating where the midway had been. "And the tent was right about here." He took a step forward, as if centering himself perfectly.

Arthur couldn't tell for sure, but he nodded anyway.

"Gimme the rocks, Jimmy."

Jimmy handed the rocks to their father and stepped back. "They said lay 'em on the ground, right Arthur?"

Arthur nodded, trying to remember exactly what the lie had been. His mind had been racing that day in Oklahoma, and half of what he'd told his father was a fog of memory.

Randall placed the pair of Orange Rocks side by side at his feet, spacing them about a foot apart. "Got another two hours or so 'til sundown, so we'll just wait and see what happens. See if anyone shows up."

"What do you think'll happen, Pa?" Jimmy asked nervously, pretending he wasn't in on the whole ruse.

Randall slipped a cigarette from his breast pocket and struck a match. He lit the end and inhaled, closing his eyes as he did, savoring the moment. It was the first and last time Arthur had ever seen his father smoke.

"I think we'll get Ruby home," Randall said, a calmness in his voice that scared both boys.

No one said a word for an hour, and as the sun began to dip, a chill took over the air, and Arthur stood to retrieve the sweater he'd left in the truck. It was still forty-five minutes until sundown (the arbitrary time when Arthur had said the 'abductors' would arrive), and now Arthur prayed none of it would occur. He hoped the twins had been wrong about what they saw and heard, that the trigger to bring forth the ancient witches of the Tompiros was all a myth. Maybe Ruby was indeed the prize they'd wanted all along. And now that they had her, they wouldn't be coming again. At least not for another century or two.

Arthur grabbed the sweater from the truck and returned to the spot of the tent, and as he walked up on his father and brother, he saw Jimmy kneeling in the dirt now, hunched over the stones.

"What are you doing, Jimmy?"

"I, uh, I was just telling Pa I thought maybe the stones should be touching."

"What?"

Jimmy shrugged nervously, and then he nodded as he adjusted the stones again, positioning them so they were adjacent, the way he'd remembered them in the altar.

"I know it was you boys that did this."

The words came from Randall Richland as a defeated proclamation, and for a moment, Arthur thought his father had suddenly been inhabited by the witches, the way Glenn Flannery and Sherman Caswell had. But as he looked to his father, he could see that his face was clear and solemn, meeting Jimmy's gouging stare first, then Arthur's.

"Didn't for sure until today, when Jimmy came out with the stones."

"What do you...mean?" Arthur asked half-heartedly, giving an exaggerated furrow of his brow.

Randall snickered at his son's attempt to sound bewildered, and then he said, "If that pair of freaks in Oklahoma had given you these rocks at the time we were there, like you told me they did the next morning, don't you think I'da noticed. Heavy as they are?" He paused. "Still, I gave you the benefit of the doubt, that maybe you'd snuck 'em by me somehow." He nodded toward his younger son. "But then Jimmy come out carrying them to the truck this morning—saw you boys from the window—and then he insists on coming along with us today. And here he is now, arrangin' 'em just so." He searched his sons' faces for final proof, but neither boy looked back at their father, which was all the proof he needed. "Don't know what you boys know for sure, just that you got hope in somethin'. And if it means there's a chance I'll get Ruby back to your mother, then I'll go all the way to the end with it."

Jimmy and Arthur continued to hang their heads in shame, and Arthur suddenly felt a rush of regret at what he and his brother were prepared to do. He couldn't know for sure if what the twins had told him would happen, of course—there was plenty of reason to suspect not—but the very fact that they were willing to try was itself a mortal sin.

"Pa, we can't stay," Arthur called now. "Those ladies at the fair, they couldn't know anything. We'll find Ruby another way."

Randall Richland looked at Arthur now with an expression as warm and rueful as Arthur had ever seen from the man, one that suggested he knew he was the lamb, and that the wolf was on its way. He took a drag on the cigarette and then exhaled. "I bet there ain't one," he replied with a smile. "So let's just hope this one works."

"Pa, I—"

"It's alright, Arthur." He nodded once and then looked at Jimmy, nodding again, as if to give his younger son the same assurance.

THE FIRST SIGN OF THE storm came as a single tumbleweed, rolling from the east in a lazy bounce, hopping across the spot in the dirt where the stones had been arranged by Jimmy minutes earlier. And then a whistle like the steam warning of a distant train pierced Arthur's ears. He looked to the east, the direction of the sound and the road and the rising wind, and for a beat, he could see only the snaking curve of the dirt lane winding toward the horizon.

And then, just in front of the horizon, perhaps a half mile from where they stood, Arthur saw a cluster of black balls, hundreds of them perhaps, appearing along the skyline like an approaching stampede of buffalo.

And then the forms began to rise, lifting off the street as if by some magical breeze, swirling into a tight vortex toward the sky. Arthur saw now the black forms were tumbleweeds caught in the tempest, forming a kind of miniature tornado, a churning mixture of thistle and stone that raged toward them now like an invading army.

"Look at that!" Arthur said, not quite convinced of his assessment about what exactly was occurring, though he knew precisely what it portended.

Jimmy and Randall turned in unison toward the whipping twister, which had quickly added sand and dirt and God knew what else to the cyclone, giving the tunnel of wind a thick, opaque appearance.

"Boys," Randall announced in his deepest of tones. "To the truck. Right now!"

Arthur and Jimmy paused just a moment, espying a last glimpse of the approaching storm, and then they followed the command and sprinted to the truck without a word. Randall lingered a moment longer, and then he flicked his cigarette and took off in a light jog behind them, and within seconds of the three Richlands entering the cabin of the truck—Randall in the front, brothers in the back—the twister began to pass over them, whooshing above and around them like an overflowing river of dirt and debris.

Tumbleweeds slammed into the truck like oversized dust balls, clattering against the windows with cottoned ferocity.

As the hollow bushes collided, Arthur thought of that day with Ruby in Downes', and how the storefront window had seemed destined to implode under the onslaught of the storm. But the glass had held that day, just as he knew it would now. At least at first glance.

At least until the Skadegamutc arrived.

Another minute or so passed and the entire truck was enveloped with dirt, buried beneath the loam of the New Mexico desert. Only the sound of the storm registered now, as there was zero visibility beyond the inside of the glass.

Arthur put his hand to his chest and turned to his father, who was staring straight ahead, his eyes vapid and searching.

"I've lived in these parts all my life," Randall said. They were the words of man who knew his time left on earth was short.

Arthur gave no response to this, but he didn't need one.

A moment later, the storm passed.

As silence fell once more on the fairgrounds, Randall continued his gaze forward, and neither boy said a word for several moments, perhaps hoping their father would simply start the engine and drive them home, to reset their lives once more, and then approach a solution for finding Ruby another day.

And though Randall did turn on the truck, it was only to activate the windshield wipers. And when he flipped the arm of the wiper, that was when they saw them.

Chapter 30

Standing where the stones rested were two of the Skadegamutc, the final two that still existed on the plain of men and machines and dust and rubble.

They had come to claim their sacrifice, one they no doubt hoped would be waiting in a state of horror. Their mouths hung wide like the jaws of fiery piranha, their eyes solid and giant, gaunt, burning with a heat that could only be generated from a furnace in hell. They were facing the truck in perfect alignment, watching, waiting, wavering like flames on a pair of enormous candles. Their electric hair flowed wildly outward, while each of their naked, undefined bodies was like the outline of a menacing star.

"It's a sacrifice, is it?" Randall asked. "Guilty for innocent?"

It hadn't quite occurred to Arthur in such a straightforward way, that the reason why Ruby couldn't be used by the demons, or be killed by them—the reason why, according to Maggie, she wasn't even really scared—was because of her purity. The Skadegamutc had a thirst for punishment, but they couldn't punish those who had committed no sin.

"I think that's right, Pa," Arthur said, his voice a crackling whisper.

Jimmy couldn't speak at all, so spellbound was he by the terrible figures which had appeared like haunted divinities above the stones. And they were growing closer with each second that passed, though their approach was incalculable, their movement unnoticed.

Randall nodded in response to Arthur, and despite the sacrifice he had so willingly agreed to, there was fear in his eyes, in his heart. He swallowed and reached for the door, and as he did, Arthur reached forward and grabbed him by the arm.

"Pa, you don't have to," he said. "Don't. Please. I...I don't see Ruby anywhere. What if...we don't even know if this is true. This part of it anyway. It could all be a trick."

Randall frowned and nodded, acknowledging the possibility, and then, as if some pressure that had been built inside for decades was suddenly released, he grabbed his son by the back of the head and pulled him to his chest.

With this sudden, unprecedented show of affection from his father, the Skadegamutc's spell on Jimmy was broken, and he turned now toward the embrace. And then he burst into tears.

Arthur allowed the arms of his father to devour him, and he wished he could stay there forever. But when his father released him, he looked at him with fresh tears in his ducts and asked, "Why did you do it, Pa? At the garage that day?"

Randall looked at Jimmy now, but there was no malice or blame in his stare. Rather, it was a look of realization, a flash of harmonizing memories as a montage of events from that day fluttered through his mind in crystalline order. He understood it now. The immoral compulsion that had driven him to abuse that girl—an urge which he had yet to comprehend, despite having explored it in the quietest, most honest moments since that day—was fated, necessary, one which had to occur in order to bring him to this day, to arrive not only as a suitable replacement for his daughter, but as one who was willing to die in her stead. Randall too began to cry now, for the first time since he was twelve years old.

"Because I'm a sinner," he answered, his lips pressed tightly in regret. "And I'm sorry for all I put you boys through. Your whole life. You're good boys. And I love you both."

Randall opened the door now, and as Arthur grabbed for his arm once more, he turned and hugged him again, this time pulling Jimmy in, squeezing them both with an effort that could only be born of love. And then he released them and quickly exited the truck, standing and facing the encroaching demons with his chin high, his cheeks riverbeds of tears.

"Tell your mother I love her too," he said, not taking his eyes from the monstrosities ahead of him. And then, before he closed the door and walked away, he added, "And Ruby."

Randall Richland closed the door and took a step forward, and without turning back, he shouted, "Don't wait, boys!"

Neither boy had ever driven a truck before, but Jimmy knew the basics better than Arthur, and he instinctively climbed up to the driver's seat. He hesitated, however, his hand on the key, his eyes fixed on the landscape beyond as he watched his father walk bravely toward the sizzling fiends.

The Skadegamutc were barely twenty yards out from the truck now, and though their father had ordered them not to wait, there was still the matter of Ruby and her return. Of course, there was no guarantee she would be returned at all; what they knew of the exchange was a single word—*Sacrifice*—and the name of their father as the one to be martyred. Beyond that, they could only hope that some honor existed in this deranged deal, some required reverence to truth that was necessary to maintain order in the world. It was a monumental assumption, of course, and yet it felt accurate to Arthur, the only way things could go.

"Wait," Arthur said, "don't go. Not yet." And then he added, "But if you can't look, Jimmy, then don't. I understand."

Jimmy *didn't* look. Instead, he buried his face in his hands, quietly at first, and then he began to weep, sobbing the way his mother had that night at the kitchen table on the day Ruby was taken.

But Arthur kept his eyes bolted to his father, watching without blinking each move he made, knowing it was he, Arthur, who would be responsible for his death in the end. He had lured him here, and though his father knew the way it would go in the end, Arthur had set the wheels in motion.

Randall Richland stopped a step or two from the looming creatures, and then he pulled his Bowie knife from its holster, holding it upright for just a beat before slicing the large blade first across his right wrist, and then, quickly, across his left. He stood like a sculpture for several seconds, perhaps one that depicted some brave pioneer who had died during the settlement of the American West. And then the knife fell to the ground, and seconds later, Randall followed, dropping first to his knees, and then forward, collapsing face down beneath the vermillion witches.

The devilish entities hovered and sparked above the dying man like demons awaiting the payoff of a soul, and within minutes, the last of the life of Randall Richland finally spilled upon the dust.

Then, like a bucket of water tossed upon a campfire, the Skadegamutc were gone.

Chapter 31

"And Ruby?" Chris said the name like it was enchanted, as if everything in his life going forward depended on the answer to this question.

Arthur shook his head. "Despite what my father told us, not to wait, we did anyway. For over an hour inside the truck, and probably another two on the spot of the oddities tent where the stones had been placed and the witches appeared. But she never showed."

"What?" Chris was baffled now, and it felt as if the air in his lungs had been sucked clear with a vacuum. He already knew that Ruby returned, eventually, but if it wasn't from the practice Arthur had just described, then he was back to square one. "Never showed? Then it...it *was* a lie that Ruby would come back that way?"

Arthur frowned as if a point had been missed, but he gave no direct reply. Instead, he returned to his most recent segment of the tale, that of his father's sacrifice. "Do you understand what I've told you, Mr. Boylin, about what my father did in the end?"

Chris shrugged, defeated. "That he killed himself to resolve his own guilt?" he replied sarcastically. "Yeah, I got it."

"No! That wasn't it! He was a sinner! Just as he said he was!" Arthur put his hand to his chest and took a deep breath, and then he closed his eyes, regrouping. "But his sin was also a gift. One that he couldn't atone for directly, per-haps—not with the migrant girl or her family—but that he could still use nonetheless, as his legacy for what he had done."

Chris once again felt that he was losing Arthur, and that all he had endured in his effort to find Jaycee had been a waste. "I don't understand."

"It all happened the way it did for a reason. The event at the garage. The fact that Jimmy was there with him that day, helping him fix the truck that would take us to the fair. And that my brother heard the distress in that family's voice, the voice of the girl, and then passed the story on to me so that I would be a kind of witness to it as well. Don't you see? If we didn't know about our father's sin, we would never have brought him to the fairgrounds that day, even if I had be-lieved with all my heart what the twins had told me."

Chris scoffed and shook his head, which was pounding now with confusion and frustration. And though Arthur's theory was one the man had obviously thought a lot about, it was also rather outlandish, not truly matching up with the timeline. "But that incident, at the garage, it happened *before* Ruby was taken."

Arthur nodded and gave a soft smile, once again pleased at Chris' attention to the details of the story. "It's not some-thing to understand in linear terms, Mr. Boylin. I'm not a religious man, Christian or otherwise, even now, after all I know to be true in the world. And, I suppose, what I know lies beyond it. But I know this much to be true: there is a god—and whether He is Jesus or Allah or Brahman or whoever it is Zoroastrians believe in, I don't know—but He made my father sin that day, as a way to bring Ruby home."

Chris hadn't the energy for philosophy or religion, and though on some primal level he perhaps believed Arthur—who had spoken his words with perfect clarity—Chris didn't care about Arthur's father. Not anymore. 1939 was a long time ago, and he wasn't invested enough in Randall Richland to worry about granting the man clemency. All he wanted from the story was Ruby's return, and how it was relevant to finding Jaycee.

Jaycee.

They had driven east on 412 for over an hour now, and as he saw the sign which read: *Oklahoma state line: 40 mi.*, he knew he was getting close to the spot where his daughter had disappeared.

"I need to know now, Arthur," Chris said, his voice cold, on the edge, indicating he just might steer the pickup into a telephone pole if he didn't get an answer soon. "Tell me about Ruby's return."

Arthur exhaled and nodded. "Just remember what I told you about sins and sacrifice," he said. "And about the will of God."

Chris shrugged and shook his head. "Fine."

Chapter 32

Arthur saw her first, standing beside the church, her head slightly cocked, her arms hanging limply by her sides. She was wearing the same dress she'd had on the day of the fair, though that was only evident by the cut and length; the color had turned from that of daffodils to the forlorn brown of rotting wood. The color of demise. The color of New Mexico in autumn.

It was Ruby. Arthur had no doubt on that. But her face was a blackened image of his sister's, the color his father had often worn on his own face, entering their house after a long day at Chester's. For a moment, Arthur thought he was seeing the ghost of Ruby, and that she had risen from the dead, from the very graveyard where her father was being buried currently.

The story of Randall Richland's death had been a simple one, at least in terms of the details. He had brought his boys to the fairgrounds to help him look for Ruby one last time, and when they found only the desolation of the American Southwest, the pain finally reached its threshold, and their father had killed himself on the spot, too despondent to carry on. They had left his body where it lay, and, after gathering the Orange Rocks, Jimmy and Arthur drove the six hours to home, squaring their stories along the way. And once there, they told their conjured lie to their mother, who took the news of her husband's death with a certain crushing stoicism, listening to her sons as they spoke without hearing their words or comprehending their meaning.

And when they had completed the tale—which included real tears and emotion, though not the Skadega-mutc—their mother's eyes flickered, and as she scanned the faces of her boys, Arthur saw distrust in her gaze, suspicion that all he and Jimmy had just described to her was a lie. But Arthur knew it wasn't the lie of her husband's death that burdened her, it was that of Ruby's disappearance, that her sons were keeping something else from her, knowledge that might explain her daughter's disappearance

But none of that mattered now. It was three days after her husband's death, and Dotty Richland's daughter had returned.

Arthur rubbed his eyes and quivered his head, trying to remove whatever mental debris might be fogging his senses, or the fracture of some memory of Ruby that was producing her apparition. But then the rumble of the funeral guests began to grow, and soon his mother was pushing past Arthur, past the grave site where her husband was to be interred, past Father Kerrigan and Chester Sutton and a handful of other Clayton residents whom Arthur's mother, by only the loosest of definitions, considered friends.

And then she was running toward her daughter.

Arthur imagined the thoughts of Dotty Richland in that moment, and he knew in her mind there could be only prayer, the deepest of hope casting upward to God that what she was seeing was real.

Ruby took a step forward, toward her mother, and when she was only steps away, she fell to her knees in an almost perfect rendition of Randall Richland's final collapse on the site of the tent of oddities. But Ruby wasn't dead, just exhausted, and Dotty was atop her instantly, enveloping her like a starfish on a clam.

Laurie Hickman folded in a heap, fainting, while Father Kerrigan made the sign of the cross, all the while whispering, "In the name of the Father, and of the Son, and of the Holy Spirit. Amen."

The remaining attendees at the funeral stood stunned in disbelief, including Jimmy and Arthur, who, after a moment of realization, looked at each other and began to cry.

Chapter 33

"Where was she?"

Arthur nodded. It was the logical question, of course, one that would haunt Chris Boylin for much of his remaining life. And he knew the answer he was about to give would be less than satisfying. "She was...okay. Healthy. She still is as far as I know. Lives somewhere in Europe. Austria, I think. Or perhaps she's moved since I spoke with her last, which was seven or eight years ago."

Arthur shrugged, knowing the question of *'Why so long?'* was brewing in Chris.

"Like Jimmy, Ruby needed Clayton to be a faded memory, and that included fading the people who lived there. I doubt she even remembers the incident now, she was so young; but the scars are there. I've no doubt about that." He added, "And I've never blamed her for leaving home. I just thank God every day she came back when she was five."

"But *where*? *Where* was she?"

Arthur shook his head and grinned. "I understand your frustration, Chris. But I have no answer to that question. Ruby could never describe it, not at the time and not years later. We questioned her for months—Ma and Jimmy and me—but the more we asked, the less she seemed to say. Eventually Ma just told us to knock it off. Ruby was back, and that's all that mattered to her. All that should matter to us.

But...every once in a while, when it was just the two of us, I would bring it up with her again, delicately." He paused and put his hand to his chest, monitoring the beat of his heart, and then he said, "But all she could tell me about where she went, in those rare moments when she was willing to explore it, was that it was dark. And warm. And that somewhere in the distance she could hear screams."

Chris swallowed and his face flushed to pale as a tightness formed in his chest. He took a breath, trying to manage his composure.

"But *she* wasn't going there, Chris. To that place in the distance. And she knew she wasn't. Not Ruby. And not Jaycee either. I believe that. I truly do. And when you do get her back, don't press her to tell you about it. Just be happy to have her there. With you."

"When?" Chris managed to say, fingering a tear from his cheek.

Arthur ignored the question and stared back out the windshield. "Are we close?"

Chris shook himself back to the moment. "Close? To what?"

"The site of the accident. The place where your daughter was taken."

Chris looked confused, but he scanned the area, noting another landmark that showed they would be upon the spot in minutes. "A few miles."

"Will you be able to find it? The exact spot?"

Chris nodded. "Of course. The guardrail hasn't been fixed. I know exactly where it is." He paused now, and then he gave a crooked look to his passenger. "What are you saying, Arthur?"

Arthur smiled and looked down at the rocks by his feet.

Chris followed his gaze and said, "You want to try to summon them?"

Arthur chortled. He wasn't sure he had ever used that word in reference to the witches—*Summoned*—but now that it had been spoken, it sounded precise. "You've been following the story, Chris. You know how it has to end."

"But...the sacrifice? Who will...?"

Arthur remained quiet, peaceful as he stared through the windshield to the unfolding world beyond, and then he pulled a straight razor from his pocket. It wasn't the exact one Roger Desormeaux had used in the corridor of Stratford Manor, but it was the same make and model, taken from the supply closet during the chaos earlier that morning. But this one was new. Cleaner. Sharper.

"No, Arthur. Never. I can't let—"

"This was why you came to me, Chris." Arthur smiled and turned gently to the man. "It was God's will. Just as it was Jimmy witnessing my father's sin."

"But...it's...it's not the same as that. You just listened to my story. *I* came to *you*."

"It doesn't matter how it happened. All that matters is you found me. From the internet or intuition or however, it makes no difference. Just accept that it was to be."

"But what about the voices? I never heard your name. Nothing ever spoke to me."

Arthur shook his head. "You didn't need it to. You didn't need direction from any voice. You had me to guide you to the answer. Someone who'd already lived the story and new how to bring it to an end."

Chris was silent, absorbing the reality of what he was being asked to do. Finally, he said, "I can't."

Arthur chortled. "Can't what, Chris? There isn't anything for you to do. Except to collect the stones when it's done. And then to find your daughter. Find her. I can't tell you how. But do it."

Chris let the proposition weigh heavily on his mind as he drove in silence for four more miles, and when he finally came upon the spot of the accident, he considered driving through, to not give Arthur the choice. It was Chris who was at the wheel, after all, he who was in control, and if he didn't want to stop, there wasn't much Arthur could do about it.

But when the guardrail appeared in the distance, the splayed, twisted metal, replete with extensive scrapes of red and black paint seemed to scream at him to stop, so Chris pulled over and shifted the truck to park.

Arthur bowed his head in relief. He sat silently in the passenger seat for several beats collecting his thoughts, and then he said, "I don't know where she'll be when she returns. And I suppose, if I'm completely honest, I can't even guarantee she'll come back at all. I only know what happened with Ruby. That she appeared. There was no clue I could ever find as to why it happened when and where it did. But she was there. Just as I described." He sensed the desperation in Chris. "Just watch for her. Look for her." He paused. "And one more thing..."

Chris looked at Arthur expectantly.

"When this is over, soon after it's over, I need you to promise me to return them."

"What?"

"The Orange Rocks. Return them."

Chris shook his head. "I...where? How?"

"The Tompiros Burial Grounds is a protected site in Clayton now. A kind of museum, I think. Or a tourist spot. I don't know what it looks like exactly, I haven't been since it was finally completed. It took them decades to finish the excavation, and then to build the facility, and now that it's been open to the public for several years, it can't be much of draw anymore. If it ever was at all." He shrugged. "Clayton is a different place now, but it's still the middle of nowhere." Arthur leaned forward, searing a stare into Chris' eyes. "Replace them. Put them inside the altar if you can. I don't know how much difference it will make now, but I think it will."

"Why did you never take them there?" Chris asked. "Or at least try?"

Arthur sighed and stared toward the roof, as if trying to remember the reason. "I always planned to. I even tried to once in the mid-fifties, a few years after I found them in an open lockbox in Jimmy's trailer in Spokane. It was after his funeral when I was going through his things." He breathed a heavy sigh and continued. "I put it off for a while, stalling I guess you'd call it, but then I took them to Clayton, right to the spot of the Ditches. But when I arrived, the dig was active, heavily monitored at the time; there was no way to just walk into the Hollow and return them properly. And I knew if I'd simply handed them over to some graduate student, they would have ended up in some university lab and then a museum in Santa Fe or Las Cruces."

Chris waited for more, and when nothing was added he asked, "And later?" Chris wasn't letting Arthur off that easily.

Arthur shrugged. "I thought it was over, I suppose. Or at least I hoped so. Jimmy was dead, so there was no one else. And even before he died, they had already come for my father. The revenge—or whatever it was—was complete. I figured that was the end of it. So, I just...kept them. They were the only thing I had as a memento of my brother." He paused now, searching, trying to excavate the deepest truth from his heart. "But I guess I always knew. I knew they weren't truly gone. I couldn't tell you how, just that I did. So, I kept them covered, sealed in a chest in my home, and that's were they stayed for fifty years. Until the day I moved to Stratford Manor."

Chris wanted to say more, to ask additional questions about the stones, or say thank you for what he was prepared to do to save his daughter. Or even to plead with Arthur to reconsider. But the die, it seemed, had been cast, and nothing Chris could do now would overturn what was to be.

Arthur opened the door and began to shuffle toward the guardrail, and seconds later Chris was behind him, his arm around the old man like a friend, supporting him as they strolled down the empty interstate.

Chris led the way to the exact spot where the Tacoma had rammed the metal barrier, and then he stopped, nodding once, indicating they'd reached their destination.

Arthur scanned the area like an architect on a homesite. "This is more precise than we were in Albuquerque," he said, nodding. "This is going to work, Chris."

"What do we do?" Chris asked.

"We wait. We place the rocks, and we wait."

The two men sat on the street with their legs crossed, and as the hours passed, they talked about things unrelated to missing sisters and daughters. Arthur told Chris about his own son, Daniel, whose death he blamed himself for, though he never quite explained why. But Chris knew the reason. He admitted that he missed him every day, several times a day, even with his mind degenerating as it was. And Arthur spoke of his dementia as well, which he admitted to playing up on occasion, though not as often as he once did. And then he gave the veiled suggestion that his imminent death would be a blessing in this regard, sparing him the ravages that lie ahead.

They cried and laughed and listened as neither man had to anyone in years. A car passed on occasion, but no one stopped. No one cared. All the while the stones sat blandly in front of them, touching lightly, just the way Jimmy had arranged them at the carnival site in 1939.

And then the wind began to blow. And the sky, which had been a clear blue for the last several days, turned the murky color of swamp water. And, within minutes, it looked as if night had fallen over Interstate 412.

Chapter 34

The storm descended quickly, arriving first as a brisk breeze across the flat plain, and then swirling into a whirlwind, whipping brush and twigs and earth into a funnel of energy.

Arthur stood alone by the guardrail, the stones at his feet, his eyes closed in concentration, knowing he would need the fullness of his faculties to carry out his intentions.

Arthur's companion, whose name he suddenly couldn't remember, had returned to the truck in which they'd arrived (though from where, Arthur couldn't recall), and then had backed the vehicle up to a point twenty yards or so from the site of the accident, the site where the demons would return. At least Arthur prayed that was true.

Arthur didn't know how it all worked exactly, in terms of the possession and one's proximity to the creatures, but he'd seen the attacks of the residents at his home, as well as from Sherman Caswell, so he'd had a lifetime to formulate his theory.

A person under the spell of the Skadegamutc, he'd determined, would, in a blind rage, search for a life to take. And anyone near that person was a target.

And when there is no one nearby, Arthur thought, *the victim is the one who is spellbound.*

Death. For the first time in his life, Arthur felt at peace with the idea. He knew he was near the finish line, he could see it right before him, and all he prayed for now was that his life would have purpose, that his soul would be repaired. *She had to return*, he thought, though he could no longer remember the name of the girl, or if it even was a girl for whom they'd come.

His mind was beginning to fail. His memory was sliding quickly from the folds of his brain like a piece of driftwood over a frozen waterfall. It needed to happen soon. Now.

And then he could feel them, the heat of the approaching malevolence behind him, and as he turned toward the sensation, he raised his eyes to a string of orange lines that had suddenly formed in the body of the storm. Arthur shielded his eyes from the gust as he watched the outlines of the Skadegamutc rise from the dust like lustrous eels, forming the pair of witches that had been loosed into the world so many decades before. In a moment, the bodies were fully formed, their identical feminine outlines unchanged since the first day he'd witnessed them over six decades earlier.

They moved toward Arthur without hesitation, advancing at a rate more quickly than he'd remembered when he was twelve, when he had watched from the back of a pickup truck as they infected the mind of his father, murdering him with his own hands.

Arthur latched on to their empty eyes now, shifting his glance back and forth between the twin pair of rotten apricots, and at once, the fulvous orbs cast him back to that day inside the Hollow, to the etchings of evil that had littered the wall of the altar room, shining like terrible totems of fire.

And then, as if a heavy blanket were suddenly draped across his brain and had begun to press down on the nerves of the organ, Arthur was lost in the world, ignorant of his surroundings. In a moment, he'd forgotten why he was standing in the desert at all. He'd forgotten the name of his mother. Of his son. Of the town in which he'd grown up. His own name. His life.

But not everything.

With all that his brain was unable to process in that moment, he still knew the moniker of the approaching wickedness—*Skadegamutc*—and of their intention to ruin and steal, manipulate and kill. It was the only thing they knew to do. The reason for their existence. The duty for which they'd been originally summoned by a starving tribe centuries earlier and which they had carried out for hundreds of years. Perhaps longer.

Arthur closed his eyes and waited for his mind to succumb to them, praying that it would happen now, before it was too late.

But it wasn't to be. Despite the power of the Skadegamutc, they were no match for Arthur's dementia, the disease winning the moment easily, making his mind oblivious to the attraction of the villains.

The witches quickly moved past him, through him, like the shadow from a flock of giant birds. His lack of cognizance was protecting him from their infection, making him unsuitable as a vehicle for the ancient witches' appetites.

But there were others to be found in the area, victims with a healthy sense of awareness, brains that were exposed and uncluttered, available for consumption, and the

Skadegamutc headed for the pickup truck parked only steps away.

"No!" Arthur choked out. "No!" And then, not quite understanding the context of the words, he added, "It's me you want!"

But the Skadegamutc continued drifting forward, and as Arthur turned with them, he could see through the blast of debris a man standing just outside the truck, appearing there like a phantom, his chest bowed and willing, the pose of someone prepared to accept whatever was to come. His form looked familiar to Arthur, vaguely, though he couldn't have said where he'd seen him previously.

But the man's eyes were locked on the Skadegamutc, Arthur could tell that much through the gale, and this gave Arthur hope. His memory was nearly gone, but his mind in other ways was functioning still, including processing the images his eyes were seeing. And that meant there was a chance. He just needed to get to the truck in time.

The fresh gale was working against Arthur, relentless now as it blew from the northeast into and across his face. But he took the first step toward the pickup truck anyway, and when his body moved forward with the effort, he took another step, then a third, and after adjusting his pace and posture for the force of the wind, he was suddenly striding with the plod of a dinosaur toward the truck and the radioactive witches that hovered there.

And then there was a break in the dust and the churn of the atmosphere, just for a moment, and Arthur, who was only steps away now, saw the stranger lift a short knife beside his head and bring it to his throat.

Arthur could remember nothing else from his life but a single name, and he screamed it with every fiber of force he possessed as he ran toward the man.

"Ruby!"

Chapter 35

Tears streamed down Chris Boylin's face as he crossed the city limits into Clayton, New Mexico. He noted first what he imagined was once Chester Sutton's shop, but which had now been turned into a Sunoco station, probably at some point in the eighties, he guessed. The town was nondescript otherwise, with a pair of fast food restaurants and a small grocery store, as well as a large church that seemed to be the anchor of the town now, which, to Chris, despite not being a religious person himself, felt right to him.

He guided the Frontier down Main Street through the middle of the town, and when he arrived at an antique shop, he spotted a small brown sign with white lettering that read: 'Native American History Site,' and just below that, a left-pointing arrow with '.05' beside it, indicating the Ditches were a half a mile down the narrow road.

Chris followed the sign, and when he pulled into the grassy parking area of the site, there was little to indicate any attraction existed there at all, other than a small white building which acted as the visitor center. Chris exited the truck and stared at the surroundings, the place that had once been Ty Sampson's farm but was now a preserved piece of the Native American West. It wasn't at all how Chris envisioned it from Arthur's stories, but that was so often the case when one matched words to reality.

Chris walked to the building, which had a sign that read **Closed** on the window beside the door. He tried the door anyway, but, as expected, it was locked. On either side of the structure, however, there was only flat land as far as the eye could see, and nothing aside from a wooden fence with a Keep Out sign on the gate to prevent someone from passing through. And beyond the fence were the Tompiros Indian Burial Grounds—the Ditches—so Chris hopped the fence with ease and strode the fifty yards or so until he came to the first of the unlikely holes. He stopped there a moment and replayed in his mind Arthur's story of the day he and Jimmy had arrived in the spot together, and then he continued on the cobblestone path that had been built for the visitors and which ran along the rim of the unused gravesites. When he reached the last one on the left—Crater 7 as Jimmy and his buddies had named it—he stopped and stared inside.

Chris recognized the entrance to the Hollow by the stones that were stacked by the base, but, as Arthur had described, the opening was hidden from above. The area around the site was bordered off with fencing, and an information plaque had been erected detailing the significance of the grounds. The sign indicated that a secret tomb was below, inside the burial site itself, and below that was a room that had been used for sacrifices. No entrance was allowed, however, which was another rule Chris was about to break.

He jumped into the hole and slipped through the opening that led to the Hollow, and once inside the cave, he crawled on the path that led to the short flight of stairs, descending them and working his way back to the altar room. All of it had been clearly marked by the excavators, but even if it hadn't been, Arthur's description would have allowed Chris to find it easily.

A wooden gate had been constructed in front of the altar room, and though it was nailed shut, it appeared flimsy, and with a couple of heavy tugs, Chris removed the barrier and was through to the chamber.

The altar itself was smaller than Chris had expected, but Arthur's description had been from a child's perspective, so it made sense that he'd imagined it as bigger. Yet, despite the size, the top of the altar was heavy, and with more effort than he'd imagined would be needed, Chris shoved the cover forward, exposing the empty chamber beneath.

He saw four stones at the bottom, just as he'd expected. The formation of three that Arthur had seen when he first looked inside, and the Orange Rock of Ralph Brater, who had returned his in 1939, days after his aunt was murdered.

Chris unzipped his backpack and pulled the Orange Rocks from it. Jimmy Richland and Bucky Mason's rocks. The boys had stolen the stones from a sacred ground, unknowing of the consequences, and that act had gone on to ruin their own lives as well as others whom they loved. But now was the time to atone for that act. To give a certain peace to a careless deed of mischief.

Chris took a deep breath and leaned into the altar, placing the stones at the bottom of the tomb as Arthur had described, so that each of the added stones touched the original but not each other.

He stood up straight now and stared a moment longer into the chasm, noting the symmetry of the arrangement, all six rocks in perfect formation. He considered the other three rocks for a moment, the ones that had been left undisturbed, and he wondered what would have been if Jimmy and his friends had removed those as well. For the briefest of moments—perhaps influenced by the Skadegamutc—Chris was tempted to find out, and he had to look away from the trio of rocks and banish the thought.

And then with a nod to himself, as if he had honored his duty properly, Chris stepped to the opposite side of the altar and pushed the lid back into place, sealing the spirit of Skadegamutc inside.

That was the hope.

Chapter 36

It was over. All of it. And now that it was done, it seemed to have been for nothing. At least that was true when it came to the death of Arthur Richland. It had been nearly a week now since Chris had killed Arthur, having used the blade of his utility knife to carve a gorge into the man's neck.

Chris didn't remember the attack, and when he had opened his eyes and was back in the world, he was leaning against the guardrail, his knife in the dust by his side. It was coated with dirt and pebbles, items which had been fossilized in place by Arthur Richland's dried blood.

Arthur's weapon, the blade from the nursing home, Chris tossed into a patch of desert shrubbery.

Acting almost on instinct, Chris had placed the handle of the knife in Arthur's hand and then gently dragged the man's corpse to the side of the road, all the while expecting someone to speed by and spot the murderous activity, and then to call in the crime, the truck and the plate number, ultimately sealing Chris' future.

But no car passed during the time he was awake, and somehow Chris knew one hadn't during the time he was unconscious either. The storm had closed the interstate, insulating him from witnesses.

But now that Chris had rendered the sacrifice, killing a man who had given his own life for the chance of bringing back a stranger's daughter, he knew Jaycee wasn't coming home. They had waited too long. Or it was all a myth to begin with. Not the Skadegamutc, of course—he had seen too much not to believe—but the sacrifice itself. The exchange. Perhaps they never wanted Arthur at all. Maybe it was Chris they had coveted all along, to punish him for the multitude of sins he'd committed over the course of his unfulfilled life.

Or perhaps Ruby Richland was exceptional. The sole beneficiary of the witches' mercy. Maybe they had simply taken Jaycee as another victim, and she was with the monsters now. Screaming.

Chris almost couldn't breathe now as he drove, and suddenly his thoughts went to Calista. He hadn't spoken with her in almost two weeks, and he knew the next time he did it would tempt violence, a conversation that would be impossible. How much would he tell her about what he knew? Any of it? All of it? What would be the point, really? In the end, she would think he'd lost his mind.

But even his estranged wife didn't matter to Chris anymore. Not really. Neither the hatred she felt toward him or the pain she was suffering. Perhaps one day he would care again, when his own pain subsided, though the truth was that that day might never come to pass. Not in this lifetime.

He wiped a tear from the corner of his eye, then another, and then he began to bawl from a depth in his gut he never knew existed. His first instinct was to pull the truck over and let the deluge spill from his soul in giant waves, until he was depleted, numb. But for what? It didn't matter. He would just drive now. Drive forever. Drive until he fell asleep and ended up in a deep ditch on the side of the road, hopefully

CHRISTOPHER COLEMAN

with his neck snapped, the accident in a place where no one would ever find him.

He put his head down on the top of the steering wheel and continued to weep, and then he began to slam his hands into the rubber ring with the wildness of a rabid animal, trying to undue the tragedy that had devoured his life over the last month. He kept his foot on the gas, pressing down now, careening the pickup down the arrow-straight road of Interstate 412, the same stretch he had driven a thousand times now it seemed, searching for Jaycee.

But now he prayed for the storm again, and for a truck as large as the Penelope's Pickles semi to suddenly emerge again, just as it had all those weeks ago.

But this time he wouldn't brake. He wouldn't swerve.

He lifted his head now and began to scream, gripping the wheel in his hands and pulling it toward him in jarring yanks, truly intending to pull it from the steering column if that were physically possible. He would try.

And then in the distance he saw a road sign on the right shoulder of the road, a speed limit sign, he supposed. And just beyond it was a large rock, large enough to be classified as a boulder, he guessed, surrounded on all sides by a sprawling patch of prairie grass.

And there was something atop the boulder, a smallish figure that looked to be a jutting extension of the stone, like a bush or a small tree had suddenly grown from its core.

Another eighth of a mile and soon he could see it was a person, a girl, sitting in the center of the stone, her head cocked slightly to the left, her arms hanging limply by her sides.

Chris stopped crying, an instinct of his body to keep his eyes clear.

And then he began to laugh.

Epilogue

Brandon Locklear noticed the footprints immediately, the heavy footfalls of a man who had made no attempt to hide them. He followed the sneaker steps, tracking them as his ancestors had tracked prints for millennia, following them beyond the empty burial sites to the last of the seven ditches, where the sacrificial rituals had occurred beneath the ground in the hollowed-out portion of the earth.

The tracks that led inside the cave were obvious as well, and Brandon stepped down into the crater and entered through the gap, lighting the flashlight in his hand instantly.

Inside, everything appeared as he knew it to be, the ground smooth and stable, the torch holder undamaged. He crawled carefully forward to the stairway that led to the basement, and then quickly descended the stairs and strode cautiously to the Room of Sacrifice.

And that was when he saw it.

The latticed door—which had been erected years ago when tourists were still permitted inside the cave, allowing them an outside view of the Sacrifice Room—had been dislodged, and it now rested broken against the jamb of the doorway.

Brandon lifted the door aside and stood at the threshold, watching, listening. But the room from that vantage looked as it had the last time he'd checked on it, two days earlier after the end of his shift.

"Mischievous white boys," he said aloud, though in his mind that explanation felt amiss. It was too clean and undisturbed inside the cavern, on the entire site generally. Had it been naughty high schoolers who had damaged the door, there would have been other signs. Beer cans. Food wrappers and cigarette butts. Graffiti. And Brandon couldn't see any evidence of a hate crime, some symbol that would have suggested violence or intimidation.

And then he noticed it, the slightest displacement of the altar's cover, the wooden slab of the crypt not quite lining up with the base.

He stepped inside the room and stared at the top of the relic from above, and then he bent at the waist to get a view from a flatter angle. But it was unnecessary; he already knew he was correct in his assessment.

Brandon gently pulled a pair of latex gloves from his back pocket and slipped them on, and then with a heave, he pushed the top of the altar forward, exposing the chamber below as he shined the beam of his flashlight inside.

Except the contents of the chamber had changed.

Instead of four black rocks on the altar bottom, there were now six, the single stone on the right side having been added to with two additional rocks.

And then, despite a voice deep in Brandon's mind instructing him to leave them as they lay, he reached down and picked up the two new additions to the crypt, holding them high as he studied them in the dim light.

He smiled at the sight of the stones in his hands, his new treasures, and then he looked around cautiously, wary, as if there were someone watching him in the dark chamber ten feet beneath the surface of the earth. He slipped the stones under the flap of the satchel on his chest and placed them inside, and then he climbed the stairs and exited the Hollow, returning to the surface of Crater 7.

And as Brandon Locklear walked confidently back to the visitor's center, a smile across his face, storm clouds began to gather in the west.

THE END

DEAR READER,

Thank you for reading THEY CAME WITH THE STORM. I hope you enjoyed it. I'd be grateful if you would leave a review for it on Amazon. It doesn't have to be long. A simple, "I liked it!" is enough. That is, if you did like it, which I hope you did! You might also enjoy the They Came with the Snow series and my standalone novel, They Came with the Rain.

OTHER BOOKS BY CHRISTOPHER COLE-MAN

THE GRETEL SERIES
Gretel (Gretel Book One)
Marlene's Revenge (Gretel Book Two)
Hansel (Gretel Book Three)
Anika Rising (Gretel Book Four)
The Crippling (Gretel Book Five)
The Killing of Orphism (Gretel Book Six)

THE THEY CAME WITH THE SNOW SERIES
They Came with the Snow (They Came with the Snow Book One)
The Melting (They Came with the Snow Book Two)
The List (They Came with the Snow Book Three)
The Ghosts of Winter (They Came with the Snow Book Four)

THE SIGHTING TRILOGY SERIES
The Sighting (The Sighting Book One)
The Origin (The Sighting Book Two)
The Reappearance (The Sighting Book Three)

STANDALONE NOVEL
They Came with the Rain

Printed in Great Britain
by Amazon

84235606R00203